Before Tim had opened the passenger-side door, he took Brandi into his arms. He could barely control himself as he pressed her against the truck, kissing her as if he had just come from the wild. His arms wrapped tightly around her as he pressed his body hard against hers. Brandi was warm against him despite the coolness of the evening; and she felt utterly fantastic against him.

Brandi held onto him for dear life, not remembering if she had ever felt that wonderful before. Her kisses were as feverish as his, matching him tempo for tempo. Having him so close to her, ignited memories of their first night together. She slowly broke the kiss, and stared into his flushed face saying, "I can't believe I'm in your arms again."

Indigo Love Spectrum

An imprint of Genesis Press, Inc.
Publishing Company

Genesis Press, Inc.
P.O. Box 101
Columbus, MS 39703

ISBN-13: 978-1-58571-207-6
ISBN-10: 1-58571-207-8
Manufactured in the United States of America

First Edition

Visit us at www.genesis-press.com
or call at 1-888-Indigo-1

A TASTE
OF TEMPTATION

RENEE ALEXIS

Genesis Press, Inc.

ACKNOWLEDGMENTS

First, and certainly foremost, I want to thank God. For without his blessings, there would be no book. Thanks also to my parents, my friends and family. All of you have given me something that makes me unique. To Deborah Schumaker, my editor at Genesis Press: you are more valuable than you know. Thanks for putting up with my tantrums. To the Greater Detroit Romance Writers of America, you couldn't have been any more supportive—thanks. Last, but definitely not least, to my fans who have supported me with my previous books. I love you!

Renee Alexis

CHAPTER 1

Parson's Lecture Hall was filled to capacity; Brandi knew why. She had heard about this professor, how good he was, how he played no games when it came to his class. She wanted that kind of discipline in order to keep her scholarship. Her other professors were virtual academic stereotypes: middle-aged, graying, pot-bellied. Tall, dark and handsome would be a nice change. Her ex-boyfriend, Eric was exactly that. However, Eric had zero ambition, and fully expected his good looks to get him over, no matter what. Eric was, in a word, shallow. For Brandi, those negatives were compounded by his having slept with one of her best friends, graduating from just being shallow to being a dog. She had dumped him immediately.

Her mind drifted back to an evening a month ago at Manhattan's newest nightclub, The Entrapment. She and some friends celebrated her emancipation from Eric Fontaine and her winning the Seymour Scholarship. There was a man in the club who was tall, handsome and magnetic. She hadn't been attracted to a white man since having a crush on her gym teacher in 6th grade. Their eyes had met the minute Jacob walked into the club. Everything about him—his light brown hair and tall slender frame were orgasmic. She had felt like a traitor for having seen beauty in one outside her race. But this Jacob made her forget all that. Those deep-set hazel eyes of his mesmerized her right into his bed that night.

She pushed aside memories of her Jacob encounter since he flat-out told her he wasn't into relationships. So she turned to the class syllabus. She could tell the class was going to be a killer. A fifteen-page syllabus! *Isn't it just like an older man to give everyone the life histories of all the classic authors and poets?* This professor must be expecting some heavy-duty studying from his students. Like it or not, there was nothing she could do about it because the class was a prerequisite to retaining her scholarship money. She quickly put the paper away and her mind returned to ditching Eric.

Her best friend, Tiffany, breezed into the room, her upbeat personality on full display. "What's up, girl? Anxious about seeing Polaris?"

"No, I'm not anxious about Polaris. You know how most professors are, sixty years old and balding!"

"Polaris? Girl, please! He is fine, let me tell you. Why do you think I busted the pavement the first day of registration to get this class? He has all the women following behind his tight little butt."

"Then he's not sixty or balding?"

"If Timothy Edward Polaris is sixty let me just say this; he carries it well, damn well. The guy can't be any older than thirty-two, but from his credentials anyone would think he's older."

"Yes, yes, I know. He's the king of the world, right?"

Tiffany looked around the crowded, noisy lecture hall and smiled. "Your sarcasm is actually on the mark. It's packed in here because the man knows his stuff. He didn't graduate from Princeton with two degrees and tons of writing awards by not knowing his stuff. The guy's a heavyweight."

"How do you know all this about the guy?"

"Look, if you study something, you tend to know it well. I have studied him like he's a course being offered here. I know everything about him."

Brandi shook her head. "I don't even believe you. Some people study everything about bridges, sciences, math, etc. But you, you study Polaris?"

"You will, too, take my word for it. He has the sexiest hazel eyes you ever wanted to drool over."

Hazel eyes! Jacob has hazel eyes, not that I'll ever see them again, but I can dream. But thoughts of him will get me nowhere. She forced her mind off him. "Finally, a handsome *young* instructor. Well, that's a perk of sorts, since we have to sit in here for three hours."

"It's all cool, girl. Polaris will rock this class, and you will be damn glad for it." Her eyes widened. "Oh, yeah, are you still gaga over that man you met in the club?"

So much for shutting out thoughts of Jacob. "Please, don't bring him up."

"Why? I thought you liked him. You told me that when you called to tell me everything."

"Almost everything. I did like him."

"Did?" Tiffany leaned in closer. "What's your deal, girl? You said he's fine and that he was sweet to you, so what's the problem?"

"Tiff, you know what the problem is. I have thought about my actions that night and I feel ashamed. Plus, I would just make matters worse for myself by dating a white guy."

"That doesn't even sound like you. Color never mattered to you before."

"It has, though never in a negative way. I never let anyone know about it. I just feel bad knowing how much I love the brothers, then backsliding and going for a white guy. Besides, you know my dad, Kelly, Marco, and the rest of my friends and family. You know how rigid they are on this subject. I'm just not ready to deal with questions about why I'm with a *white boy.* And you know they would call him, *boy,* Tiffany."

"It's a big deal to them, but hey, they're not dating Jake, Jock . . . what's his name?"

"It's Jacob. Now get it right."

Puzzled, Tiffany dropped the subject. "It's all cool. I'll leave you alone, but don't ask me for any tissue when you start drooling over Professor Sex Machine."

"Does he really look that good?"

"You may not want to go by me. I'm the one who doesn't have problems with *white boys,* so how would I know?" She held up a finger. "Correction, I don't have problems with boys at all . . . or men." She turned in her seat. "So, you're going back to Eric, aren't you?"

Brandi looked annoyed. "Can't let it go, can you? You, of all people, know Eric and I are a done deal. We don't want the same things. Besides, he's not ready for a woman who could end up making more money than he does. He doesn't want that, or a family. No! He and I are done."

"Jacob whoever could give you those things?"

Brandi dropped her notebook back onto the small desk. "Cool it, Tiff. He and I are also a done deal. Besides, he didn't give me a number. Now will you cool it about that?"

"Fine, but you'll change your mind about white guys when you see Polaris, because his butt is so . . . so, ooh, I can't even describe it."

Brandi clenched her teeth. "I don't have a race issue, Tiffany. Besides, don't you still have a thing for Stuart?"

"Will you hush? I can't have screaming orgasms over Polaris when you mention Stuart!"

"You've finally hit rock bottom."

The back lecture doors opened and Timothy Polaris started walking down the long aisle. From behind, Brandi could tell he definitely wasn't sixty. As she looked at the slender professor with the light brown crew cut, she saw a resemblance to Jacob. The tall, well-built frame was the same. *I've got it really bad. Now Jacob is everyone to me.* Thinking she could be losing her mind, she quickly squashed the thought. She felt relief as she kept watching him. *No, definitely not him—I hope. Besides, what would Jacob be doing in Parson's lecture hall?*

Tiffany nudged her slyly. "He's looking better and better, isn't he?"

"Until I see his face, he's just another professor."

The professor turned to face the crowded lecture hall and began speaking into the microphone. Brandi lifted her head and her jaw dropped. She couldn't believe her eyes. She looked at the closed circuit television set near her. "Tiffany, that's him. Look."

Tiffany peered at the monitor. "Are you sure that's lover-boy?"

"As sure as I'm sitting here." She saw the skepticism on Tiffany's face. "I know you don't believe me, but I'm sure he's the one."

"Frankly, I don't believe you, but if that's the daydream you want to have, go for it."

"Whatever." Nothing mattered to Brandi. She was face to face with the one man who had taken her body to heaven and her mind—south! Reality quickly set in. *My God!* Mind in overdrive. His voice confirmed everything.

"I'm Timothy Polaris, and this is English Comp 812." He smiled as he spoke. "If you're at the wrong university . . . well, sorry, you're stuck with me for a minute, I guess." He waited for the laughter to subside. "Before I go over the roster, let me explain a little about the course. It covers 16th through 20th Century literature from the best in American lit to England and the rest of the world. It's a long course lasting from today, August twenty-eighth to December eleventh and attendance is mandatory every week since the course moves fast. Take plenty of good notes. There is a mid-term, papers and the final exam, which is half of your grade. The first three weeks of the course will concentrate on 16th and 17th Century authors. Midway, I expect to get into the middle 18th century. Everyone with me so far?"

Brandi knew that smile was definitely the same smile that had dazzled her at The Entrapment. "No, this has to be a mistake," she whispered to herself. "Why is he here?" She nudged Tiffany. "This can't be him!"

Tiffany looked at her as if she had lost her mind. "It's him, girl. It's Timothy Polaris though, not your dude from the other night." Back to Tim: "Told you he was *tight*, didn't I?"

Brandi ducked in her seat so he couldn't see her. As he continued, all she could see was the sexy man that had turned her out, an entire night and well into the next morning. The more she thought about having slept with her English professor, the sicker she felt. She had worked way too hard to get into Madison to have it all suddenly come crashing down. Sleeping with a professor was not the best way to start a course of study. Sleeping her way to the top wasn't about to happen.

For the past month, the very thought of Jacob Wells made her smile. Now thoughts of him brought on emotions far different from the ones he had aroused in her that night. Shock and embarrassment washed over her. She couldn't look at a man who represented unwanted friction in her life. She grabbed her books and ran out. Tiffany was able to stop staring at Polaris long enough to see Brandi run from the lecture hall.

Tiffany caught up with Brandi, who was huddled in a corner in the main hallway. "Are you okay?"

"No, I'm not okay. I can't go back in there."

She took Brandi's shaking hands. "That is not your lover, Brandi. There are a lot of people who look alike in this world. I'm sure that's the case here."

"I'm not. He's too much of an exact replica. He would have to be a twin because everything is exactly the same, from the shape of his head to his shoes. Everything, Tiff."

"He's is our professor, nonetheless. Isn't he everything I told you he was?"

"That and more."

"Okay, I'm missing something here."

"You don't understand."

"You're right, I don't! Girlfriend, women don't run *from* Polaris; they run to him."

"That's . . . that's him, Tiffany. That's the same man from the Entrapment, no matter what you say."

Tiffany frowned. "Still on that, I see."

"Yes, I'm still on that because he is who I was with. No doubts."

"You didn't say his name was Tim when you called me the next day."

"I said his name was Jacob Anthony Wells, but apparently that wasn't his real name. Don't you understand? He . . . he lied to me— lied, like all men seem to do. 'Jacob' and Polaris are the same person." She looked desperately into her buddy's face. "I slept with Timothy Polaris, and didn't even know it."

"Maybe you're right, since you're so dead sure about it. I guess you would be since you were able to get a good look at him from the monitors around the room." She leaned against the wall. "You got a good look at him somewhere else, if you know what I'm saying."

"I do know what you're saying, and it's not bringing a smile to my face. Not this time."

Tiffany covered her face and took a deep breath. "You lucky heifer. Don't you know that women would give up organs to sleep with him? They transfer from other schools to get him." She rested her books on the floor and smiled into Brandi's less-than-eager face. "Dang, girl! You've made history and don't even appreciate it."

Brandi stared at her in amazement. "You really don't get it, do you? I have slept with my professor, not a great way to start at the one school I've wanted to attend since seventh grade. Even worse, he lied to me. Haven't I had enough of that with Eric?"

"First of all, you didn't commit a mortal sin. Professors need love, too. True, it shouldn't be done if he's *your* professor, but it happens."

"How do you know?"

"Women talk, Brandi. I see and hear all kinds of things because my nose is always into someone's business. I admit to that, proud of it, actually! I would consider it myself if Polaris as much as looked at me, which he never has, I'm sorry to say!"

"Be serious. This is terrible. I could lose everything I've worked for. Winning the Seymour is not an everyday thing. Besides, he could lose his job, too!"

"He won't let that happen, girl, and you know it! Timothy Polaris is too smart for that. The guy has a nightlife, apparently. Because he's a college professor doesn't mean he has to stay home and grade papers all night. It makes sense to use a fake name. I know dudes who do that all the time, not that they have to. Yet, they do it. So does he, apparently."

"He lied to me, Tiff!"

"I know. I'm not saying the lying part was cool, but he had his reasons. You could still have a relationship with him."

Brandi's voice dripped sarcasm. "Really now; do tell."

"If you like the dude, you'll figure something out." Tiffany couldn't suppress a devilish grin.

"Why are you smiling at me like that? Let's go so I can face the music, very unsettling music."

"Not just yet. I need to know something."

"Yeah, like what?"

She lowered her voice. "What was it like? You know, being in bed with Timothy Polaris?"

"Are you crazy? That's personal."

"I tell you about my conquests."

"You always volunteer details like they're notches on your belt or something."

"A girl's got to be proud of something, right? Come on! You're holding the key that every chick on campus would pay big time for."

"This better not go any further than this little huddle you've got me in." Her eyes took on a dreamy look. "For lack of better words, it was out of this freakin' world! I never knew sex could be like that. With Eric it was on the verge of boring. I could balance my checkbook while Eric and I were in bed, but with Polaris, every nerve ending was on fire!"

"He looks like he's great at everything, especially sex. A man who looks like that can't help but jam. Come to think of it, don't you think he looks like Prince William? I bet he can jam, too."

"Right, when the tabloids aren't chasing him." She looked at her watch. "We had better get back in there. My dreams are over!"

"You'll figure out what to do. Just believe that you will."

Brandi grabbed her books and walked toward the lecture hall. "There's no solution to this problem."

"You're not going to see him after sharing a night with the only man you seem to care about?"

"He made it clear that night that it was a one-time thing."

"And you were okay with that?"

"I had to be."

"But if you like him . . ."

"I just said what could happen!"

"So you're going to sit there day after day, remembering what you two did and not even try to make anything else happen?"

"Yep."

"Have you changed that much?"

"Again, yep. I can't ruin things for both of us, and apparently I can't trust him, anyway."

"I think it's because he's white. Your attraction to a white man scares you. You don't want it out of the closet."

"That's not it! He was white the other night, and I wasn't scared then."

"I just don't get what the urgency is."

"Things have changed. Despite knowing what's in his pants, I still have to get an education from him."

"Sure wish I could experience what's in his pants because he's fine as hell, girl! You're lucky."

"Glad someone thinks so; I sure don't."

Tim had completed his course overview and was announcing the scholarship recipients when Brandi and Tiffany walked back in. Brandi and Tim's eyes locked briefly and his mind kicked into maximum overdrive. *Please tell me this is not Brandi Miles.* The other name on his list of recipients was Joseph Drake; surely, that name didn't match that lovely face. He looked at the name again. *This can't be happening to me.* He squared his shoulders, trying to keep what little composure he had left. "Are you Brandi Miles?"

"Yes." She stood frozen in her tracks. Tiffany had to force her into her seat. She stared at him open-mouthed, unaware of everything in the room other than the man talking to her. His voice was so real to her, as if she had heard it just the night before. He was impressive, memorable. She could still feel him making love to her as no man ever had. How his body moved through hers with powerful force. *He would be the one, wouldn't he?*

Tim forced himself to look back at the paper in his hand. Yes, there was a red star next to her name. He cleared his throat. "Welcome to Madison Tech, and congratulations on the Seymour Scholarship."

Brandi felt hyperconscious of herself and her surroundings, as if everyone knew what she had done with him. She knew she was being paranoid. People were looking at her because it took mega brains to even apply for that scholarship, let alone win it. She knew he was aware of her intelligence based on their conversation that night. However, she hadn't mentioned her schooling, and he had failed to inquire. Turns out to have been a bad move for both of them.

Throughout his lecture, his eyes came back to hers. Something that was normally so easy for him, such as teaching sophomore composition, suddenly was not very easy at all. He wanted to get out of there and never return. The fact that he was paid handsomely kept him there. Now Brandi would keep him there. He didn't like the idea of having slept with a student, but couldn't change it. His only recourse was to pray that it would stay between them.

Keeping his mind on track and away from the beautiful, five foot seven-inch, slender natural brunette who had rocked his world was the only ticket to his sanity. Continuing his lecture on 16th-century authors, he wrote several names on the board then turned to the students. "I've listed a few names for you. This is an easy question for anyone who has read the first two chapters. I've also given you some clues as to the major authors of this time period, but some names have been left off. These are the prominent ones for this century, and you should know all. I need a volunteer to come to the board and fill in the rest. If you know, raise your hand. Reading the first chapter was a requirement, not an option, as indicated in your syllabus." Arms raised high as he scanned the room. Brandi's was one of them. He knew she could answer the question; after all, she had won the Seymour, but he was reluctant to call on her. She kept her hand up and he caved. "Yes, Miss Miles?

"I can do that, Dr. Polaris."

Tiffany whispered in disbelief. "After all that crap you and I went through in the hall, now you decide to get all up in his face?"

"I know the answer, Tiff, that's all."

"Please come up and fill in the missing authors, Miss Miles. Remember this is for 16th century, not the following one. The next few chapters are on this century as well. It's a hard chapter to follow. It's like a chapter within a chapter, if that makes any sense."

She remembered how direct he was, the type who usually got what he wanted, at least for the night she was with him. However, she was quite sure that he hadn't *wanted* her showing up in his class after what they had done together. She felt skittish as she approached him, as if he might bite.

Nonetheless, she knew the answers and wasn't going to let anyone or anything get in the way of the A she knew she had to get. She took the chalk from his hands and filled in the correct answers, sensing his closeness, smelling his Burberry's Classic after-shave. He smelled like sex, wonderful sex, incredible sex, and it was making her mind race. She just wanted to finish and get away from him as quickly as possible before her body language betrayed her. There was still one answer, and he expected it from her.

As Brandi worked, he secretly eyed every caramel inch of her frame. Yes, she was definitely the one from the club; sensual, flawless complexion, like honey-butter and just as soft. Her small frame fit perfectly against him and he remembered craving every minute with her. It was a body worth dumping his 'no women allowed beyond sexual contact' mission statement. Almost. It was the relationship part that wasn't allowed. And Brandi Miles looked like a relationship waiting to happen. When he came back to reality, Brandi was almost finished filling in a wrong answer.

He took the chalk from her shaking, sweating hand, and filled in the correct name of the missing author. "This is excellent. You've got Anne Bradstreet, 1612–1672, Roger Williams, 1603–1683, Robert Beverly, 1673–1722, Daniel Defoe, 1660–1731, my personal favorite. You missed Mary Rowlandson, 1635–1678. Very good, though, Miss Miles. You were closer than expected with the correct response. I'm glad to see you involved, and remembered the women. They were very important during this era, an almost beginning to the women's movement. Now I know why you received the Seymour."

When Brandi returned to her seat, Tiffany whispered in her ear. "You belong to him, and you know it."

"Drop it. Yes, Polaris is very sexy, but he's also very off-limits, as you well know."

"Fine. It's dropped for now, but I know you won't be able to leave it alone. I've known you since eighth grade, remember?"

"Tiffany, please."

"Okay, I'll cut you some slack." They were both silent for a few seconds, but Tiffany couldn't let anything rest. She kept on in a sly undertone. "I didn't know you knew those authors the way you do. He likes smart women."

"Didn't you hear him? I *should* know what I'm doing in here. I received the Seymour, after all. Besides, how do you know he likes smart woman?"

"He told me."

Brandi teased. "If he likes you for being smart then he should love me."

"He does love you. Know what I'm saying?"

"Yes."

Brandi spent the rest of the class trying to avoid looking at him, but he was so beautiful, so interesting. He made even the dullest of English lit fascinating. He was enthusiastic about it, born to teach it, and to make sure his students appreciated it as he did. For those reasons as well, Brandi couldn't take her eyes from him; he was the most exciting instructor she had ever seen.

After class, Tiffany pulled Brandi's sleeve. "You were mesmerized by him. You seemed to be in a trance over even the dullest of parts."

"It's not dull with him."

"Yes, and for obvious reasons."

"I don't mean that."

"I know what you're saying; he is very good. He even has me lit up. So, you going up to talk to him, or is that brain of yours still on lockdown over 'the situation' you're in?"

"Are you kidding? I can't go up to him about that! Both he and I know what we did that night, and it's a sticky situation."

"You need to get over that and talk to him. He's a man, not a boy, Brandi. He understands how the world works. Besides, if you talk to him, you could clear everything up."

"Yeah, maybe, but it won't be easy. This man saw me naked, for Christ's sake. He saw every inch of me, and now I have to act as if nothing happened? How can I do that? I don't know how to get out of a man's bed one day and pretend nothing happened the next. I'm used to relationships."

"Then have one with him and get it done. I wish that were my only problem." She nodded in Tim's direction. "Look at him, Brandi. Women crawling all over him, but he keeps looking over here at you. You could at least talk to the guy."

"Okay, okay, I'll talk to him, but only because you may fall apart if I don't." Clearing the air with him was a good idea. But it took Tiffany to make her do it.

CHAPTER 2

After the entourage of women left, Brandi approached him, reminding herself that Tiffany was right about clearing the air. She cleared her throat. "Dr. Polaris?"

Without looking up, he responded, not knowing exactly know what to say. He quickly got his head together. "Yes, Miss Miles? What can I help you with?"

"I need to talk to you."

"I know you do." He stood to greet her, lightly resting his hands on his slender hips. "Both of us need to talk about some rather serious circumstances." He looked at the clock, then back to her. "Now is not a good time."

Her thought processes were a jumble as she looked at him. "I can't believe this is you in here."

"Neither can I. This really took me off-guard . . . the last thing I expected this morning."

"I understand. What time can I come back today?"

"After class is good; I have a prep period at three. Is that a good time for you?"

"Sure. I'll be getting out of physics and can head right over."

He moved a little closer to her, so close that she could see the tiny laugh lines at the corners of his mouth. The dimness of the nightclub had hidden just how good looking he was. Looking at him in the light of day, she saw that he was beautiful, but wrong for her in every conceivable way.

His voice brought her back. "Well, then, is there anything else?"

"No, nothing that can't wait."

"Then I'll see you. I need to finish this coffee. I have a sudden need for extreme caffeine." He sat back and picked up a stack of forms.

Directness seemed to be his preferred approach. When he ended things, he really ended them. They had their fun then it was gone. Just like that, just like now.

There was a bandage on the side of his forehead. It seemed like a trademark, and it was a sexy one, a bad boy's. She walked to the door without mentioning it.

"Brandi, our time together a month ago was out of this world, for lack of a better term. I just wanted you to know that."

"It certainly was, Dr. Polaris. God, I've gotten so used to calling you Jacob. I don't even know what to call you now."

"For our purposes it should be Dr. Polaris."

"That'll be hard since I know you as Jacob."

His eyes shifted a bit. "I am sorry about that but . . ."

"I'm sure I can handle saying Dr. Polaris, but it's your trademark that gave you away today. I wasn't going to mention it, but . . ."

"Trademark?"

"The bandage. How did you get that bump on your head?"

"Someone pulled a costly move last night."

"And, as usual, you took care of him, right?"

"How do you know that?"

"Remember, you and I talked about it after we danced? I asked you what happened." She started smiling.

Becoming more and more bewitched, he added, "And . . . ?"

"You said the same thing, that someone pulled a costly move."

"That's my stock answer."

"I see that now." She slung her book bag across her shoulders. "I guess I'll be back by three."

"Yes, I suppose you will, Miss Miles." He watched her walk out, remembering their evening, how he kissed her, how incredible she tasted—like the sweetest of wine, and how much he knew he liked her. She was both smart and dazzling, attributes he had never experienced with just one woman. He hadn't expected that dazzling woman to greet him in English Comp. He moved the pile of papers aside, feeling a migraine coming on. He hoped the rest of the semester wouldn't go as badly as the first day of class.

The cafeteria doors opened and Tim walked out carrying two cups of coffee and a bagel. Her eyes followed the sexy young man with light-brown hair that shined golden highlights who had made her night two weeks ago seem magical. Jacob didn't exist, and who was left in his place? A man she really didn't know and wasn't sure that she had wanted to know, despite the fact that she adored him beyond reason. But who was he, really? She didn't know the answer. She now thought she should have had some clue before sleeping with him. Everyone makes mistakes on occasion, not to say that he was a mistake. However, he sure as hell was going to find out who *she* was.

It was 2:55. She had decided to give him a little time to drink his coffee to get composed before she traipsed in there lowering a bomb on him. At exactly 3 o'clock, she walked in. "Dr. Polaris you said it was okay to . . ."

He hadn't looked up, but knew her voice. He had hoped she would get skittish about the meeting and decide to not come, yet there she was. He looked up putting on the best smile he could muster. "Sure, Miss Miles, come in. Just finishing a little lunch; I hardly get a chance to have anything on the first day."

"Coffee and a bagel is lunch?"

"It is today." He wiped the whipped cream off his hands. "Now. To the matter at hand. Please have a seat."

While he finished the last of his bagel, she sneaked a look at him. Few men were considered pretty to her, but he was at the top of the list. Woman could fall for him solely on the basis of his looks. He looked rich, too, as if he had been born with a tennis racket in his hand and a lake in his backyard. She had definitely fallen victim to Timothy Polaris's looks and charms.

He finished one cup of coffee and lifted the lid from the other. "One thing puzzles me, Miss Miles."

"What would that be, other than my behavior on July twenty-third? By the way, that was not really me."

"I don't mean that. I didn't have a bandage on the night I was with you. How do you know about this bad-boy image I seem to have?"

"You told me. I thought you were a contractor. They often get hurt on the job. I didn't know you were a professor."

"I know you didn't."

"I assumed Timothy Polaris would be like all the other instructors here, older and ordinary looking."

"Is that how college professors are supposed to look?"

"Apparently not all of them; there was a bandage that night. You probably forgot."

"Really? Where?"

"Your lower left hip. I saw it when you stripped for me."

"Indeed, you're right, and it was fun, lots of fun. I get in jams often, Miss Miles. I take hits everywhere, it seems. The Entrapment has turned out to be the biggest jam yet. Not that you were a mistake but . . ."

"That's the main reason I'm here. As I said before, the woman you were with that night really wasn't me. I don't make it a habit of going home with strange young men."

"I liked who she was. She was intriguing, extremely beautiful. But you're right, smart women don't normally do that. I could have been anyone, and you could be dead by now."

"But you're not just anyone, are you?"

"Apparently not."

"That night wasn't my smartest moment. I wanted you to know that I . . . I was out of sorts, getting rid of a boyfriend who was holding me back, getting the scholarship. I was celebrating everything, it seemed. Then I got crazy. I saw you, well, you know the rest."

"I do, and as I said, I enjoyed your company very much; however, if you're here to further this relationship, then I'm afraid I'll have to decline, despite the fact that I don't want to. My habits have a way of running away with me." He moved in closer to her. "Brandi, this could get both you and me into some serious trouble. What I do with my nightlife has never gotten me in hot water, but this was close. You understand?"

"I agree. What I . . . we did was foolish. Winning the Seymour Scholarship has been my goal since I learned about it. As you well know, it's hard to get and easy to lose."

"I'm well aware of the Byron Seymour Scholarship. You had to have been on your toes to have won it."

"I'm the first African-American woman to get it, and the fact that I might have done something to jeopardize my keeping it scares me."

"Losing it for any reason would be devastating."

"I just wanted to clear things up with you so you wouldn't think that I was just some stupid girl chasing after you. I want to further my education, so you really don't have to worry about me trying to make trouble for you."

"That's good to know."

She couldn't help but smile. "I hate to admit this to you, but no man has ever made me feel that wonderful, that feminine. It was glorious. You took me to paradise, and I didn't want to return. I've never known anyone like you, and I do cherish that."

"Indeed, it was paradise. I don't regret being with you that night either, despite where I work."

"My body still shivers at the thought of you." She watched as he rolled his sleeves to the elbow, exposing hints of those well-muscled arms that had held her close that night. The way his eyes had looked so deeply into hers made her want him that much more, again and again. He was perfect, almost.

"You were like no other woman, Brandi. It took me a half-hour to get the nerve to approach you. When I saw you dancing, all I wanted was for you to dance with me, under me, on me, all night, all morning. I never thought you would be here with me now. It scared me when I saw you in class today."

She wanted to approach him to say something to make him feel better about the situation, but knew it would not solve anything, only would make matters worse. If Timothy Polaris were to touch her one more time, she would give into feelings she knew could ruin them both. "I would never tell on you, never. I promise you that. But why did you have to lie about being someone else? I don't think that was necessary."

"It was necessary. Saving my ass around here is always necessary. As I said before, my nightlife has not caught up with me until now. Madison probably doesn't give a good damn what I do at night. Bringing students home and having something go wrong in a relationship—well, that could cost the university. Could be a scandal if it's the wrong student."

"I'm not the wrong student."

"I'm not saying you are. My point is that it takes a lot to get a teaching position here. Also, I didn't graduate Princeton with two degrees at the age of twenty-three to have my career go down the toilet over an affair."

Cool words, Mr. Tim. I'm sure I feel on top of the world now! She suppressed hurt feelings his words caused. "Believe me, I understand what you're saying. I feel the same way."

"It's hard to stop doing something you've been doing for years. I lost my marriage . . ." Bringing up his crappy past life was painful to hear . . . and inappropriate. He sat on the corner of his desk. "The fact of the matter is this: My life is my life, Miss Miles, and . . ."

"You may call me Brandi."

"Fine, but not in front of anyone. There are things that just can't end overnight, Brandi, although they should."

She had gathered something about an ex-wife from his conversation that night. But asking him what happened in that marriage could turn him off even more, causing him to think she was trying to get to him somehow. That she didn't need.

"I believe you won't cause a ruckus, Brandi, so don't worry." He sat back, and stared at her. "Both times you've entered my life when I least expected it. Had I only known the other night . . ."

"You wouldn't have slept with me, right?"

"Right."

"I wanted to be with you. Only that night you weren't Timothy Polaris, were you?"

"On any given night, I have no idea who I am."

"I know who you are now, and I really like him. I liked 'Jacob', too. He was sweet to me."

"That's the only way to behave around a woman." She was definitely a woman to him, but a very unwelcome woman. At that very minute, his only thought was to take her back into his arms and finish what was cut all too short. Her eyes said that she was feeling the same way. He couldn't do that to a student. He worked to give students his best, and that's what he wanted to give her. Suddenly he felt he couldn't live up to the job—suffering from want of her. He took her delicate hand into his. "Look, Brandi, we really shouldn't discuss this anymore. I can't be with you because relationships and I don't work."

"I can say this: It'll be hard looking at you and realizing we can't, shouldn't, be together."

"You're sweet. I knew that the minute I met you."

A knock at the door startled them, and they both turned see a beautiful Asian woman entering. Tim immediately released Brandi's hand and stood, smiling. "Hey, Monica, I didn't know you were in." He turned to Brandi and introduced the slender woman to his troubling student.

"Monica, this is Miss Miles. She's the recipient of this year's Bryon Seymour Scholarship."

Monica Shang extended her hand, looking curiously from Brandi to Tim. "So, you're the one. Congratulations, that's a prestigious scholarship."

"Thank you, I worked hard."

"I'm sure." She returned to Tim. "I didn't mean to break in on anything."

"You didn't."

Brandi looked at him, wondering if everything they had discussed was just idle conversation.

Monica continued. "I'll leave you two alone. But Tim, I need the contract for the spring trip to Niagara Falls. We'll want to get to work on getting that trip under way early. You know how that fills up."

"Sure. Five minutes. Miss Miles and I are about done."

"Fine. It was nice to have met you, Miss Miles." Then she left, turning so fast that her long dark hair bounced against her face.

Brandi's attention returned to Tim. "Co-worker?"

"Yeah."

"She likes you."

"Not a chance."

"She does. Take my word for it."

"She should like me. I sign her extra-credit reports."

"I don't mean that way."

He sat back down, feeling aggravated by her suggestion. "No. She's engaged."

"Whatever, but she likes you the way I do. Face it." She collected her book bag. "I should go, you've still got lots to do, I'm sure. I'm glad we had this because I don't need anything distracting me from my work here. But if anything could, it would be you."

Tim just stared at her, not really knowing how to respond, except to issue his usual invitation to his students. "I'll be around if you need any help with my class."

"Good, because I know I'll need help in your class. I'm great with writing, but bad with focus sometimes."

"That happens."

"Not for you. I know you've won literary awards awards. Maybe you could help me with my writing. I'm actually better in math, if you can believe that."

"Anytime, Brandi; just call my office or come by."

She left feeling better about the situation, but still sick over the fact that her loving *Jacob* was now a memory.

Tim relaxed, but did not feel good about their meeting. He still wanted her, but didn't know why. He and relationships were done, but he also knew she was way more than a one-night stand; they now shared a past, an enjoyable one, and he appreciated her intelligence. He loved how she truly made him feel like a man in bed, but it was over. She was his student. Remembering how lovely she looked in that yellow tank-dress made him regret being her teacher.

He sat there thinking about his failed relationships, and about why they were painful to him. His ex-wife, Charlotte, gave him the most horrible four years of his life. His family life as a child had been a nonstop nightmare. This was usually brought on by thoughts of his brother, whom he hadn't seen in years. This time Greg wasn't the cause, although they'd been at odds forever it seemed. He still didn't know why because what happened really wasn't his or Greg's fault. Opening that can of worms was something he avoided at all costs. All he knew was that if he didn't keep his protective shell in, he would go mad in no time.

Brandi had just gotten behind the wheel of her Escort when she heard Eric calling her. She thought she had seen the last of him a month ago when he, in his fake-sincere voice, pleaded with her to return to him. Instead of taking off, as she was tempted to do, she decided to hear him out one last time, hoping he would have something honest and civil to say, though she knew that was a pipedream.

She stared up at him through the half rolled-up window, afraid to roll it all the way down. Knowing him, he was likely to try to reach inside and grab what was no longer his. "Eric, what do you want?"

He wiped his sweaty brow. "Man, running after you these days is some feat."

"Again, what do you want with me, Eric?"

"Just to talk."

"I know what your conversations are about lately: nothing! I frankly don't have time for it today, and I've got to pick up the rest of my books. So, if you don't mind . . ."

"I do mind. Brandi, I just want to talk."

"I had a feeling." She laid her backpack on the opposite seat. "Look, this hasn't been a banner day for me, and I don't need you making it any worse."

"We can't end like this. I've invested too much time in this relationship for you to leave it."

"There it is again. It's always about you, isn't it? What about me? The only thing you invested in the relationship was laziness, infidelity, and lack of commitment—three things I can't stand. Now you want to talk! I don't think so, not this day, not any day. I'm gone." She started to raise the window, but he grabbed it.

"Brandi, please."

"Don't *Brandi, please,* me. I've had it with you. Go and talk to Stacey Neal. Wasn't she the one crawling all over you, practically in front of my face? I've been going through the motions pretending you and I were happy, and I have figured out why I stayed with you—to please everyone but myself. You and Stacey were stabbing me in the back the entire time. I was the stupid one still trying to make it work. I must have looked like a complete fool to everyone. I sure feel like one now."

"Will you stop for a minute? I'm sorry, okay? I knew I was wrong, but it just happened. You know how Stacey can be."

"Don't you dare blame her alone. You were a willing participant. She was my friend, Eric. How could you have done that to me?" She cranked the engine. "Leave me alone. Go on with your life as I have."

"She's the one who kept after me. I didn't force her. Can't you just give me another chance?"

"I've cursed her out already. Is it your turn now?" She turned up her CD player, hoping the singer's voice would drown out his. She could still hear him talking as she drove off. His dull voice echoed in her head. "Brandi, please, let me make it up to you."

How many times in the past had he screwed up, and she had forgiven him? Too many times, and this was it! Eric was actually the last man on her mind. What haunted her was not being able to be with a man she found absolutely incredible—Timothy Polaris. The time they were together, he treated her as no man ever had, but he could be the ruin of her scholastic ambitions. *For the sake of a career, I have to give up the man I've dreamed about. That sucks big time!* Tears ran down her cheek. Tim would never be hers; he wouldn't allow it. Neither would society because of his race. Trusting another man after Eric would also be hard. It was mostly a color game, but the outcome seemed all black!

Even a cool shower couldn't relax her, and an unusually hot autumn in New York didn't help. She fanned her face, but couldn't decide if her flushed appearance was due to Eric or to Tim. The latter seemed the likely cause. But he was clearly a no-no in her life.

Her father called her from downstairs. She knew he had been worrying all day at the police station about how his *baby girl's* first day had gone. She didn't know why she had moved back into her parent's house from NYU's dorm to save money for school in the first place. Her parents meant well, but her whole life was changing in ways they could never understand. They still saw her as a teen who was hog-wild over Eric, failing to see her as a grown-up.

"Up here, Dad."

He poked his head through her bedroom door, a wondering expression on his face. Finally he said it. "Well?"

She had no appetite for talking about her less-than-perfect day at Madison. She took a deep breath. "Madison was okay. I know that's what you're getting at."

"Just okay?"

"It was a drag, but I know it will get better. It just didn't start out the way I thought it would."

He walked over to her and began massaging her shoulders. "Madison is the only thing you've ever thought about as far as school is concerned."

Now the names 'Jacob' and Timothy Polaris were the only things on her mind; he was the man who opened her eyes to the real world. Suddenly, the world wasn't a pretty picture anymore.

To ease his mind, she spoke up and fixed the problem he had assumed she had with Madison. It was not the school it was the man there teaching English Comp 812. "Dad, Madison is fine. It's the books. They'll cost a fortune."

He kissed her cheek like the princess he thought she was. "Is that all it is? Baby, we'll get the books. Money is not a problem because your old man is police . . ."

"I know, Queens' chief of police."

"This Saturday we'll make a day of it, just you and I. We'll get the books, then go for your favorite, seafood pizza."

"I'm dieting."

"How can someone who wears a size six be on a diet?"

Even she had to smile at that one. "Okay, one slice, but that's it."

He walked to the door, pausing with a questioning look on his face. His reflection was in her mirror. "Are you okay, Dad?"

"Yes, but I still need to talk to you about something."

"Sure."

"It's about Eric."

She retrieved the brush. "Dead subject. Your words normally enlighten me. Why now are you bringing him up? I would just as soon puke."

"I know you would, and I sincerely understand. It took all the power I have not to kill him."

"Then why are we still discussing him? You aren't suggesting that he and I start seeing one another again, are you?"

He sat down on the bed. "Why would I want that for you? A man who sleeps around on my daughter has no place in my house or my life. But as you know, his father and I are good friends. Peter feels really bad about this, but he's worried about his son, too."

"What for? They know he's a louse. They raised him."

"True, but Peter sees what this break-up has done to Eric. He mopes around, hardly goes out. He's basically depressed."

"Then he should find comfort in the loving arms of Stacey Neal, as he has done many times before."

"I understand, Brandi, but can you be civil to him?"

"Come on! Is this what you want?"

"I want you to do what you think is best. I told Peter that I would run it by you and see how you feel about it. Look, baby, I'm not asking you to do it if you don't want to. He messed up royally, and the only reason his back is not broken is because his father begged me not to do it. Peter and I go way back, before you and Eric were even thought of. We don't want strife between the families."

She couldn't help but smile. *Strife between the families?* "This sounds like *The Godfather*! I don't know about this. He really took advantage of me, made me feel like a fool. I feel bad for him, but he messed up, not me. I like Mr. Fontaine, but this is a little too much to ask. I've gone on without Eric."

"Is there anyone else?"

"There was, but he and I aren't seeing each other anymore."

"Who was he? Do we know him?"

"No. He's white, and I know how you feel about me dating other races."

"Brandi, now wait a minute . . .

"Isn't that true? Had I brought him around here, you would have burned the house down to get rid of him. Besides, *he's not into relationships,* or so he says."

"Nothing is wrong with staying within your own race, Brandi. Is it so bad to want that?"

"No, but it is wrong to practice racism. I just can't understand how you can work in that station with cops of all races knowing how you feel about them."

"We work well together, and they don't come into my house to date my daughter."

His statement angered her, even though she had heard it before. "Dad, I love you, but that's backwards."

He wondered what was wrong with his baby girl. She had never bucked him before. "Brandi, who was this man you didn't want to bring around here?"

"Just a guy; a guy who liked me and I liked him. It didn't last long." She knew they could never have a relationship even if she transferred back to NYU. He had made his point very clear.

Her father had not given up. "I only want what's best for you. I don't want you with Eric. Despite the fact that I would prefer you date black men, I know you will do whatever you want to do—you always did." He kissed her forehead. "At least be civil to Eric when he's around. Can you do that for me?"

"Okay, okay, whatever." All along, she knew she and Eric were 'not happening'. Same for her and Tim.

The following Tuesday, Eric showed up in Tim's lecture hall and took a seat behind Brandi and Tiffany. He put his books on the floor and nudged Brandi. "Hope I haven't missed too much of his lecture."

She thought her eyes had deceived her. She caught herself staring at him. "Eric, what the heck are you doing here?"

"Can't a guy get signed into class without someone getting suspicious?"

"Yeah, but not if it involves you."

"I've got to get back in school, Brandi. I can't sit in the house all day."

Tiffany interrupted. "Shut up, for crying out loud! I can't concentrate on dream boy with you two going at it. You want him to put you out?" She glanced at Brandi. "Yes, he would put you out, too, if he had to. We have a test coming up and I plan to do well, both of you cool it."

Realizing Tiffany was right, Brandi turned to Eric. "Since you are almost two weeks late, the least you can do is shut up and listen to the guy."

Eric whispered in Brandi's ear. "I'm sure you and Tiffany have cornered the market listening to him. I can see drool on your desks."

"Do I need to move?"

"Sure, get closer to him. Isn't that what you want, anyway?"

At that, she grabbed her books and moved down a few aisles. Tiffany looked at Eric. "Happy now?"

"Maybe." His heart did not feel happy that Brandi moved, but he did not follow her. Instead, he glared at Tim, who seemed to have captivated everyone but him.

CHAPTER 3

Brandi and Tim exchanged glances during class, but nothing more. Every time she looked into his honey-colored eyes, she felt herself melting, remembering how they were together. They seemed like a perfect match. Yes, Tim had it together with a great career, looks, and probably a ton of money to go with that career. But he was still a man, and the men in her life were known to fabricate things. She wanted to trust him, but the *Jacob* issue was still that—an issue.

She had wanted many times to talk to him after class, discuss how she was hurt by his name pretense, even though she understood his reasons. But she didn't. Things were already bad enough, no need to make matters worse. She had stayed clear of him, fearing that being close to him would send her into orbit. Each day she practically ran from his class to avoid confronting him. Friends noticed her unwillingness to hang around after class and questioned her about it. Her only response would be, "I hate being late to class, and you know my other courses are across campus." It was a cop-out and they knew it. So did she, but it had to suffice for as long as her excuses sounded faintly plausible.

For Tim, his problem wasn't that Brandi was African-American—she was desirable to him no matter what, but he had to avoid her. He would not go out of his way to see her, but her in his presence every Tuesday and Thursday caused him to treasure those days. She always sat in one of the last rows in the lecture hall. He knew why—avoidance. He had to live with it, and given his history with relationships, he wasn't about to subject her, or anyone else he cared about, to the kind of life he had led for so long. He had to see her, though, and on *that* day.

Time was up and Brandi, as usual, tried rushing past him to get away, but she had a test to turn in. Eric was headed her way and she quickly got in line despite the dread she felt. Eric caught up with her. "Did you pass the test on your own, or did your Mr. Tim help?"

"Take a hike, Eric. How well did you do, since you've been in here only a week?"

"I can handle pretty boy's tests. Let's get something to eat. I'm hungry."

"Go alone. I've got things to do."

"Like what, him?"

"Could be." She walked off and caught up with Tiffany, leaving Eric at the back of the line.

That day, she was destined to see him because no way was he going to take that exam from her without saying something to her; she knew him too well for that.

Others were ahead of her. She could see him calculating how long it would take her to get to him. She had always been one to face up to reality. She couldn't survive the remainder of the course without speaking to him. He would surely notice if she gave her exam to someone else to turn in. He would get to her later no matter what. That's how professional he was.

Before Tiffany turned in her exam, she glanced at Brandi. "I know what you're doing by letting everyone ahead of you. It's about time you faced him."

"Am I that transparent?"

"In a word, yes; even he knows it."

"Just turn around and give him the paper, Tiffany. You see his hand reaching around whoever that is in front of you."

"Should I wait in the hall for you, or do you plan on spending the honeymoon in here with him?"

"I swear, if you embarrass me . . ."

Tiffany turned away from her, smiling into Tim's face. "And how are you today, Dr. Polaris?"

"I'm great, thanks. Yourself?"

She looked back at Brandi then answered, "Peachy, just peachy; glad the exam is finished, though. I'm sure I didn't do as well as *others,*" casting a glance at her cringing friend.

Brandi rolled her eyes. *I hate her!*

"I'm sure you did quite well, Miss Jackson." He reached around for Brandi's exam. Tiffany moved on, winking at her as she left the room.

Brandi placed the two-page written exam on 17th century authors into his hand, and glanced around the room. "Hello, Dr. Polaris."

"Hello yourself, stranger. How are things?"

"Busy."

"I've noticed you haven't taken time to say anything to me after class. Is everything all right?"

"Sure."

He looked at her, clearly not believing her.

"Really, I'm fine; just lots of work to do."

"Madison will keep you busy, and now with the Seymour, you really have to stay on top of your class load."

"Right, an A-B average is hard to maintain."

"Exactly! That's why I wasn't happy with that C paper you turned in last week." He took the last few papers and waited for them to leave.

"Tell me about it. I wasn't happy, either."

"I think you could benefit from tutoring, at least temporarily."

She put her books on his table. "I am being tutored."

"By whom?"

"One of the student teachers working in Crosby Hall."

"There's a great tutorial lab in the Mathaei building. Brian Douglas runs it. Miss Shang helps at times. He would be glad to help. Why didn't you come to me about this before writing the paper?"

Because the very idea of you puts me in meltdown. "You've got your own stuff to deal with."

"Yes, but I told you to come to me if you needed help. I think there are other reasons you didn't come to me. Am I right?"

That was the truth, but she wasn't in the mood to deal with it, so she lied. "Really, I've just been so bogged down with other things that I . . ."

"You can't let that C stay on your record."

Passing his class was a must, and she needed him to help her do it. Tim had won awards for his writing, and getting his help would be a small price to pay. Sitting next to him and concentrating on things other than sex would be her cross to bear.

"I'm just not interested in 17th century literature. Do you think you could give me some pointers?"

"You've got me; I've told you that before. I also know that you'd rather not be around me."

"No, the problem is that I do want to be around you. I need the help, though, and you can give it. I don't know how to write a good paper on that subject."

"Your problem is focus, maybe a little lack of interest. You picked a good subject, but you didn't fully explore it, manipulate it, make it work for you. I can show you how to do that despite how boring you may think it is."

Indeed, you can, Timothy. Even his words were provocative to her. He managed to use the very words that made everything on her stand to attention. She needed his help, but wanted his passion. "I'm good with punctuation and all."

"And you'll become good with the rest of it. Trust yourself. Trust me."

"That's also hard to do." *In more ways than one.*

"You have to do this and do it well. It's a core minor that you had to select in order to pass into the advanced lit department. Do you want my help?"

"Do you think we can . . . should?"

He moved closer to her, lowering his voice even though the door was closed. "Brandi, listen to me. Both you and I know that we can't let anything get in the way of my career or your education. Yes, I still like you, and I still remember what we did. That will never be forgotten because it was incredible. It's over, though, and I know you have self-control because you've shown it to me the last three weeks."

"I know, but . . ."

"There are no buts, Brandi. Either we do this or we don't. I would like to help you. That grade can't stay there. You're too smart, and I know you can do the work. The Seymour is not easy to get, and it's not easy to keep. I would hate to see you lose it when I can prevent that . . . if you'll let me."

She looked sincerely into his eyes. "You're right."

"I'm free this afternoon. Thursdays are my light days, if you can call four classes a light day." He smiled, crossed his arms across his chest. "So, how 'bout it?"

"I would like that. But I already have the bad grade. What about that?"

"We'll start from this point just this once."

"And you'll drop the C?"

"Yes. You'll redo it with my help and go from there. Is today good for you?"

"What time? I have a lecture at three."

"Then come after that. Say at five?"

"That's workable. I have such a heavy load, and it's hard to juggle everything."

"You can do the paper; you're smart enough to redo it in a timely fashion. That C was just a lapse. For the most part your paper was okay. Fine-tuning and a little more interest will help you a great deal." He walked her to the door. "Bring the thesis statement. We can work with that. Come to my office in Fischer, and Brandi, don't get into a jam again and not tell anyone. If I can help you, you know I will."

"I sure need it, in more ways than one."

After letting her out, he leaned against the door. *God! Tutoring her. How deep into this mess am I going to sink?* He wiped the perspiration off his forehead and tried to get the most beautiful woman he had ever seen off his mind. He knew it would be hard, and would be until she graduated. He didn't know if he could take putting her off for that long. A relationship was out of the question, but he knew he had to have her—somehow!

Tim's last lecture for the day was across from his office in the Fischer complex. She arrived early and decided to wait at the door near his office. But the heat was stifling in the hallway. So she decided to find in an empty chair in his lecture room and wait there. She looked inside; he still hadn't dismissed his English theory class. The heat from the inside of the room hit her. It was fierce, despite the air conditioning, which apparently was not working at peak capacity. She braved it like the rest did and took a seat in a corner to wait out the last ten minutes.

Tim was working at the board when he saw her from the corner of his eye. She had kept her word, but he was uncomfortable with fact that he would be alone with her. The last thing he needed was temptation. He knew he was weak . . . weak for her, but he had stay at a safe distance matter what was put in front of him.

He watched briefly as she relaxed in her seat. Her tight-fitting ivory skirt was just above her knee. With each move she made, the skirt rose higher, exposing some of what he had witnessed. He was losing it. His eyes darted from the clock to her. She was a walking dream that he needed to be near—but a dream with a mind that intrigued him even more because he loved smart women. A white silk blouse clung to her; her sleeves were rolled up, exposing more of her skin. The things a smoldering autumn did to a woman's clothing.

For Brandi, time moved just as slowly. The more she looked at how the hot breeze ruffled his shirt, the more she wanted him. His shirt had only two buttons undone as he tried to look as professional as possible in that heat. It was the kind of heat that would be followed by rain at any given moment.

Finally, class dismissed.

Once the last student had gone and the door closed, they stood facing each other in silence, trying to muster the strength and the nerve to be with one another.

"Sorry the session lasted longer than expected."

"No, I was early."

"Give me a minute to erase everything. I try to leave the lecture hall clean for the next instructor. Take a seat; I'll be right with you."

Her head dropped slightly. "Brandi, are you okay? You look a little out of it."

"I'm fine. It's this heat."

"I've never seen it this hot here in October. It's crazy. Can I get you some water or a Coke, something to cool you off?"

She walked to the chair near his desk. "Really, I'm okay."

"Let me just get this stuff off here, and we can go to my office. It's cooler there. By the way, did you remember to bring the thesis question?"

There was no response. He turned in time to see Brandi falling against the chair. He grabbed her and put her arm around his neck to steady her. "Brandi! Brandi! Come on, snap out of it."

She looked into his eyes; eyes that made her feel even more lightheaded.

"I should take you home. You can't drive like this. Here, sit down and let me get you something to drink."

"No, no, I'm fine. It's this heat. Besides, we have my paper to go over."

"Not today. You're not well. You need to go home."

Her body was limp; her head rested on her shoulder. He eased her into the chair, the scent of her hair filling his nostrils. Her body felt so good next to his, making him yearn for her. Once she was in the chair and appeared more, steady he took a bottle of water from his briefcase, handing it to her.

"Thank you. Can I just sit here for a moment?"

"As long as it takes; don't rush."

"I don't know what happened. I just felt so weak."

"Relax, and don't think about anything. Sometimes things like that happen, especially in this heat."

"I need to go. I'll take the water with me in case I feel weak again." She stood but stumbled back into his arms. Her eyes searched his as she stood erect. She felt his hands tighten around her waist, helping her to stand. Their faces were inches apart; her hand reached to stroke his cheek. His strong hand grasped hers. She could feel his heat, his strength, and wanted nothing less at that point than all of him.

He became a willing participant, moving closer to her, wanting to kiss her so badly he could actually taste her. Reality knocked. "Brandi, don't. We can't do this here, and you're weak from this heat anyway." He held her hand tighter, staring into her dark almond shaped eyes. A knock on the door shattered the moment.

Thank God! He backed away from her and managed a breathy, "Come in."

Eric came in waving a paper in his hand. "I forgot to give this to you, Dr. Polaris."

"I shouldn't take it. The test was due earlier today, Mr. Fontaine."

Eric smiled smugly, looking at Brandi as he handed the test to Tim. "Hey, Brandi. What's shakin'?"

"Hello, Eric."

Eric took his eyes off Brandi long enough to ask Tim about the test. "I've had so many things on my mind. I didn't mean to walk out with the test. Will you still grade it?"

"This time." He walked over to Brandi. "Drink the rest of the water, then maybe in a few minutes I can take you home."

Eric heard the exchange. "Did I interrupt something?"

"No, you didn't. We all need to get out of here."

Ignoring Tim, Eric walked over to Brandi. "Are you okay?"

She walked over to the door, Eric on her heels. "Yes, I'm fine. Dr. Polaris, thanks again for the water."

Tim followed behind her. "Are you sure you're okay to be leaving now?"

"Yes, the water helped. I think I was just really tired."

"I'm sorry about all of this, Miss Miles, but we can reschedule for tomorrow, same time."

"Could we?"

"Sure. What's another day? But you should go home and lie down. This heat is bad right now; you could get really sick. Have you had anything to eat?"

"Lunch earlier."

"You need more than that. It's almost five."

"He's right. I can walk you to your car, Brandi."

"I can do it alone, Eric. Thank you just the same."

"Maybe it's a good idea to let him walk you; if he doesn't, I will."

"I can do it, Dr. Polaris, thanks."

He watched Brandi walk out with Eric still on her heels. He sensed tension between them, but didn't know what it was all about. He grabbed his briefcase as Monica Shang came in.

"Tim, do you have time today to look over the book request form? We really need those for the writers retreat this spring."

"I know." He walked towards her. "I can look over it as we walk."

"Was . . . was that Brandi Miles I just saw?"

He answered without looking at her. "Yes. Why?"

"How's she doing with the Seymour?"

"Fine, as far as I can tell."

"I wasn't aware that she had this class."

He looked up from the paper he was scanning. "She doesn't. She's in trouble in my writers comp and asked for some suggestions."

"I could tutor her, since I oversee the tutorial lab. I would hate to see her fail."

"She's too smart to let that happen." He and Monica were walking down the corridor leading to the parking lot when they heard bickering. Normally the halls were filled with student chatter, but it was past four o'clock and he knew just about everyone was gone. He stopped dead in his tracks, thinking he had heard Brandi's voice.

"What's wrong, Tim?"

"Shhh . . . Something's going on. I had better see about it."

He and Monica turned the corner to see Brandi pressed against the wall; Eric was blocking her way. Tim cleared his voice.

They turned and saw Tim and Monica staring at them.

Tim eyed Brandi suspiciously. "Is everything okay, Miss Miles?"

At that, Eric dropped his hands and let her pass.

"Thank you. I'm fine now." She gave Eric a smug look and walked off.

He kept his eye on Brandi as she passed and headed for the parking lot. He glanced at Eric, who was giving Tim a hateful stare. Then he walked off.

Tim walked on with Monica at his side. "I should make sure she gets to her car. She was sick just moments ago."

"Good idea. Not many men would do that."

"I only want to make sure she doesn't have a relapse. Can I sign the papers in the morning?"

"Sure, we have a few more days, but I do want to get those in as soon as possible." Tim followed Brandi into the student parking lot, and saw her get into her car. He tapped on the window. "Brandi, I think I should follow you home."

"I'm not sick anymore. I can make it."

"Okay, if you're sure you can."

"I think I can."

"You think so? That's not good enough. Let me get in on the other side. You can take me to my truck in the faculty parking lot."

"That's really not necessary." She didn't want Timothy Polaris in her car, in a closed-up place, a tight-fitting place. It would be too tempting, but she could see he wasn't taking no for an answer and she reluctantly pulled the lock up on the other side.

He got in, fastened his seat belt. "I know this is highly irregular for a student to be driving a teacher around, but I'm concerned about you. Suppose you pass out while driving?"

"It won't happen."

"It could, and that's why I'm going to trail you home."

There was no bucking him. She did as told, and waited until he started his truck and pulled up behind her.

Brandi turned into her driveway and got out; he parked and walked her to the door. "I feel better now that you're home safely. You need to go in and rest. Take the rest of the evening off."

"What about going over my paper?"

"You can do that with me tomorrow. Now, will you go in and take it easy?"

This is not fair! He cares for me; he's polite, sensitive and gorgeous. Why can't I have him? She forced a smile for his benefit. "Sure, I'll go in and take it easy, but it'll be hard. I'm used to working on something, not lying in bed waiting for my parents or my brother to cater to me."

"I'm sure in this case you can manage." He looked at his watch. "I have to go."

Brandi watched him leave, holding back tears for as long as possible before running to her bedroom.

Tim realized he was getting in way too deep for his own good. He had never followed a student home. He hated the idea of falling for another woman, because it could only spell trouble. Frustrated, Tim couldn't wait to get back to the safety of his home in Queens Jamaica Estates district, far away from Brandi Elaine Miles.

Brandi couldn't even remember if she had turned the ignition off in her car. All she did after leaving Tim was collapse on her bed. Almost falling into his arms had made her examine her real reason for staying at Madison. Surely, the scholarship could be transferred to another school. Then there was Eric. She knew him, and he would stop at nothing to make her life hell. As she rubbed her tired eyes, her mother tapped on her bedroom door. "Brandi?"

"Yes, Mom?"

"Can I come in for a minute?"

All she had wanted to do was sleep, not answer any questions about her day. She dried her eyes, trying to look as normal as possible. "Sure, Mom."

Mrs. Miles immediately saw the pain on her child's face at once. "Brandi, have you been crying?"

"No. I don't feel well. I think it's the heat."

"The heat's never gotten to you before."

"Always a first time."

Mrs. Miles sat on the bed next to Brandi. "Okay, now tell me what's really wrong."

"Everything."

"Like what?"

"Eric finally showed up in class, and he's been a pain in my butt ever since then." Say anything to hide the real truth behind her tears.

"Maybe you're reading too much into this because of the problems you two have."

"He's a cad, and wants to further his education about as much as a drunken fool does. He's following me, keeping track of me, even though I broke it off with him over two months ago."

"With him sleeping around, I was glad you got rid of him. You deserve better."

"I know I do. We don't want the same things. I want a career and someone who doesn't cheat."

"That man is out there. Don't you want a career and a family?"

"Yes, but when the time is right. I don't want to run around with a baby in each arm, and chasing behind another. That's all he wants—someone to be a slave to him."

"I would hope your father and I raised you better than to settle for that."

"You did, and that's one of the main reasons I broke it off with him. There's too much that would drive us apart. I want someone who's going to be good to me, someone I can be good to and make a life with. I want someone who wants me the way I am, not the way he wants me to be." *I want Tim!*

"That's the thing I want you to strive for, Brandi. You don't have to take things from a man just for the sake of having one. You're worth more to yourself than that, aren't you?"

"You and Dad have always made me think that."

"That's what we want for you, and Brian also."

"I can take care of myself. I don't need a man to do that for me. But when the time is right, well, I would like to give my all." She wanted to give her all to Tim, but wasn't about to start that train of thought again and become depressed.

Mrs. Miles walked to the window. "Men are funny people. They don't see things the way women do. Just know that your father and I are on the same page as you on this Eric thing."

"I'm not going back to him, but Dad wants me to be civil to him to save he and Mr. Fontaine's relationship."

"Jeff doesn't want to make you do anything you don't want to do, but he and Peter have been friends forever. They're always in one another's face, either on the golf course or at the games. Nothing will break them up, not even Eric."

"I want to date other people, and Dad dislikes other races. I couldn't bring anyone here who is not black."

Mrs. Miles stared questioningly at her daughter. "Is there someone you're not telling me about?"

"I thought so, but now I'm not so sure."

Mrs. Miles moved closer to Brandi. "Who is he?"

"No one, Mom. Can we drop it?"

"No, apparently he's someone you want to be with, but aren't, for some reason."

"I didn't want to talk about him, but I suppose you can see him on my face. His name is Tim and he's . . . white, Mom. How could I have brought him around here with Dad being a racist and all?"

"Brandi, your Dad is not a racist."

"Really now? Then what would you call not tolerating your daughter dating a white man?"

"He had a hard time growing up around white people. He was the only black student in school until Theresa and I got there. Times were different for blacks back then."

"Not all white people are bad."

"No one race is all bad, Brandi. Your father's a hard nut to crack. Don't ask me why."

She eyed Brandi. "What's going on with this man you're interested in?"

"Nothing, and that's the problem. He didn't want to further the relationship. He had his reasons."

"Married?"

"No, just not into relationships, so he says. The thing is, he and I are not together either, and Eric and I are definitely through." She looked at the clock on her dresser. "It's getting late and I have studying to do."

"Are you sure you and this Tim guy are over?"

"As sure as I'm breathing. Take my word for it." She switched gears but ultimately left the conversation about Tim, one way or another. "Anyway, Dr. Polaris is going to help me redo my paper since he's a published author. I can get a better perspective from him."

"Good. Concentrate, do what he says, and you'll be fine. Dinner will be on shortly. You sure you're okay?"

"I'm fine."

"If you'd like to talk, you know where I am."

"I will. Thanks, Mom."

She watched her mother leave the room and then lay back on the bed. The last thing she wanted to do was concentrate on English Comp. That would bring her straight back to Timothy Edward Polaris. She was doing everything possible to free her mind of him.

CHAPTER 4

Eric gets everyone's attention by arriving forty minutes late. And he got every female's attention with his incredible good looks. He knew his dark brown eyes were lady-killers. As for Tim, he just checked his watch and continued his lecture.

As fine as Eric was, Brandi didn't understand why she would be so attracted to Tim. But he was not your typical 'pretty boy.' He was sexy, fine, sensitive and intelligent, a combination she had not seen in anyone. This attraction bothered her and caused her all kinds of problems.

Eric found a seat in the row directly behind her, the better to watch her like a mother hen would. However, to Brandi, he was a jackal on the hunt. There was nothing protective about him.

It was not long before the females in class were drawn back to the magnetism exuded by Tim.

Eric had said not a word during the lecture, but tried getting to her afterwards. She was surprisingly civil to him, having thought about what she and her father had discussed. Had it not been for the Stacey Neal thing, she may have been still dating him, but for how long, she did not know.

He caught up with her leaving the lecture hall. "Brandi, wait up."

"What is it, Eric?"

He lowered his voice. "Look, I know you're pissed at me, but can I just talk to you for a few minutes?"

"I don't know. There have been a lot of bad words exchanged."

"I know and I'm sorry. I'm sorry about everything. I'm not any good without you. Why do you think I enrolled in this class?"

"You shouldn't have done it for my benefit, but yours, to further your program."

"I'm here for that, too, but I can't help missing you. Yes, I screwed up, I admit that. I want to make it right with you this time. You're my girl, and I want what our parents have with each other—a lifetime."

"That's a lot to hand to me right now, and quite frankly, I'm too busy to even fathom another relationship, especially with you."

"We can start slow. Anything you want, Brandi, I will do it to get back with you."

She looked at her watch, then back at him. "Look, I can't talk right now because I have to meet with Dr. Polaris about something. Maybe we can talk later. I'm not promising anything, though. I will at least hear you out—again."

"When?"

"I don't know; take your chances."

Without adding anything, she walked towards Tim's office. Eric watched for a minute then walked on.

By 2:30 that afternoon, Brandi was standing in Tim's office, holding her C paper and looking around the spacious room. Only PhD's get the big offices, she thought to herself.

He rushed in, "Sorry I'm late; someone stuck a knife in one of my tires."

"Really? Are you okay?"

"I'm fine. It's my baby I'm concerned about."

"Do you know who did it?"

"I have some ideas, but that's another story. I'm glad you came so we can get started on your paper. You want anything to drink, coffee maybe?"

"No thanks, I just want to get this paper over with."

"You sure you're up to it? After yesterday . . ."

"I don't know what was wrong yesterday, but thank God it's over."

"Fine. Let me see the thesis." He removed the lid from the Starbucks foam cup and began sipping his coffee. "Glad you like Defoe as much as I do."

"I don't, not really, but I did enjoy *Moll Flanders*."

He surveyed the text briefly. "The thesis is general. Maybe you can concentrate more on what aspects you liked about the book and character. You centered more on the book itself—like a synopsis of it. That's not what I wanted."

"I really didn't understand what you wanted. I thought I did when I sat down to write the paper."

"Why didn't you tell me? You know I would have gone over anything you were having problems with."

"I know, but I just didn't want to impose." *Or be close to a man who would have nothing to do with me.*

Brandi picked up the paper, sighing. "I don't know what to do with this, Tim."

"I think it would be good if you decide what you want to focus on, character or plot."

"I like characterization."

"Male dominated. Let's go with that. What do you really know about *Moll Flanders?*"

"Well, the book is generally about a woman's survival in late-17th century England. It was mostly a capitalistic society. Because of that she took to drastic measures just to survive."

"Right. So center on the person. Moll herself was way ahead of her time. She had to be exceptional; think of the measures she took. She was a complex character who adored having all the things women yearn for."

"You really love this period, don't you?"

"It really gets me going. I like it, studied it a great deal. Same can be true for you. You're smart and you know a lot about literature, Brandi. You simply need to fashion your papers to meet your professors' expectations."

"I've never been fond of 16th and 17th century fiction. Can you skip me to 18th century?"

"You're extremely smart; I know you can do this. If I let you skip ahead, others will want to, and they may not be as ready as you are. You don't want me doing extra work, do you?"

"No, I don't." *Only for me, with me.*

"Think about your point of view for the paper."

As she thought, Tim's mind wandered. He thought about what they did after dancing the night away at The Entrapment. He hated thinking about her, but couldn't help himself. Brandi's body was off-limits to him, and the sooner he got that through his head, the better off he knew he would be.

Her voice intruded, bringing him back to reality, a *Moll Flanders* reality. "There were struggles; she was complex, as you said."

"You seem to like her complex aspects as much as I do. As you know, Moll was orphaned, forced to fend for herself at a very young age." Moll's life made him think about his own young life, and what he had to do to survive in foster homes. Thinking of what happened in one of those homes caused him to go off track.

"Are you okay, Tim?"

"Sure. Why?"

"You zoned out for a minute; like you went somewhere else."

He straightened in his chair, disgusted that his past still haunted him. "No, I was trying to get a better feel for the character."

"Are you sure? We can reschedule?"

"Really, I'm fine."

Naturally you are. Tim represented a whole different side of her brain that she still wanted to explore, but didn't feel comfortable doing so. He was that large gray area that she had no control over.

As she listened to him rattle off the complexities of Moll's life, her mind wandered, too. He was so incredibly knowledgeable to be as young as he was. He would be hard to get over, and constantly reliving that evening with him didn't help. His sexual gifts were way beyond anything she could have imagined. "You are so incredible to me, Tim." *Oops!*

His eyes met hers and he put his pen down. *Why am I here with her? Both of us are falling apart.* "Brandi, don't do this. We are here to concentrate on your paper—only that."

"I'm sorry. It just slipped out."

He massaged his left temple. "Maybe this was a bad idea. You know we can't be together, and continuing this will only make it worse." His mind hadn't been on Moll Flanders, either. Brandi was a real struggle for him, but for the sake of her schooling and his career, he could not falter. "Can we do this, or do I need to refer you to Miss Shang's tutorial?"

"No! I . . . I'm sorry. I didn't mean for anything to come out. I'll be okay; please don't stop tutoring me, Dr. Polaris, I really need to pass your course."

"Don't get upset. I didn't mean to get on you, but I don't want us to get into trouble. You will pass my class, Brandi, but it's going to take a lot of work, not only with the books but being professional as well. You understand, don't you?"

"Yes, but it'll be hard trying to keep my mind off you. Tell me that you also understand."

"You know I do. Now, is it going to be me or Miss Shang, plain and simple, Brandi?"

Her voice dropped. "I want you."

That hit him hard. Her answer had more than one meaning—for them both. His voice softened: "I'm sorry if I scared you. Are you okay now?"

"I guess so."

"Good, then let's explore Moll Flanders in more detail. Moll also had sexual issues, Brandi. There were instances of incest, homosexuality, prostitution, and multiple lovers. That could be one aspect of Moll you could address. What do you think?"

"That might be a good angle, because there's a lot of that throughout the book."

"Right. You could explore how her personality fit into all of that and what made her explore those issues. You'll have to dig into Moll's personality to make this work. Do you have any resources?"

"Just the book, but I could go on line . . ."

"I've done that for you; got some things that might be helpful. I also found some of my old notes. You can use them if you like."

"You did all of that for me?"

"Sure. I pulled them out last night. I said I would help, and I am."

He handed her the package. "You should start on this as soon as you can, and if you need me again, you could call me. Here's my cell and the office numbers."

That wasn't what she wanted, easy access to him. Her mind would go a mile a minute until she dialed him. Restraint would be the key, and from what he said he had to help her use it. He seemed different from Jacob, perhaps because she was getting to know him in a different light.

"Another paper is due in three weeks. Can I call on you again for that one if I need help?"

"Yes, but you won't need me; everything you need is already inside you. Just use it."

"When do you want the paper?"

"The sooner the better; couple of days, maybe. I'll edit it for you if you like—give you extra input before it's due."

Silence. They were okay as long as they were talking business, but the minute it stopped, the awkwardness set in. Brandi grabbed her backpack from the floor. "I heard you're thinking about that assistant coach position for the Madcats this year."

"Maybe, but I think I have too much on my plate for that. They knew I did some coaching at the high school level."

"Cool. I'm on reserve cheerleader squad since I was late for try-outs last spring."

"I didn't know. I haven't checked the rosters. I'm sure you'll get your chance to show Madison what you have."

"Sure hope so." She checked the clock on the wall. "Better get over to Thorndyke. He's a killer on people coming late to his lab. Thanks for the info." She looked at him strangely. "Are you okay with me calling you Tim?"

"I guess, but not around other students."

"Good I'll make the paper a good one . . . Tim."

"I know you will. You're incredibly talented."

She smiled. "Are you trying to say you like my mind?"

"Definitely."

"So, how's *Moll Flanders* coming along, Brandi?"

"Good, actually. I have the paper right here."

"Didn't take you too long."

"That information you gave me was so helpful. Thank you so much for that."

"Anytime. Now, let's see the paper." She watched him while he read, smiling at times, agreeing at times on her comments about Moll's strong and willful personality. "This is nice. You really captured Moll's persona from what I've read so far. She was rough, uncouth, but basically a victim of the times. I think your paper is going to be excellent. You have put in more in about her personality, and how that way of life affected her."

"You know all of that already?"

"I read quickly. From the first two pages, I knew you were on the right track. I'll read it later, then record it."

"You think I may have gotten my A?"

He smiled at her. "Brandi, I haven't read the rest of it. I'm sure your A is on its way."

"I just hope you'll say that at the end of the paper." He watched as she grabbed her backpack. "Are you in a hurry to leave?"

"Not really. Why?"

"There are some things I would like to discuss with you."

That rattled her, thinking he still had issues about her blurting out her inner thoughts to him the other day. "What's going on?"

"There's a lecture being held in White Plains weekend after next. There will be discussions on William Bradford, Defoe, all the writers from that era. I was wondering if you'd like to join me? You can take your own car and follow me if you like."

"White Plains? That's a distance. I'll let you know. Besides working with the adult literacy program on Fridays, I also work at the bookstore every third Saturday."

"Maybe you can get out of it that day. I really think this will help since my class is centering on the romance and renaissance eras. Certainly, your papers in the near future will center on some of those authors. Might be good for you."

Being up there with the renowned Timothy Edward Polaris and fighting to keep her distance would be hard. Tim brought on a lot of drama that she was not in the mood for.

"Let me know what you want to do. By the way, you'll be at this weekend's Special Olympics fund-raiser, won't you?"

"I wouldn't miss it, and we'll beat out Rutgers for top donations."

"We always do. Good luck with your paper, Brandi. I'm sure you did everything I wanted you to."

He exhaled once he was alone. Why did he feel so out of sorts in her presence? The only answer was that she was incredible in every thinkable way, and she learned so fast. He knew her paper was good just from reading one section. Everything was good about Brandi, but she was still that awful taboo in his life. The way his life was, he would only make her miserable, and she would end up leaving him anyway after learning about of his past. No, he couldn't let anyone into that ever again. It was his to deal with and his alone. He walked into the oppressive heat with her still on his mind.

When Tim reached the multi purpose area of Miller Hall, Monica was already there, counting the minutes. He rushed in. "Sorry I'm late, truck issues. What's up with the supplies?"

"The list for the textbooks and note pads are all wrong. Where were you when the order came in? You were supposed to be here a half-hour ago."

"I was caught up with Miss Miles, helping her to get a paper together."

"Brandi? Is she still having trouble?"

"She's on that scholarship, Monica, and if she goes below a B average she can kiss it good-bye."

"She'll work it out." She quickly cast Brandi's problems aside, "Here, take a look at these. We can't use them, Tim, and they have to go back."

"Couldn't you have done this without having paged me? You teach here and use these, too. Send the requisition back to the company with my signature and they'll . . ."

"It would get done faster if you contact the company, since you're the overseer of the project." She was seething and it showed, even though she tried her best to rein in her anger. "I'm sorry, Tim. I didn't mean to . . ."

"Monica, what's the real problem today? You don't normally act this way when an order is wrong."

"Nothing is wrong; I just got upset about this damn book order."

"There's time, and don't get so mad about it. We've never had this problem with Ameriquick before. Calm down." It surprised him that Monica had not seen signs of Brandi written all over his face. He always felt hot and rushed after seeing her. If Monica ever found out what had happened between the two of them, he knew his goose would be cooked. The university would find out.

He signed the requisition and returned it to her. "Is the rest of the equipment as we ordered?"

"Yes, thank goodness."

The peeved look was still on her face. "Are you sure you're okay?"

She slouched into the chair and gave him a little *forgive me* smile. "I'm fine, Tim, just sick of fighting with Myron over wedding plans. I'm really sorry about snapping at you."

"It's okay. Better to have someone who stays on my butt than to have someone who doesn't care. Right?"

"Yeah, and thanks for not ripping my head off. I know about your brawls."

"In the past, and I never hit women, Monica."

"I didn't mean that."

"I'm trying to stay away from the bars."

"Good boy."

"I do need dinner. Want to come?"

"Not tonight, Tim. Myron and I are going out."

"Good, that might be what you two need; get the friction off your backs."

"It wouldn't hurt you to go out once in a while with a nice young woman."

"I'm done with relationships, Monica."

She stared at him. "It's too bad you think that way. Love is an awesome thing."

"Yeah, for everyone but me."

"One day you'll change your mind, when the right person comes around." She gathered her books and walked out.

Brandi immediately reentered his mind. The right woman for him was Brandi Miles, though he thought he could never do her justice. He hadn't known why he had broken down and impulsively invited her to the conference with him. Yes, he knew she could benefit from the information, but he would be spending that time with her. His heart was being pulled in two directions, and there was no middle ground.

CHAPTER 5

Justin's was one of Eric and Brandi's favorite places to dine while they were together, and he figured it would be just as good a place to make up.

Brandi, on the other hand, didn't know she was there to make up with him. He had been so nice to her, she figured the least she could do was meet him halfway. Their conversation let her know that he still hadn't matured enough to even consider reconciliation.

When Eric went to refill his soda, he saw Tim sitting at a corner table. He smiled devilishly when he returned to Brandi. "He managed to find you, didn't he?"

"Who?"

He pointed to the back of the restaurant. "Your boy Dr. Polaris is sitting back there. What's he doing following you?"

She saw Tim cutting into his steak. "He is not following me. This is a public restaurant."

"He has it bad for you, Brandi. He's always smiling and looking at you during his lecture."

"You're imagining things. Besides, what would you have him do, hold a knife under my neck while growling at the class?"

"Other cavemen do; why not him?"

"He's our professor, Eric; he's supposed to be friendly. He is not a Pleistocene man, which is how you're beginning to sound."

"He certainly is that, and you hover around him every possible chance you get, like you're waiting for him to knock you over the head and drag you into a cave."

"I told you he's helping me with my papers, and that's all it is."

"Let a tutor help you."

She looked at him as if he had finally turned into the caveman he had accused Tim of being. "I already told you he can give me a better perspective on my papers, since he's teaching the class. Why can't you understand that?"

"Because there's more to it than that, and you know it."

"I don't know or care what your problem is with him; I can only assume it's that D you got on his last test. Don't take it out on him."

"Why are you protecting him? You're into white dudes now?"

"Don't go there. It never solves anything. All it does is bring out ignorance." She threw her napkin on the table. "I need a bathroom break, if that's okay with you—master! You and I are going to try and have a normal conversation when I return; if not, you can leave right now. Understand?"

He pushed his plate away. "Oh, I see how it is. You would never talk to *white boy Floyd* that way. And here you go basically flying in the damn air to get to him, but I had to work my butt off to get you to come here with me tonight."

"Exactly where is all of this coming from? I'm not the one who messed up our relationship. Dr. Polaris did not sleep with my girl-friend. You did. So get off of his back!"

"Bringing that up again?"

"Darn right. When or if you become Mr. Perfect in my life, then you can talk to me like this. Other than that, don't push it. I didn't come here to get into this with you."

"Then tell me this, Miss Brandi, queen of the freakin' universe, who did he sleep with? Better yet, who would he like to sleep with? Yeah, he looks like the type to get some of that black blood and sip on it until he's drunk from it. Then perhaps go home to his pretty white wife and do it all again."

"Drop dead, Eric!"

As Brandi hurried away from him, he realized he had put his foot in his mouth. That wasn't the way to get Brandi back in his life—if that was to ever happen again.

Getting away from Eric consumed her, but as she approached Tim's table, all thoughts of Eric vanished. "Dr. Polaris, I thought that was you."

He stood, taking her hand. "Miss Miles, how are you?"

"Fine. Eric and I were out and decided to come in. I saw you and wanted to say hello. Thanks again for helping me with the paper."

"No problem."

"It was an A, exactly what I need."

"The paper was actually very good. It flowed, and I like how you centered on Moll's personality, helping the reader understand her instead of her tactics." He looked across at Eric who was staring at him. "Are you two okay with one another? I've heard you two going at it a few times before."

She shrugged. "He and I disagree on everything, it seems."

"Are you two dating?" He backed off realizing he was digging too deep. "Sorry, I didn't mean to ask that."

"No, that's okay. We were dating. He has issues to work out but he's . . . well, he's Eric. What can I say?"

His eyes cut to Eric's. "Just be careful. He has a bit of a temper."

"What do you mean?"

"He didn't make the final cut for the basketball team, and he walked out, slamming the door and mumbling obscenities. I chalked it up to his immaturity."

"I'm sorry he did that to you."

"What for? It wasn't you."

"I don't know what Eric's deal is, but his words and actions have always gotten him in trouble. Anyway, I should let you finish your dinner. I wanted to say hello."

"Glad you did."

When Brandi returned from the bathroom, Eric was gone.

Tim stopped her. "Brandi, I saw Eric walk out after paying the bill. Is he waiting for you in the car?"

"I don't know. We didn't make any arrangements."

"Check it out. If he's not there, come back and I'll take you home."

She smiled, "He's there, Tim. Eric wouldn't do that."

"You're right. Enjoy the rest of your evening, and I'll see you in class Tuesday."

Moments later, Brandi walked back into the restaurant alone. She walked to Tim's table and slid into the booth.

Tim knew what the deal was. "He's gone, isn't he?"

"You were right. I may need that ride after all. I can call my father if it's a problem, though."

"It's not a problem, Brandi."

She watched as he ate, stuffing everything the way most men do. Still, he managed to look incredibly sexy.

It was as though he read her thoughts, and he deliberately wanted to block them before they got the best of him. "You want a soda or something?"

"What I want is to strangle Eric. Thanks, I don't care for anything. Don't hurry with your dinner."

"I'm almost finished, and I really don't need that key lime pie I was eyeing."

"Don't be silly; have it. You're in great shape, so a little slice of pie won't hurt you."

"Only if you'll share it."

"No way; one bite and it shows up the next day."

"You're beautiful one way or another."

She hadn't expected that, but thanked him anyway.

His waitress approached, eyeing Brandi as if she were a deadly snake. "Is everything okay, sir?"

"Yes, I'll take the bill."

She scribbled out the bill while eyeing Brandi, then walked away with an attitude.

Tim noticed the reaction, but Brandi quickly calmed him. "It's okay, Tim. She's a jerk."

"I won't have that from her, or anyone else."

"Screw her, let's just go. Don't leave a tip."

"I don't plan to."

Brandi was mostly quiet on the way home. At times, Tim took a stab at engaging her in conversation. Forced close to him in a Mercedes Coup wasn't helping her situation. Their bodies were so close she could smell his cologne. It intoxicated her, intensified her craving for him that much more. "What are you wearing? It smells wonderful."

"John Varvatos."

"Really? Eric wears that. It stinks on him, though. It has something to do with body chemistry. Each man is different."

"I'm glad you like it."

"Very much. It smells great on you."

Their conversation was getting way too personal. He said nothing further. He pulled into her driveway and unlocked the door. "Home sweet home, Miss Miles."

Thank goodness! It felt as if she had been holding her breath the entire time, fearing what she would say to him. Deciding to keep quiet was her only shot at staying sane around him. Suddenly, something as simple as holding a man's hand was the hardest thing in the world. Knowing that, she knew she had to leave him, and leave in a hurry before the inevitable happened—a kiss. "I had better get out of here."

"Yes, I think you'd better." He pushed her door open further. "You have a good night. Don't worry about me with Eric. He will only test my waters so far. Besides, I'm not the coach he has a beef with."

"Eric has a beef with everyone." She got out, looking back inside at him. "Thanks for rescuing me."

"Anytime." Once she was safely inside, he sped off. His hand felt the perspiration on his shirt. His damp clothing wasn't from the heat outside, but from the heat inside–inside his heart. He wanted Brandi more than he could stand it, and something had to be done about it, but she didn't know what.

Mid-October was a repeat of September, warm and humid, perfect timing for Madison's annual car wash fundraiser. Everyone was excited and buzzing around getting the teachers' parking lot ready for the event.

Brandi put in her time, along with other student volunteers who didn't have Saturday jobs. The weather was great for her cut-off jeans and new tank top, just perfect to clean up a parking lot that normally housed over 250 faculty automobiles a day. Tim would be there, having volunteered to take on the fund-raiser this year.

Upon hearing she would be near Tim's station, Brandi made every effort to switch with someone. The other night in Tim's car could have turned into a big mistake. Wanting to kiss him was more than a whim, and she had spent half the night tossing and turning from thinking of him. The entire thing was Eric's fault for having left her at Justin's. Riding up to White Plains with him would be just as hard as dealing with him at the carwash. But attending the seminar would be a smart move in terms of passing his class. She felt stuck in Tim's face today, and the upcoming weekend, too.

She couldn't switch with anyone, therefore she and other students were put in charge of towel drying every vehicle in the lot. She saw Tim, Dr. Malone, and a few other faculty members getting all wet. She tried not to look his way, but then glance and see Tim in a damp shirt puckering in all the right places. It was exciting, and frustrating at the same time.

They were making loads of money. Madison had the undisputed reputation of pulling off great fund-raisers, especially the car washes. Lots of well-off parents and students supported the school's efforts because it was it was known for its academic excellence. Then there was Tim. For the last three years, he was the one for whom those women in the luxury cars showed up. Anything to get a gander at Timothy Polaris in wet clothing. They were only too glad to shell out the cash for his cause.

Brandi watched the antics from her station: women handing him lots of cash while students tried dousing him and others with water. Tim finally became a victim of the bucket prank. He was drenched from head to toe, and looking at him with everything sticking to him made her feminine core ache for him. His wet, cold nipples poked through the material, and the bulge pressing in his jeans packed a mean punch. As she watched him flex he flex to shake off the extra water, her mouth went dry.

A honking horn interrupted her daydream. Eric sat behind the wheel watching her watch Tim. The look on his face told her that he well award of the object of her gawking. "I see you've found the entertainment."

"Dry up."

"Cute, considering what you're doing."

"After what you did to me the other night, don't even think of talking to me, jackass."

"I admit that was rude, but going gaga over white-boy Rick was also rude, don't you think?"

"I don't. I was saying hello to the guy. You were the one seeing what wasn't there, now make like a bee and buzz off."

Dr. Moore approached her with an armful of towels. "Miss Miles, take these over to Dr. Polaris before the poor guy freezes to death."

With little enthusiasm, she walked towards Tim.

Eric heard the exchange and smirked as Brandi walked away with the towels.

The sight of Tim wet with everything sticking to him almost made her stomach churn. Dropping the towels into his arms and scurrying away was her only recourse. "Here. Dr. Moore told me to give you these before you die of pneumonia."

"They got me good this time, didn't they?"

"I guess." Her eyes stared into the distance, never meeting his.

His head tilted to the side, "What's wrong today?"

She hadn't been short on purpose, but Eric always managed to bring out the worst in her. "Nothing."

She headed back, but he stopped her. "Someone's got your dander up. Now what's wrong?"

Nothing could make her face him. Instead, she stared at the students running about. "Just a bad day, Dr. Polaris; I'm not feeling well."

He moved in closer to her, but not close enough to rouse suspicion. "You look wonderful, if you don't mind me commenting."

"I do mind."

A compliment from him should have set her world on fire, but the last thing she needed to hear from him was how good she looked.

"Thank you, Dr. Polaris, for the compliment. I should get back to the other side."

"Wait. Don't let him get next to you like that."

"What do you mean?"

"Eric Fontaine. I saw him over there."

She had to look at him. "What can I do? I certainly can't date you, now can I?"

He didn't understand her shortness with him and wasn't in the mood for it. "You're right. You do need to go back to your station."

As she walked away she felt guilty about her behavior. Nothing was his fault, and she had taken it out on him. He was only trying to make her feel better, and she had rebuffed him. She threw her towel down and ran to the ladies room, practically in tears.

The following Monday, there was no one in his room after class. No students stopping by to say hello, no women pretending to need help just to get close to him—and no Brandi. She had stayed clear of him, and he knew why.

The letter he had received from the literature department at NYU inviting him to an interview dangled from Tim's hand. He had liked their program, and taking the job would definitely free him to be with Brandi—if he could handle a relationship. But he didn't want to leave, didn't feel it was fair to himself to leave because of a woman. He had invested three years at that school and had loved every minute. No, he couldn't leave Madison. His life was there. Getting Brandi out of his head would be dreadfully hard, but he could do it.

He thought about Brandi nonstop, no matter how hard he fought against it. No matter how many times he paced the floor trying to find other things to think about, his mind always returned to her. Madison Tech and Brandi were double-teaming him; one he wanted to run from, the other he wanted to run to. His head began to ache, so he left without putting grades on the last batch of student papers.

The cheerleaders were practicing in the gym. Brandi was one of them now that McKenzie Miller had transferred to Princeton. Their routine was almost perfect, and Brandi really added to the team due to her cheerleading experience in high school. The gym doors opened and Tim stepped inside. All eyes were on him, all except Brandi's.

He watched her routine. Her prowess was breathtaking, her technique flawless. All he could see was a blur of red and white tap panties fitting her like a glove, making him feel the pressure in his pants. He turned to leave, but everyone ran to him for his opinion on the outfits—except Brandi. Mrs. Washington clapped her hands. "Ladies, let the man breathe; he's not a toy. Hit the showers." She turned to him. "How are you today, Dr. Polaris?"

"I've been better; just tired, Mrs. Washington."

"You saw part of the ladies' routine. What do you think?"

"It was excellent."

"They'll be ready for the game by Thursday, Dr. Polaris." She turned and saw Brandi walking back into the gym. "Miss Miles?"

"I need to talk to Dr. Polaris."

He nodded, "It's okay."

Both watched Mrs. Washington leave the room before facing one another. Brandi looked down at her red and white clad feet. "I'm so sorry about the other day. I was rude to you for no reason. Forgiven?"

"I forgave you the second you said it."

"I appreciate that. It's been really hard for me with Eric always in my face. Hiding how I feel about you is worse, though."

"It'll work out, Brandi. Trust me."

"How? Everything seems so impossible."

"Right now, I can't say how it will work itself out, but it will. I actually hadn't planned to come in here today."

"Didn't you want to see our routine?"

No! "Sure, but I knew I would see it at the game. I couldn't work because I was tired, but something is on my mind and I need to clear it with you."

"With me? Why?"

"I was out of place complimenting you the other day. I was out of place to assume anything about Eric."

"You were right on target. Screw him. But why do you feel you were out of place complimenting me? I liked it, even if I neglected to tell you."

"You did everything right. You weren't supposed to take kindly to me telling you how great you looked. I didn't tell the other ladies how good they looked."

"Did I do something lately to make you feel bad about me, other than the car wash thing?"

"Brandi, the point is that we are student and professor, and I feel that I'm crossing the line with you a lot."

"What do you mean?"

He leaned against the bleachers, his head tilted back in frustration. "Look, all I'm saying is that we need to keep this professional. I've been getting a little too close, giving you extra notes when I haven't given anyone else any, taking you home after Eric ditched you . . ."

"Would you have left me in that restaurant?"

"Of course not, but I should have let your father pick you up."

She dropped her pom-poms to the floor, staring at him as if he were crazy. "Tim, what's going on with you?"

"All I know is that sitting in that car with you the other day gave me ideas that I should not be having now that you're my student. I know how we feel about one another, and it can't work, Brandi. It can't work for many reasons."

"Tim, I'm not trying to have another fling with you. I told you that wouldn't happen."

"I know you did, but all I'm saying is that we really need to be more careful. Eric knows that I didn't leave you in that restaurant. Who knows what he might be saying to everyone."

"He hasn't said anything, Tim."

"That's another thing, maybe it's not a good idea to call me that."

"I can't call you by your name now?"

"It could make our relationship harder to let go if we're personal with one another."

"You can't be serious! No one's here; no one can hear us."

"We don't know that, and I think I need to go back to calling you Miss Miles."

"Miss Miles? Is it like that now?"

"It has to be."

"I don't believe this. I'm acting as professional as I can around you, and it still is not working for you."

"It's just that I'm scared. I love my job here. I can't see myself without this job. I've worked too hard to lose it now."

"I would not be the reason for you losing your job, Tim, sorry, Dr. Polaris. I want my scholarship as badly as you want this job. Why would I jeopardize anything?"

"All I'm saying is that we should not be seen together other than for tutoring."

"Then what about the seminar this weekend? Is that off, too? I would hate to know that I took this weekend off from the bookstore for nothing. Besides, now that I know about it, I really want to go and hear those lectures."

"No, that's still on. I said I will."

"I can take myself up there. My car is not working well, but I can chance it."

"No, I won't go back on my word. Besides, you need to hear the lectures. I'm the reason you know about them, anyway."

Her eyes gazed into his with disbelief. "How can I not call you Tim when I'm so used to it?"

He wiped the perspiration off his forehead. "Fine, call me Tim, but don't ever slip in front of anyone, especially Eric. That's all the fuel he needs."

"Don't be afraid of Eric."

"I'm not scared of him! It's . . . it's just that he could cause trouble and you know it."

"It won't be a first for him."

"I know that."

Suddenly her body felt so tired, doing something as simple as retrieving the pom-poms at her feet was an effort. This was all too much for Tim to put on her, though she believed she knew his reasons. Her little display in front of him with the towels drew a few looks, namely, Dr. Moore, though she hoped he had been looking in their direction for other reasons. Yes, she knew Tim was scared, and with good cause. She had to respect how he felt and watch her own butt around him.

"I guess that's that, isn't it?"

"I don't mean to hurt you, Miss Mi . . ."

"You can call me Brandi. No one is here, Tim, and I know you don't mean to hurt me. I didn't realize things were getting so out of sorts with you. I didn't realize I had left such an impression that you have to get over me. I know how I feel about you, and I'm always out of sorts. I'm getting used to it."

"I'm sorry about all this. I need to keep myself out of clubs in Manhattan."

"If that's how you feel." She retrieved the pom-poms. "Are we still meeting in the student parking lot?"

"Just as planned. By the way, the outfits are outstanding."

"Enough to wow the other team?"

"That's an understatement."

"Careful about those compliments. They can cause trouble." She smiled a bashful smile and headed for the showers.

CHAPTER 6

The double black Durango pulled up in front of the house, and Brandi wanted to get out of there before her father woke. She didn't need to hear her father's mouth about why she was going up there with her professor. *Dad hasn't gotten the fuel injectors fixed on my car yet, so what can I do other than ride with Tim? Does he want me to walk to White Plains?* It would be hard enough dealing with a man she was attracted to who wanted nothing to do with her, but also to hear flak about it? She wasn't in the mood for it.

The minute she saw him she remembered the nightmare she had had: Tim was making love to her, then he pulled the mask from his face, revealing Eric's nasty, snarling persona. The nightmare awakened her at 3:00 in the morning and she had not been able to get back to sleep. No matter what, she had to put on a nice face and be civil to Tim. Her life and her feelings about him weren't his fault, but she still wanted him as she had never wanted any man before him.

She slid into the passenger side. "Good morning, Tim. How are you?"

"Sleepy as hell, but I'm looking forward to hearing lectures on the greats of literature. I hope you are, too."

"I am. I didn't sleep well, but I had better wake up because my next paper is on someone from 17th century lit. Remember?"

"I do. Which author are you doing?"

"Maybe Samuel Sewall. I read 'The Selling of Joseph' in high school."

"Did you like it?"

"Very much. I should read it again, become more familiar with it."

"Good idea. By the way, which high school did you attend?"

"Brooklyn High."

"Good school, great drama and literature department. I did a seminar there for the twelfth graders about a year ago. I just wish more people were familiar with the arts, to know and explore people like Fitzgerald, Rowlandson, Countee Cullen, and other great figures of literature. There's so much to tempt the minds of young people these days. A lot of it is all the wrong stuff."

"Like what?" Brandi inquired.

A sly smile came to Tim's face. "Like gangster rap."

Brandi smirked at his statement. "Yeah, like you'd know about that."

"I've heard rap before, Brandi."

"Do you own any?"

"No. I don't like it well enough to buy any."

She yawned, and leaned back in the seat. "I'm sure you know about Sinatra, Manilow, soothing, something you can't get up and do the Hustle to."

"Fine, make fun of me, but it's actually about time I did settle down to something smooth and relaxing."

"What do you mean?"

"I was wild for a long time, doing what I wanted, when I wanted to. I'm still that way, but counseling toned me down. I was really something."

"I can believe that, Tim. You're still something, but in good ways." She kept looking at him, wondering whether or not to ask why he had been in counseling. Her ambition to know any and everything about Timothy Polaris beckoned her. "Why did you have to go to counseling?"

"Well, the fact of the matter is that I didn't have a nifty childhood. My parents were people who shouldn't have been parents. They didn't take their job seriously and because of that, I stayed in trouble, fights in school, etc. Finally, I got help from Dr. Hammond. I still see her at times, just to talk over things."

"I'm sorry about what happened to you."

"Me, too."

"Still, it's kind of sexy being with a man who was and still is a rebel."

"That's a part of my life I don't want to revisit. However, I can wow you with some smooth jazz."

"No thanks. I have my guys and you have yours." Brandi pillaged through her CD case, found Outkast and put her headset on.

Tim slipped a Sarah Vaughn CD into the changer and relaxed as he drove.

They both wanted to hear the lecture on Mark Twain, one that Tim didn't know would be offered. When he looked back down at his program, he noticed there would be selected seminars on 19th and 20th century authors. Those were the ones they went to first. They sat in the overly crowded lecture hall. Tim lowered his voice. "I know everyone has read Huck Finn, but what other works of his do you like?"

"Everything he wrote, but I hate doing papers on anyone. Maybe I can do my paper after the mid term on Twain. We should be getting into the 19th century soon right?"

"The midterm is in three weeks, and the paper is due almost two weeks after. And yes, Twain would be good. So would, Melville, Poe, Walt Whitman, Thoreau, Dickinson. You have a large choice this time as compared to the 16th and 17th centuries. Besides, I have notes on those authors that you can use."

"You would let me use those?'

"Sure. I have helped you before, why not now?"

As Brandi turned her attention to the speaker, Tim wouldn't help but stare at her a moment longer. She simply took him away with her beauty and intelligence, something he was so turned on about.

Brandi turned and saw him in dreamland and pulled his ear. "What were you daydreaming about? Or was I boring you to tears?"

"Hardly that; I was thinking about how glad I am that I brought you up here."

"Why?"

"I've opened up a new world to you. I think you have a better appreciation for literature than you had."

"Yes, but more to the point, I need the A."

"That's all?"

"I do appreciate your helping me, and who better than someone who's won literary awards? And true, I do have a greater appreciation for literature, more than I thought. I am a literary science major and this is helping, but this is a grade to me as well." She knew why Tim was staring into her eyes. There was no doubt that their attraction had lasted way past The Entrapment, despite how he carried on the other day about the risks of them being together. Running into bathrooms and crying her eyes out because he was making mind moves on her was unnerving. He was the kind of man who made her wonder which she wanted more: a man who could love her endlessly, or a career that would guarantee financial independence? Tim could give her both, but not while at Madison. Thoughts of NYU crossed her mind.

She came back to earth. "I think I'll do something on Poe. I love his 'Fall of the House of Usher.'"

"It is a good one. Do you want to stay for the other lectures or take off in a couple of hours?"

"Stay for a while. I really like the authors they're showcasing."

"If you like, and we could grab something to eat in between."

Two more hours of seeing Tim in that white buttoned-down shirt with the first three buttons undone. She didn't know if she could do it. His tight jeans weren't of any help, either. She remembered his power between her thighs, inside of her body, moving through her like a raging river. He was awesome, more so than any man she had ever known. She loved and hated being with him, but the lectures were important to her GPA. "Let's hear the rest of the lectures, grab a quick bite after a while, then go home. I have a lot of work to do. Is that okay with you?"

"Sure."

Tim could barely keep his eyes off Brandi. She was the only woman he had wanted to be with on an intimate level and that bothered him.

Liking her was cramping his style and his career at Madison, yet Brandi consumed him; made him think differently about women for the first time in years.

His mother was busy tossing him into foster homes and blaming him for everything his father did to them. That hurt him, and just thinking back on it made him lose track of the speaker at hand. He had never lost track of what Brandi was doing to his heart, though!

The drive back was long, and they were both tired. Brandi slept most of the time while he drove, giving him the chance he didn't want—to concentrate on everything wrong in his life, including her. Their lunch together was fun; they talked about everything, despite the fact that he was the one that wanted to keep it impersonal. Their conversation was stimulating, nothing like how he had thought it would be—around sex and The Entrapment. No, they had steered clear of it, though it still rested in the back of his mind. He admired how eagerly she took in the information she needed to make her papers all they could be. She cherished Madison the way he did, and she was surviving it. That appealed to him. There wasn't anything about Brandi that didn't appeal to him. That's how he knew she would never leave there without her degree. How could he manage without her in his arms? He thought about the invitation from NYU. They'd been after him for years, trying to get him in for an interview. *Maybe it wouldn't be a bad idea to hear what they have to say.* After really thinking, he knew he still wanted to be a part of Madison and couldn't imagine leaving. *Suffering for two more years can't be all bad. Or can it?*

The minute Brandi heard Outkast being played on the radio, her head lifted. "The Way You Move"reminded her of Tim and how he moved with and on top of her that night. She watched his profile as he drove, liking how he moved his head to the music, loving the idea of waking up next to him. Her voice broke into the calm night air. "You like that song?"

"It has a great beat."

"You don't look like the Outkast kind."

"Looks are deceiving, aren't they? I didn't mean to awaken you."

"I like this song. I like everything by them."

"So, I don't look to be the Outkast type, huh? How is someone supposed to look who likes crazy songs?"

"Crazy! You're the last person I know who looks crazy."

"You should see me in the mornings after one of my drunken stupors."

"Do you still do that?"

He fumbled for words then realized it was always best to admit to the truth. "Sometimes."

"What makes you drink, other than what you told me before about your family?"

"Isn't that enough?"

"Sure, but you didn't drink a lot at The Entrapment."

"I was trying to impress you."

She turned the music down and moved closer to him. "You've impressed me since The Entrapment. I'm even more impressed now. I had no idea you had so much going for you. You're top dog at Madison, Tim. You know everything."

"Not everything." *Top dog, huh? How can I leave there now?*

The way he sounded made her feel sorry for him. "What happened in your family? I see something in your eyes after lecture."

"Way too many things to talk about. I never really knew my father. He was gone before I even knew him. My marriage to Charlotte was a joke."

"How long were you married?"

"Five years. I had just graduated from Princeton when we married, and I've been divorced two years. Maybe I was just too immature."

"I doubt that; any kids?"

"No. No kids allowed after . . ." He clammed up, not wanting to even discuss what led to the breakup. "Things happened that you wouldn't understand. We shouldn't be talking about this anyway."

"I would like to. We are friends, right?

"No, Brandi, we're professor and student. We both have to remember that." He turned off the freeway. "We're near my house. I would like to give you those notes, and the other papers on Twain."

She knew why he had changed the subject. That student/teacher thing. She also knew he was tired from a long day, and decided not to push it until he wanted to come to her about it. "I think I'll need those notes, because your papers are going to kill me."

"Writing is something you're good at, Brandi."

"I know. I'm just lazy."

He pulled into his driveway. She recognized the house immediately. They sat there a brief moment, silent. He didn't want to invite her in; students and teachers weren't to be seen at one another's houses. They weren't supposed to share anything but lecture time and nothing more.

Brandi wanted to go in and never come out. Tim spoke first. "Come on in? I don't want to leave you out here alone. There has been some vandals running around. My trashcan was thrown into my back window and my garage door kicked in."

"Did they damage the Mercedes?"

"Cracked the windshield."

"Really? I'm sorry."

"Anyway, that's why I would rather you come in. I know you don't feel comfortable; neither do I, but it'll only be for a few minutes."

"It's all right, Tim. We can handle one another on an adult level, right?"

He pushed her door open. "Sure." *I hope I can.*

CHAPTER 7

Everything looked as it did the night Brandi first went home with him. The house was a rather large ranch with two bedrooms, well-manicured lawn, neat. Brandi could hear his shepherd mix, Myrrh, barking in the background. She entered and tried not to think of anything else. She walked into the spacious living room and immediately went to his book collection. "May I look through these?"

"Help yourself. I'll get the papers from the bedroom."

"Don't forget the notes."

"I won't." He entered the bedroom, wishing he was carrying her in his arms to place her on his bed. He quickly shoved the idea aside, knowing it would never happen as long as they both were at Madison. He picked up the folder containing the papers—they weren't inside. "What the hell. . . ." He took a quick look around the room. Nothing!

Brandi called to him, "Are you okay in there? You're making quite a racket."

"Just looking for something. Be out soon."

"Tim, may I play your Michael Franks CD?"

"Help yourself. I can't find the papers anyway; give me a minute to find them."

As he searched the room, the phone rang and he grabbed the receiver on the second ring. It was his neighbor Anthony Haliburton from across the street. "Tim, been waiting for you to get home. Myrrh had been barking for almost two hours straight. Is everything okay over there?"

"Two hours?" He looked around the bedroom, then peeked through the shades. "Looks like everything's fine. He's been fed, so I don't know what the problem is."

"He was barking like a mad dog before."

"I'll check on him. Thanks, Anthony."

Returning to the living room, he saw Brandi looking through his CD rack. One look at her in that form-fitting jogging suit almost made him forget why he had walked back in. He cleared his voice. "Myrrh's having some kind of coronary out there. Let me just check on him. I hope to find the papers."

"You can't find them?"

"They're around here. Want a Coke or something? It's in the refrigerator."

"Oh, no thanks. It's after seven, and I should go home, shower and get going on that next paper."

"So soon?"

It was hard for her to even be there. "I hate doing papers at the last minute, so I had better get cracking. It will be due before I know it."

"Let me check on Myrrh, and then I'll take you home."

It was unlike Myrrh to bark like that unless something was wrong. He approached the barking dog and stroked his thick fur. "What's up, boy? Why the racket?" He pulled a piece of paper from the dog's mouth. There were more pieces on the grass. Reading it as best he could in the fading light, he realized it was part of one of the papers he wanted to give Brandi. *What the heck is this doing out here?* He looked at the other pieces on the grass, and realized they were more of the papers he had wanted to give Brandi. Myrrh hadn't been in the house all day for sure, nor had he taken those papers from the house. There were no signs of forced entry on either door.

Brandi was standing near the back door when he re-entered. "Is he okay?"

"Yeah, he's fine. Parts of the paper I wanted to give you were out there, and I have no idea how they got out there. Anyway, let me check a little more and get back to you. Would that be okay? I know you have to get home."

"Don't worry about it. I have all night to study."

He couldn't find the rest of the papers, but brought out the notes. He entered the living room just in time to see Brandi swaying to the music.

Their eyes met, and she immediately stopped dancing. Her brown cheeks reddened to his unspoken advances. "I got caught up in the moment. Michael Franks is one of my favorites."

"I can tell. Don't stop dancing on my account."

"Did you find the papers?"

"I have no idea where they are. I'm really sorry. They were really good and would have been a lot of help to you. I have the books, though."

Brandi walked towards him, moving so close to him that she could see the tiny laugh lines at the corners of his sexy mouth. Her voice weakened. "I truly appreciate the use of your notes, Tim."

He was nervous around her, nervous, hardly knowing what to say. "Those were good seminars, don't you think?"

"Very enlightening. Thank you for inviting me."

"It was my pleasure."

She hugged him in gratitude. Her arms encircled his neck, feeling smooth skin, and his body heat filtering through to hers.

His arms tightened around her, pressing her into the tightness of his groin. He broke from her, looking into her eyes. When he spoke, his voice was husky, his words awkward. "I . . . uh, didn't mean to hold you so tightly."

"It's okay. I hugged you first."

"I should take you home; you have things to . . ."

"Yes."

His fingers brushed against her lips. He felt her heat, her intensity. A picture of her sitting in his lecture hall flashed in his mind, and he dropped his arms to his sides. "Let's get you out of here, Brandi."

He stepped back not saying another word, just staring at her. Chest heaving, eyes searching the ground, he was a man in pain from wanting what he couldn't have. "Let's go before I lose my ever-loving mind!"

"Tim, I'm . . . I'm so sorry."

"Forget it. It was my fault. I shouldn't have brought you here."

"It wasn't just you. You know how I feel about you."

"Please don't feel that way about me, Brandi. It'll never work."

"I know. We could both end up losing it all."

"I can't have that, Brandi. I just can't have it." He saw tears in her eyes and almost reached for her hand. Touching her would start a chain reaction too hard to stop. He picked up the notes that slipped from her hand. "Don't forget this."

It was a long, silent ride from his Jamaica Estates home to hers in Brooklyn. Tim stopped the car in front of her house and leaned across her to open her door. Figuring what to say to her was agonizing, but he decided to just come out with something to try and ease her mind. "Brandi, don't let what happened stop you from getting my help with your papers. You're supposed to see me on Wednesday."

"It won't stop me, but I can't ever go back to your house again. You do understand, don't you?"

"It'll be better that way. I'm glad you went to the seminar, though. It was good for you."

She said good-bye and headed towards the house on the verge of tears.

Sounding desperate, he called to her: "Brandi . . . I'm sorry."

"So am I." She ran across the lawn and disappeared.

All he could do was sit there and give into his feelings. He could still feel her lips on his. But he knew that would not happen again unless one of them made a move. He drove off troubled. His interview with Columbia that following Monday was a definite yes; he had to get away from Madison, no matter how much he loved it there. The invitation to Columbia had been open before Brandi had resurfaced in his life.

He found himself at a bar downing another scotch. He dreaded going home to the place where he kissed her as he had never another woman. Too many fresh, unsettling memories to face. Selling his house briefly crossed his mind, but he realized that selling it would be too stupid a move even for his state of mind.

Sitting to his left at the bar was a young blonde ready to walk out with him the minute the minute he finished his drink. He kissed her on the lips, pretending they were Brandi's, but there was no comparison. Tim set the glass down, took the woman's hand, and left with her.

They headed for a mid-town motel he had frequented. He simply had no stomach for taking anyone to his house after having made love to Brandi there. He lay across the bed feeling numb and emotionless. The young woman spread eagle on top of him, kissing her way down from his moist forehead, teasing, kissing.

He usually loved women undressing him, but not this night! He looked at her face . . . and didn't see Brandi. For a split second, he was ashamed, actually feeling as if he were cheating on Brandi. Yet he let the young woman stroke the front of his pants, slowly pulled the zipper down. He suddenly took her wrists, stopping her.

She smiled at him, caressing his stomach. "Come on, sugar. I know you're not bashful; you're too sexy for that." She tried unbuttoning his shirt again, but he held her off.

"Stop. I can't do this." He moved to the side of the bed.

"Did I do something wrong?"

"No. It's not you; it's me. I just can't to this."

"Do you have a wife?"

"Not anymore."

"A lover?"

He ignored the question. "You shouldn't be doing this with a man you just met. You're too pretty for this. Go and find someone who can be a good man to you." He fished for some money in his pocket. "I'm sorry I wasted your time. Don't do this to yourself anymore."

The woman eyed him cautiously, then reached for her clothes.

Once she was fully dressed, she put the money in her purse and called for a cab. He had left before the cab arrived, telling her to not open the door until she saw the cab.

On his way home his mind went back to the events of the day. He and Brandi had such a good time listening to the speakers, then he had to ruin everything by nearly losing control. Everything always came so hard for him, including simple things like being with a woman he knew he could love. He only hoped Brandi saw him as a man who'd had a weak moment, instead of someone she could never trust again.

After their brief but steamy encounter, Brandi wasn't in the mood to do anything resembling work. She had rushed into the house practically in tears. All she had managed to do was shower and slide into her favorite nightgown. Later that evening, she lay across her bed trying to block out thoughts of Tim; nothing worked. Her Jill Scott CD only reminded her of him. Any love song brought him to mind. His kiss was so delicious, melting a hole in her. Remembering the way his body pressed against hers made her legs weak. Going into his house in the first place was a bad idea, feeling she would fall victim to her own emotions. Everything was so hard for her now that he had come back into her life. Making him part of her life even if she wasn't attending Madison, would cause her problems—*Why does he have to be white?* She knew for sure that color was not an issue for her but it was for the people she cared about. They would make her life hard in ways Tim could never dream of, and she didn't know if she was strong enough to handle the pressure that was sure to come.

Everything that happened that day gave her a splitting headache— enough to make her reconsider going back to NYU, scholarship or not! She put her pillow over her head to drown out all of the voices in her head telling her what to do, what not to do. All she wanted was her life to feel right for the first time in months.

A knock on her door startled her. At first she didn't answer, figuring it was one of her parents wanting to know about her day. All she wanted was to sleep the rest of the night; she did not want to answer any questions.

Another knock. "Brandi!" It was her aggravating thirteen-year-old brother, Brian, who had made a point of telling Tim after the last home game that he wanted to play basketball for Madison. Right. But he and Tim hit it off really well. Since Tim had been a coach before, he was used to people, especially kids, telling him that they wanted to try out. She put the pillow back over her head.

Brian knocked again. "Brandi, wake the heck up! I want some DVDs."

She didn't want to answer him, but knew he would stay there like a dope until he got an answer. "Go away, Brian. I'm sleeping."

"This early? Get real and open the door. I want Austin Powers. I know you think he's groovy, baby."

"Shut up, Brian. Or should I say, Mini Me?"

"You want me to get Dad?"

She jumped from the bed, grabbed the movie and flung the door open. "Fine, anything to shut you up. Can I be alone now?"

He stared at her weary face. "What's your deal?"

"Killing you would be an idea. I'm tired. Okay?"

"Yeah, tired of being a hood-rat."

"That's your word for the week, huh? Those hood friends of yours may very well have you killed one day—by me. Now, get out of here. Go aggravate the dog, if she is not already tired of you."

"Whateverrr."

Sometimes she hated Brian, but at least he had taken her mind from Tim.

CHAPTER 8

Timothy Polaris walking out of the administrative offices at Columbia University was about the last thing Tiffany expected to see that morning. She had been there to get her transcripts from the year before. She ran towards him, calling to him like a madwoman. "Dr. Polaris, wait!"

He turned around and smiled into her pretty face. "Miss Jackson? I didn't expect to see you. What are you doing here?"

"I took a few summer classes last year and had to get my transcripts. I'm being considered for next year's Norton award, remember?"

"Yes, I remember, and that's great. I always knew you could do it. Your grades are excellent, at least in my class. Should be no problem."

"I hope not. I worked my butt off. I remember what Brandi went through to get hers." She chose her words carefully: "Dr. Polaris. I had planned to come to see you soon anyway. I was wondering, well . . . would you write me a letter of recommendation?"

"Be glad to. When do you need it?"

"Yesterday, if that makes any sense. I'll be glad to come by your office and pick it up."

"I'll do it today, since I took the day off anyway."

"Why are you here? Don't you have enough to keep you busy at Madison?"

"They've been hounding me to come in and see what they can offer me."

"As in a job?"

"I'm thinking about it—seriously. They've been after me for two years. I decided I should at least talk to them."

"You're thinking about leaving Madison? Everyone will die."

"You're too kind, Miss Jackson."

"No! I'm serious. You can't leave us."

"I didn't say I was leaving, though it's possible. Don't let on about it."

"I won't, but aren't you happy at Madison?"

He couldn't tell her the main reason he felt the move would be good for him. True, he would miss seeing Brandi in his class, but it would free them from teacher/student complications. Getting away from Madison would give him the break he needed. Being able to step back and analyze his situation would help him decide if he could be a good man for Brandi. Given his past life, he wasn't sure that he could make any woman happy.

"Dr. Polaris?"

He turned to Tiffany. "Sorry, seems I zoned out for a minute. There's a lot on my mind today. Yes, I'm happy at Madison. It's a wonderful school, but one should check one's options, don't you think?"

"I guess. I was really looking forward to having you next semester."

"It's only midterms, and you're already thinking about next semester?"

"One should think ahead, right?"

"Right, but don't write me off so quickly. I haven't accepted the job here yet. I told them I would get back to them soon. I told NYU the same thing."

"You're really in demand, aren't you?"

"Yes, I guess so, but I don't know why."

"You're a genius."

"I am not a genius, Miss Jackson. I just happen to be passionate about literature and writing."

"You teach a good class. I would hate to see you leave." She glanced at her watch. "Gotta' go; I have Killborn in forty-five minutes, and believe me, she lives up to her name. She does *kill* us with her boring lectures."

He smiled for the first time that day. "I'll see you in class tomorrow, and I'll have your letter."

Tiffany hailed a cab and quickly slid in. "I've got to tell Brandi."

Tiffany pulled in front of Brandi's house in her father's Hummer. "Hurry up, girl. You want to be late for Wesley Snipes?"

"Give me a break. The name of the movie is not Wesley Snipes, geek!"

"Whatever, he's in it. That's all that matters to me."

"He is a hottie. I'm glad you're early. Brian is getting on my last damn nerve. You should be glad you don't have a little brother."

"I have it worse. Todd is older than me, so he thinks he's my father or something. And you don't have a sister who reports every move you make as Trina does. Give me Brian any day."

"Take him, please!"

Tiffany smiled impishly. "Speaking of hotties, guess who I saw coming from Columbia's administration building."

"Let me guess, another man you will soon be dating, right?"

"Aah, if only I could."

"Who was it?"

"Timothy Edward Polaris."

"Really?"

"Really. Guess what he was doing there? You won't like this. No woman at Madison will like it."

"He was probably just taking care of some business."

"Oh, he was taking care of business, alright. I'm not supposed to tell you this, so don't let on that you know."

"Know what?"

"He was interviewing for a job there. Please, don't tell him anything."

"What? No, he wasn't."

"Brandi, promise me."

"Okay, okay. But he was probably arranging a lecture for the school. He does do guest lecturing. Besides, he likes Madison too much to leave it."

"He likes something else more."

"What the hell are you talking about?"

"There's got to be a reason for him to want to leave Madison. Can you think of anything?"

Sure the hell can. "No, he won't leave. I know him too well. He loves that school."

"Hey, I was simply letting you know . . . for your own personal info. What do I know?"

"Way too much to be a student."

"Tease me all you want, but I think he's leaving because of you. I know he likes you."

"Yes, Tiffany, I do know."

After the basketball game, Brandi quickly showered and dressed, knowing Tiffany was waiting for her. As she walked past the men's dressing area, she thought she heard splashing from the Olympic sized pool. She wondered who was lagging behind. Since all of the players were gone, she figured it to be a member of the swim team. For some unknown reason she decided to investigate.

The swimmer was at the deep end of the pool doing backstrokes. She walked along the pool to see who it was and immediately recognized Tim's long, muscular arms reaching to the sky.

As he swam the length of the pool, she walked along, wishing she was in the pool with him—making love. After what they had shared in his living room a few Saturdays ago, she knew she was the last person Tim wanted to see without having clothes on.

She thought of the fact that he hardly had anything on and it enticed her even more to go to him. He looked good wet. Sneaking a look at him with everything at attention would be an added bonus for the day. But she wasn't there for that. Her mission that night was to find out if Tiffany was right. Leaving Madison would make a way for them to be together, but at what price?

Tim spotted Brandi midway down the lane and swam to the edge to greet her. "What are you doing here?"

"I should ask you that. Why are you in the pool?"

"I come here sometimes to work off tension. It helps me to think clearly, you know, some alone time."

"I know you would rather be alone now but I think we need to talk."

"Sounds serious."

"It is serious. Do you have a minute?"

"Sure. What's wrong?"

Seeing his navy trunks clinging to his hips made her lose her train of thought.

"Brandi, are you okay?"

Remembering where she was, she handed him his towel. "Yeah, I'm fine."

"What's the problem? I hope you're not here about what happened the other night. I said I was sorry."

"It's not that." She didn't know whether to confront him or not. Getting Tiffany in trouble with him could jeopardize their friendship, but she had to know something. Avoiding the subject until she could approach it calmly would have to do. "Did you enjoy the game tonight?"

"Indeed I did; you ladies wowed everyone. Was your family able to make it?"

"Not all of them. My Aunt Theresa said she'll come to Holbrook for that game."

"Good. I hope they win that one just for her sake. How does your brother feel about the team now?"

"He still wants to sign up, but the brat's got some growing up to do."

"Brat? Sounds like what my brother, Greg, used to call me."

"Brother? Didn't know you had one. There's lots that I don't know about you; for instance, the decision you might be making soon regarding NYU and Columbia."

He sat on the bench and dried a space for her. "What are you talking about."

"I saw Tiffany the other day. She told me about Columbia. Does this have anything to do with us almost kissing a few weeks ago?"

"I asked her not to tell anyone."

"You wouldn't have told me? You would have just left one day and not say a word?"

"Of course I would have told you, Brandi."

"Then tell me now. I deserve to know."

"I was going to tell you when I knew something more definite. Everything is up in the air, Brandi. I don't know if I'm leaving yet. It was just an interview."

"Tim, am I the reason for the interview?"

"Yes and no."

"What's that mean?"

He ran the towel over his damp hair. "It means just that. Yes, I am considering Columbia and NYU's offer, and no, you're not the only reason. I've been considering their offer for a long time. They've been offering me a position there for over two years now." The towel dropped to his lap. "You're half the reason, though."

"I don't want to be. I didn't mean to be."

"This is not your fault, Brandi. You weren't the cause of my roaming Manhattan that night until I found you. Hell, I didn't even know I was looking for you. Now that I know you, it's become a little hard to control everything."

"You still want to be with me no matter what?"

"I also didn't say I want to be with you no matter what. I can't let this get in the way of my job, Brandi. That's why I'm seriously considering Columbia now. Besides, wouldn't my being white make life a little hard for you outside of this school?"

"If I had found you somewhere other than this school, I wouldn't give a good damn who didn't want us to be together. What matters is that we're together at a school that doesn't condone students and teachers hanging together."

"Hanging together, huh? That's a good way to put it."

"That's what it is, us being together, no matter how I phrase it."

"My color doesn't matter to you?"

She leaned against the coldness of the tiled wall. "I have been battling that, Tim. I think it's because I didn't want my friends and family harassing me. I just . . ."

"I asked if *you* still care about that. Not what anyone else thinks."

"No. I don't care about that. If I did, that would make me awfully shallow. Do you think I'm shallow?"

"You're the most together woman I know."

"There's so much that you have to learn about me. I am black, and that makes me different from any white woman you've been with. You still have to learn some things."

"What do I have to learn, Brandi? You're a woman, a woman that I like even though I don't want to. Everyone learns what to do and what not to do when in a relationship. That's basic."

"That brings us to the real point, doesn't it? Do you want a relationship with me? I think it's the only reason you would leave a school you've invested some time in. Talk to me."

He rubbed his eyes with the towel, beginning to tire of the conversation. "Are you leaving or not, Tim?"

"I don't know, Brandi. I don't know anything these days but I do know the only way I can be with you is to leave."

"I feel awful about that."

"Don't! If I leave it'll be because I want to."

He wouldn't leave what he loves to make a way for them. She teased: "I know the women will miss you. You're so totally fine, Timothy Polaris."

"Wrong! I probably look like a white version of Fred Sanford."

"Maybe in your mind. Thank God you don't to the rest of the world. The fact remains, I like you, Tim. You're much more man than I realized when I met you in Manhattan. I like being with you because you're also compassionate. I like that in a person, especially men. If you left here, you know I would be after you."

Silence. Then: "You're hard to fight but well worth it. Brandi; there are other problems, though. I'm not good in relationships. They scare me."

"I don't want to scare you, just love you. Is that too much to ask?"

"No, but it might be hard with me. It will be hard."

"No relationship is easy, and I don't expect ours to be all peaches and cream. That's not realistic to even imagine these days."

"You're right."

"Then I guess I wait, and hope your decision will be best for both of us."

"Whatever the case, I hope you'll feel free to come to me for tutoring. I want you to do well above everything else."

"God knows I need the help."

"Your last two papers were great. You did a good job on Poe, and he's very hard to interpret." He stood and wrapped the towel around his hips. "We should leave before someone walks in here."

"Have we settled this?"

"For now."

She knew he would leave Madison. She was actually glad to be *a* reason, if not *the* reason. She could have her man.

"If I do leave, Eric will be happy."

"Who cares what Eric will be? He's a prude who wants everything his way. Life doesn't work like that."

"Indeed. I should know."

She didn't known much of his life, but knew some of it hadn't been good. All she wanted was to be the one to change that. As he walked to the showers, she called him. "Tim, is your house okay? I remember you said there had been another break in."

"No. I found another busted window in my basement."

"You're kidding?"

"Wish I was. Did you tell anyone that you were getting help from me?"

"Tiffany, but she's the only one. I'm sorry."

"It wasn't your fault."

"You don't think that Tiffany . . .

"Never. She's too smart for that."

"Can I help with anything; help you fix the window?"

"I got it together, Brandi. You should take off now."

She had forgotten to mention having told Eric about the tutoring. Eric was enough of a hothead, but to break into Tim's house was not like him. He had caused her trouble in the past, like parking in front of her house and beeping his horn until she came out; following her and her friends. Also making a total ass of himself at the movies one evening. Confronting Eric would only make matters worse, especially for Tim. He would go to Columbia for sure if he had any inkling that Eric was behind this.

Instead of going home as he usually did after attending a home game, Tim sat in his truck and dialed Claire Hammond's cell number urgently. He waited for the ringing then heard her voice. His words rushed out before she could finish her sentence. "Claire, it's me. I need to come in."

"Tim, I have a client coming in soon. Are you okay?"

"I don't know. There's a lot of crap going on lately."

"This can't wait until your regular appointment next week?"

"I really need to talk to someone."

"I'm checking my schedule. Hold on. . . . I can squeeze you in at six. You can be my last appointment. Just promise me you won't kill yourself getting here."

"I don't want to die, Claire. I just need someone to help me learn how to live."

"I'm here for you, buddy. Always will be."

An hour later, he was at Claire's door. He had been seeing her off and on for over ten years. He walked in, Claire's secretary, Diannah, smiled: "You can go in, darling. She's waiting."

Claire knew something different was up the minute she saw his face. "Okay, Tim, what's the deal? You don't normally make extra appointments; usually I have to track you down to keep them."

"It's about Brandi again."

"Still fighting yourself over her, I see."

"Claire, I'm still thinking about when I almost kissed her. I just can't seem to stop thinking of her, wanting her the way I never thought I would want another woman."

"But you used control then. You can use it now. You have to, Tim."

"I don't know what to do about Brandi."

"Tim, you and I have discussed what needs to be done with that situation."

"I know, and I'm working on it. Time is not moving fast enough though. She's in my face all the time, and when she isn't, I'm thinking about her."

"What have you done to put something in motion about changing this relationship, because you know it won't just work out somehow."

"I know it won't, Claire. I actually had the Columbia interview."

"Good move. What else?"

"The second interview at NYU is next week."

"Fine, those are steps in the right direction, as we discussed before. But . . ."

"I really don't want to leave Madison. I like it there."

"I know you do, but is Brandi willing to move to another professor's class?"

"She needs my classes for the honors program. Besides, I . . . I haven't really. . . ."

"You haven't discussed it with her. Am I right?"

"No. We have talked about what this is doing to us. She confronted me. Someone saw me at Columbia and told her."

"Tim, you're going to have to be more up front with Brandi. She needs to know what you're going through and when you're going through it. You can't leave her guessing. She's half of the situation. Don't be scared to talk to her."

"I am still scared. I really like her, Claire, more than I have anyone else. I'm afraid of giving her too much to handle. I should be handling this better than I am; I should be sparing her as much confusion as possible."

"You can't do it alone, Tim. I don't think she would want you to if she is as great as you say she is."

"She's incredible, and I want her to stay that way. She doesn't need any more problems in her life."

"And you do? Tim, you know the answer to your problem with Brandi. If you want her, you have to do what's best for you both. We just mentioned the solutions, the interviews. Yes, I know you love Madison. It's a good school, but so are the others. You went to one of them. Is it that you don't think you can handle larger universities?"

"That's the least of my worries. Moving to one of them is not the real problem."

"I know it isn't. What's scaring you is the relationship after the move."

"Exactly."

"Since you and I both know what the real problem is, that's what we need to concentrate on."

"How?"

"By getting to the root that started long ago, way before Brandi was born; your fear of women. Yes, you've made progress, lots of progress. Wanting to date again after Charlotte is a major step. You're willing to let someone else inside your world, but her staying there is the problem."

"I liked my one-night-stands. No commitment required."

"That is not what you like, Tim; it's what you're comfortable with."

"It worked for me."

"It was a means to an end, and it didn't work for you. If it had, you wouldn't have this problem with Brandi. Don't you see, she is your way of getting normalcy into your life. Having dozens of sex partners is not normal and you know that. Brandi triggers something in you, what you want, what you need."

"Umm, you have a point. I do want her. I like who she is, what she does, how she does it. I like everything about her, Claire."

"But it wasn't always like that, was it?"

"You know I met her in a club."

"I do know that. I also know that you two found one another again. Unfortunately, it was at Madison, but nonetheless, you two are together." She leaned forward in her chair. "Tim, don't be afraid of Brandi. Apparently, she thinks you're worth her time, and you are. You're a good man. What you and I need to work on is getting you to understand that. Do you think you're a good man?"

"I don't deliberately hurt people, if that's what you mean."

"Partly. But do you think you're worth her love?"

He sat there silently.

Claire sensed his mind was going a mile a minute. "Tim, everything that's happened in your life has helped you build this wall around yourself. You don't want to break it down and see what's on the other side. You think that wall is hiding a monster that may hurt Brandi."

"I could hurt her."

"Do you want to?"

"Of course not, Claire. That's why I'm here. I don't want to hurt her, but I hurt everyone in my life. I hurt Greg. I hurt . . ."

"I know who else you hurt, but in that circumstance, you had no choice. You will not hurt Brandi. However, if you love her and will do nothing about it, that will hurt her and she will go on without you. Do you want that?"

"No!"

"Do you feel strong enough about Brandi to make that jump to Columbia or NYU?"

"I want to now more than before. I will miss Madison."

She smiled. "I see progress here. You are not that monster you thought you were. You also realize that not all women are bad."

"I know Brandi isn't. I just don't want to hurt her."

"And you won't. Trust yourself. Above everything else, do what you are comfortable with. If you aren't comfortable with moving, we'll discuss that, but I think you know what you're going to do."

"NYU is also a good school."

"It is." She put her pen down. "Feeling better about this?"

"You always make me feel better about my life. You have that knack."

"I didn't become a psychiatrist for kicks. I want to help you, Tim. I have always wanted that. I really see some progress. You and I still need to work through some things, and it still has something to do with women. You're getting there, Tim. Call me if you need me before our scheduled appointment. If it's after hours, I'm still available to you, remember that."

"I will. Thanks, Claire. I won't let Brandi get away . . . I am still scared though."

"It seems like she could be good for you. Make a list of pros and cons about your relationship with her. If you have more pros, then you set the table for a good life with her."

"Marriage?"

"Take it slow, Tim. as I said, you're getting there, but there's still some work to be done. See Diannah before you leave. She'll remind you of your next appointment."

There was still Tim's other problem, probably the biggest one of all for him to come to terms with. Not having a relationship with his brother, Gregory.

CHAPTER 9

Eric sat several rows away from Brandi, staring and smiling at her, as usual. She hadn't gotten the chance to confront him about Tim's basement window, but certainly would later. If he hadn't broken it, he certainly knew who had. There was something different about Eric's smile today; it was meaner, nastier, as if he was into something. She put it aside, thinking it might be her imagination. Tiffany moved in beside her. "Did you finish your paper?"

"Yes, with Dr. Polaris's help. It's still hard for me to concentrate on literature when I would rather be doing other things with him."

Monica Shang entered Tim's classroom and addressed the class. "I'll be taking Dr. Polaris's class today. He was injured in the parking lot this morning and drove himself to County General. I'm sure he will be fine, though."

Brandi couldn't believe what she was hearing. She stared at Miss Shang, then looked at Eric, who had that creepy smile on his face as though he were the devil himself. She just knew he had something to do with Tim's injury and wanted to confront him, but she decided to take her shot at him later. The good thing about it was that Tim was able to drive himself to the hospital instead of having to be rushed there. After class, she'd call his home and see if she could do any thing to help him.

The minute Miss Shang ended her lecture, Brandi walked into the hall and called Tim's house on her cell. No answer. Her second thought was to call County General. Within minutes, they told her where Tim was and she was on her way, whether or not she should have been. She would think of those consequences later.

A TASTE OF TEMPTATION

Tim lay on the hospital bed, wondering who he could have ticked off enough to land him in emergency. He could think of no one. He didn't even see the culprit, as he was banged across the shoulder from behind. All he had seen was someone duck around a building. It was done so fast. Normally he would have chased them down, but the pain was too bad to run. After starting the truck, he realized the pain was too great to do that, so he slowly drove around the corner to security, where they called EMS. They told him they would investigate and do everything they could to find the culprit. With that in mind, Tim sat there with the officer until the ambulance arrived.

This is the third incident: first the flat tire, then the basement window, now this. He didn't know what was going on, but figured it was someone who knew he liked Brandi. The sheets of paper in his yard strewn around were obvious indicators.

The doctor finished placing the large bandage on the left side of Tim's upper left shoulder blade. "Dr. Polaris, try sitting up, but slowly. Your X-rays indicate only bruising, but nothing that should keep you here."

"When can I leave?"

"An hour, maybe two, but you need to go straight home and rest a couple of days, maybe go back to work on Monday . . . just to be on the safe side."

"Monday! I've got lots to do between now and Monday."

"Madison can survive long enough to get you well. Besides, that'll give you the weekend, when Madison won't be open."

"I'm busy all the time, even weekends. I grade papers, I set up trips, I . . ."

"I'm serious. It was a bad crash across your shoulder, and those can be serious if you don't watch it! Go home and stay there. Do you have anyone who can pick you up?"

That was when he wanted the luxury of depending on family. "One of the guards from campus security."

"Good. For now, lie back slowly and rest."

Tim woke up an hour later; Brandi was sitting in a chair next to his bed. He was shocked to see her; she was supposed to be in class. "What are you doing here, Brandi?"

"Never mind that. How are you feeling?"

"Better, but what are you doing here?"

"Miss Shang told us what happened, and I couldn't wait to come and see about you."

"You shouldn't have, you know how people think."

"I don't care about them, Tim. Friends see after one another. That's why I'm here. Now, no more questions; rest. When you finish resting, I'll take you home."

"The security officer can do that."

"Then I'll ride back with both of you."

"What about your car?"

"I can come back for that, Tim, now stop worrying about everything."

"You sure go through an awful lot of mess for me."

"You're worth it."

"Did you see my truck in the lot?"

"I did. Don't worry, it's okay. We'll get it later."

"But, Brandi . . ."

"Rest. End of discussion."

Two hours later, Brandi was able to convince security that she could take him home. She opened her car door for Tim and watched him slide in slowly. After she got in, she faced him. "Who do you think could have done this to you?"

Tim sat down slowly in the passenger side of her car. "I haven't any idea."

It was obvious to Brandi who it was. For now, she was concerned about getting Tim back to his truck and trailing him home.

Both Tim and Brandi saw his truck sitting there with the two rear tires flat. They slowly pulled up to the Durango and scanned it. All they could do was stare. "Brandi, why didn't you tell me about the tires before now?"

"I didn't know."

"Then it must have happened after I alerted the guards. Why didn't they patrol the area?"

"Here, take my cell and call your towing company. I'll wait here with you."

Instead of taking the phone, he slowly got out and walked to his truck as if in a trance. Brandi tried stopping him, but he kept walking, touching it delicately, as if it were a newborn.

She followed him, taking his hand. "Let's go back to my car and wait."

He reached into his pocket for his keys and opened the door.

"Tim, what are you doing?"

"I have to see if it still starts."

"It will start, Tim."

"How do you know? I have to see about this, Brandi. You know how I am about my truck."

"Yes, don't I?" She called the towing company while he inspected the truck. Something had to be done to temporarily take his mind off his truck. She knew how men were about their vehicles, but didn't know he had it that bad, bad enough to examine every scratch on it despite his aching shoulder. Then again, she remembered how Eric drooled over the BMW his rich old coot of a father bought for him. She could never fathom why a parent would give someone with Eric's driving record a new car like that one. Her hand covered his again. "I'm sorry about the truck. I know how you feel about it."

"I just wish I knew who it was around here that I ticked off."

"A past lover, maybe?" She tried not to get Tim upset by mentioning her suspicions about Eric.

"No. Even the women I dealt with had more restraint than this."

"I know you fight, visit bars and, well, sleep . . ." She didn't quite know how to say it, so he finished for her.

"You can say it, sleep around."

"Could it be one of those ladies?"

"Could be, but I haven't done that in a while."

"Really? When did that stop?"

"The night I met you."

That took her off guard, not quite expecting Timothy Polaris to stop his freewheeling ways because of one woman. That answer made her want to kiss him but knew that couldn't happen in the school's parking lot. Instead, she settled for: "That's . . . that's a good thing."

"Is it?" He looked into her flushed face, wanting so desperately to feel himself inside of her, wanting to feel the softness of her body against the hardness of his. Fortunately, for him, security drove up.

Tim approached the officer. "I thought my truck was being watched after I left for the hospital. What happened to my tires?"

The officer approached him. "Sir, those tires were flat when we scanned the area the first time."

Tim thought, *Maybe I just didn't see the flat tires in the first place.* Then he discounted that. "No, I came back to the truck because I forgot my laptop. I didn't see any flat tires. This had to happen while I was gone."

"We saw nothing on the monitor after you left, and we continued scanning the area. However, we do have someone on security tape running from the scene."

"Who is it?"

"We don't know that yet, but we're still investigating the incident." The man's eyes softened when he saw Tim rubbing his shoulder. "Are you okay, Dr. Polaris?"

"I'm tired. Look, I didn't mean to get on you. I know you and the guys are doing everything you can."

"It's no problem, Dr. Polaris. We have to get a handle on this so it won't happen again."

"I appreciate it." From the corner of his eye, he saw the tow truck arriving.

The mechanic hoisted the truck onto the flatbed as Tim and Brandi watched. They followed close behind to Mid-Town Collision, took care of the paperwork, then headed to Jamaica Estates—to a house he hadn't wanted to take Brandi back to—unless she was in his arms.

"You don't need to come inside, Brandi. We picked up my medicine, and I'm going right to bed."

"Close your mouth for once and let me do my thing. You need to eat something, and I cook a pretty good meal."

"Really? Like what?"

"Anything. Cooking and writing are my things in life, so just shut up, unlock the door, and get in your pajamas."

"I don't wear any."

She let out a slow breath. *Way too much information, Tim.* "Whatever you do or don't wear, go in and get into them."

Dreading the inside of the place because of the memories, she forced herself inside. To take her mind off Tim's bedroom, she started looking around for canned of soup. She reached inside the pantry, took out a can of 'Chunky' and heated it up.

Noise from the bedroom indicated Tim was doing everything but resting. "Get in the bed, Tim."

The moving about stopped moments later. Myrrh wasn't barking anymore, and she was left alone to tend to a can of soup and a salad in utter quiet. She looked around the immaculate kitchen. The entire house was clean, other than his basement steps, but not so immaculate for her to think he had a housekeeper. No, he did it himself; there were still newspapers and man things scattered about. She didn't see pictures of his family. She knew he had a brother, but no pictures of him. The only picture she saw was in his computer room when she nosed around. It was an ultrasound image of a baby. *His baby?*

She entered his room with the steaming hot soup, the salad, and a cup of tea. "Here it comes, and you had better have clothes on, Tim. I'm not playing." He had fallen asleep with the covers pulled over his shoulders. As she walked in, she couldn't help but notice how cute he was bundled up like a baby in that big bed. That bed that they had made love on that night. She touched the covers, then realized she had to get the hell out of there before her emotions ran amok.

She wrote him a note and left it on his dresser. There was a letter there addressed to a Mr. Gregory Polaris with Tim's return address on it. Being the snoop she was, she had wanted to read it, knowing it was to his brother. He seemed so sad the few times he even mentioned his brother, and she wanted to know why. The letter was already sealed, so she left it alone.

Leaning over Tim, she kissed his forehead, then left. His hair and skin made her hands tingle, nervously for and because of him. Eric once had that effect on her. That was now a distant memory. Though he was supposed the 'right color' for her, he still didn't have what it took to drive her mad with passion. She looked in on Tim again before leaving. "It would take you to make me feel like a woman in bed."

She took her keys from his dining room table and saw a note to himself: "Tell Brandi about the November 'Hands On' presentation."

"What the hell is that?" No matter what it was, she knew she wanted to go, if for no reason except to be near him.

Near the door sat a Halloween pumpkin filled with candy to be handed out that night. A smiled brightened her face; so, he was a softie at heart. He was the kind of man women waited all their lives for, but she hoped she wouldn't have to wait that long. She moved the plastic pumpkin aside, stepped into the fading sun, on her way home.

Later that night, Tim warmed up his soup in the microwave. He had wanted to hand out the Halloween candy to the kids, but was too out of it. Then he looked into the now-empty pumpkin and realized Brandi had done it for him. In her own way, Brandi was systematically doing everything it took to make him fall harder for her. But he knew she wasn't even aware of doing what she was doing. Being kind and gentle came naturally to her, it was her way.

Eric sat down on the porch next to Brandi that Saturday morning. "Why didn't you come inside? From what I could gather from your phone call, it's urgent."

"There's a breeze out here; besides, what I have to talk to you about needs to be said out here instead of where your mother can hear us— she hears everything on purpose, Eric."

"Why are you jumping on Mom suddenly? She's cool, never disturbs me when I need my privacy."

"Whatever, Eric. I'm here because we do need to talk."

"Coming back to me?"

"I said we need to talk, not do something totally stupid."

"So talk. What's on your mind?"

"Oh, don't worry. I have plenty to say."

He leaned back stretching his legs out. "This sounds like a permanent 'see ya'. Am I right?"

"I am not here about us. I'll get to the point. You know where Dr. Polaris lives."

"I beg to differ. I think this is about us, now that I hear his name." He noted her grim expression. "Yeah, okay. I know where he lives. Why?"

"You were there that night, and I know it. There's a window broken in his basement, and a paper was taken that he wanted to give to me."

"First off, I wasn't there, and I didn't break any damn window. Second, if I was stupid enough to do that, would I admit it to you?"

"You might, if you thought it would throw me off. I know your sly, stupid games, Eric. How do you even know where he lives?"

"You know where he lives, why shouldn't I? Maybe we should tell the rest of the campus where this good ole boy lives."

"Just shut up! You're beginning to look as sickening as you act. Dad told me to be civil around you, but I can see that's impossible. I know where he lives because . . . well, because he had the papers for me." A half lie was better than telling Eric anything he could use against her.

"Brandi, he could have given you those at school." The snarky smile returned. "I think my idea was a good one: tell everyone where he lives. That way he could have the entire chick population come to him, right?"

"I'm sure Stacey Neal would be glad to be one of them. She can't be getting any 'real action' from someone as dull as you are. Then again, you're both dull."

"You're going too low with that Stacey crap. Lay off. I told you how it was with her chasing me."

"Eric, the point is that I'm not the one in question. You are. You have made it a point to find out where he lives, and for no reason. It's not like you're trying to get his help, although you need it way more than I do."

"Depends on the type of *help* we're talking about."

Gracing him with a response to that went against her grain, so she stared at him.

"You want the truth, Brandi? The truth you shall get. I followed you Friday. You rushed out of class so fast that I thought something was wrong with you instead of Mr. Timothy. When you got to the hospital and didn't come out, I waited and waited."

"Wait! You followed me?"

"I said I thought something was wrong. Brandi, I care about you. That's why I followed you. I followed you from the hospital back to his truck, then to his house. You stayed in that house an awfully long time, I might add!"

"Then if you knew I was okay when you saw me outside the hospital, why did you continue to follow me?"

"Because *he* was with you, Brandi! Why were you gallivanting around town with him? He is not your type, and you know it. Don't you remember? It has something to do with a *white thang.*"

"Grow up, Eric." She walked to her car then turned back to him. "He needed my help because someone attacked him. But you know that already, don't you? He was hit hard enough to require days to rest. You know that, too, don't you? Sure you do."

"Again, if I had done that, would I tell? Get real, Brandi. I did not touch him, and you shouldn't either. That could get him in trouble."

"Who would know, Eric, unless someone told? Who would tell? You?"

"Possible."

"Nothing to tell; I haven't touched him, either." *Not today, anyway.*

"Brandi . . ."

"Bye, Eric. I'm history."

He called to her again. "I didn't break any window, Brandi."

"Sure you didn't. Can't you tell from my voice that I believe you? Sheesh!"

He watched her drive off.

CHAPTER 10

That next game brought in a jammed-packed crowd, including Brandi's family. While scanning the crowd for her aunt, Brandi spotted Eric sitting with Stacey, both of them staring at her. *The nerve of him bringing that heifer to my game.* Both Eric and Stacey were staring at her. She could feel their eyes penetrating her, assaulting her. Eric had always been no good, but bringing Stacey there took him to a whole new level.

Forcing her mind off them, she looked at her parents just as her Aunt Theresa arrived and joined them. Theresa was in her early to mid-thirties and was more like an older sister than an aunt; Brandi could talk to her about anything, including her feelings for Tim. She spoke of Tim to her aunt several times, having received good advice about waiting on him to make the move to another school—if he would. Brandi also knew Theresa wouldn't care about Tim being white. Men were men in her book.

Giving a final wave to her family before the start of the game, she and the other cheerleaders did their final drill. She wanted to be extra good to show up that damn Stacey, though she really no longer cared who Eric dated.

Tim entered the gym and sat in the front row to get a good perspective of the game. Brandi smiled when she saw him and waved to Theresa again, pointing to Tim and mouthing, "That's him."

Minutes before the game Brandi quickly walked to Tim. "I'm glad you could make it."

"Wouldn't miss it. It's *our* Madcats and I have to support them, and you cheerleaders as well. Knock the other team dead tonight."

"We plan to, but . . . could you possible do a favor for me?"

"Sure. What do you need?"

"My Aunt Theresa is here, and I would like you to meet her." She lowered her voice, "I told her how hot you are, though you don't believe that you are."

"I would love to meet her. Besides, I've had that request once tonight already. Connie's mom wants to meet me. I'll come over the minute I finish with them."

The evening was not turning out to be as enjoyable as he had hoped. Sure, Brandi and the other ladies looked great doing their routine and getting the crowd excited, but that was part of the problem. She looked too good, so good in fact that she had taken his mind from the game. The Madcats were losing already 74 to 89, so that was a total wash. There was nothing to keep his mind occupied—other than staring at a beautiful, off-limits woman. Had he not promised two of his students that he'd meet their families, he would surely have left to drown in thoughts of which university position to accept, since they both offered a contract.

By game's end Tim definitely felt a migraine happening, but stayed nonetheless to fulfill an obligation. The absolute last thing he wanted to do was act like a gentleman when he felt like a troll. An idea hit him: go to his favorite retreat, the pool, and work off some steam in the water. No matter what he did, however, Brandi would still be on his mind.

After the loss, the team and cheerleaders headed to the showers, and the spectators to the gates, all except the two families who stayed to meet him. He met briefly with Connie's family first, saving the worse for last, Brandi's. The group was awaiting him on the bench, and he slowly headed over.

Brandi met him halfway. "You don't have to do this. I know you're not feeling well."

"How do you know?"

"I can see it in your eyes. Is this related to the accident the other day?"

"Not this one. I told you I would meet them. It's not a problem."

She was finally introducing Tim to her family. They walked over to the bleachers and stopped dead in front of her mother. "Mom, this is the man who saved my literal neck in English lit."

He took Mrs. Miles' hand. "I can see where Brandi gets her looks."

"Thank you. You're too kind, Dr. Polaris."

"You and your husband have a wonderful, smart daughter." Extending his hand to Mr. Miles was more than a notion for him, but did it for Brandi's sake. "Good to meet you, Mr. Miles."

Feeling much the same way Tim had, Jeff reluctantly shook hands, but stared into Tim's eyes. The face was familiar, but from where, he wasn't sure. "Tough loss today."

"Yes, but they're a good team. We've won the last three out of five. We'll recover just fine." He looked over at Brian. "Still want to come and play for us?"

"I could have helped the team win today!"

Brandi shoved him. "As if! You remember Brian from the other game?"

"I certainly do. Don't worry, Brian, you'll make it."

"Yeah, if his mind grows as fast as his body does; that may never happen, though."

Tim smiled at the exchange between Brandi and her brother, wishing he and Greg had that kind of relationship—any kind of relationship. He turned to Brandi's aunt. "You must be Theresa. Brandi has mentioned you before."

"Sure hope she did me justice, Dr. Polaris."

"More than you know."

Theresa looked over at her stiff acting brother-in-law and caught him rolling his eyes. "Brandi has mentioned you as well, and it's nice to finally meet you."

He released her hand. "Thank you. It was my pleasure to have met you all."

Brandi kissed her mother's cheek. "Give me a few minutes to shower."

As they walked, Brandi noticed Tim going the same way she was. "Aren't you going home?"

"I need a dip in the pool. That always relaxes me."

"Is something wrong tonight?"

"No, it's just that the water helps to relax me. It has healing powers."

"Yes, it does. Enjoy it, and I'll see you in class tomorrow."

Still sitting on the bleachers, Theresa sighed in a wistful voice. "What a hunk! Imagine soaping him up."

Brian smiled at his aunt, but his mother was disapproving. "Theresa, please. Brian's here, watch your mouth."

Jeff also had something to say. "We don't need you corrupting our boy."

"Oh, be quiet, Jeff. He's almost fourteen. To keep my sister happy, I'll close my mouth." But several seconds of silence was about all Theresa could manage before getting back to Tim. "He sure is a hottie. No wonder Brandi has it bad for him."

Mrs. Miles spoke up. "What do you mean?"

"Anyone can see she likes the guy."

Jeff butted in again. "So long as it stays a crush."

Both his wife and Theresa turned to him and, in unison, said, "Cool it, Jeff."

Instead of getting into his usual lecture the following Tuesday morning, Tim briefly read over his notes, then looked up at his class. He held a pile of papers in the air. "As everyone is well aware, Madison is going to a writers retreat in Niagara Falls next April. Your essays will be submitted to the literature department there. The top papers will be presented at the end of the retreat. You will want to do your best on this. I can't stress this enough. If you need help, you know you can make appointments to see me or Miss Shang. Are there any questions?"

There were no questions, so Tim continued. "As you also know, not everyone will qualify to go. The hands-on presentation in two weeks will determine who will be going. Today, you will be submitting samples of your writing. You will select a topic from the list on the board. This is something like a pre-test to see who will get to participate. Spaces are limited since other schools are competing. So I need you to do well today. Miss Shang went over part of this the other day in my absence. Any questions before we get started? No? Okay, you have one hour to show me what you can do. Make this good, people. I want Madison well represented."

After the exercise, Brandi stayed behind to talk to him about the next paper due, and the retreat. "Do you have a minute?"

"Sure. You need more information on the retreat?"

"I'm set with that."

"How do you think you did today?"

"I think I did really well."

"Good. What can I help you with?"

She was taken aback by his professional tone, since no one else was there. "Do you have any notes on Charles Dickens? I've decided to do my paper on him."

"I do, but since you did so well on your other papers without my help, other than the first one, I think you can do it again without me. Bookstores have a wealth of knowledge on Dickens, as well as other great authors. Which of his books are you doing it on?"

"*A Christmas Carol.*"

"I was hoping you wouldn't pick that one."

"Why not?"

"It's been done to death in movie after movie. There's got to be nineteen thousand movies on that book."

"That's why I'm doing it. I need notes so I can dig deeper into the characters. I've seen it so many times, I know it by heart. Even the

Flintstones have done one." She hid her face behind her folder so he wouldn't see her laughing.

"I still think you should do . . ." He thought about her comment. "The Flintstones, Brandi? Come on, at least graduate to X-Men if you like cartoons. I'm serious, though. Do something that hardly anyone does—something that's not been on television."

"I guess that rules out my second choice, *The Time Machine*?"

"It won an Academy Award in 1960 for special effects; everyone has seen it. I want you to think beyond the box. You have a good mind; use it. Go on-line for information. As I said, bookstores and the campus library are good sources. Dickens is very easy to find. You haven't needed my services for some time, and I only tutored you once. That means you can do this without me. Right?"

"I know what you mean."

"I'm sorry, but you're too smart to take the easy way out. Use that beautiful mind of yours to your advantage. I have some things that you can use but you'll have to come to the office for them. I don't want you in my house again."

"What?"

"I don't mean it to sound mean, but I don't want to risk your safety. Something is going on there, and I don't know who is behind it." He closed his briefcase. "By the way, don't tell Eric anything else about what we do."

"What do you mean? I haven't told him anything, other than you tutored me once on a paper."

"Even that's too much. I don't trust him. I think he can and will try to use anything to get me—or you for that matter—in trouble. I would just feel better if you said as little as possible to him about me."

Keeping her own suspicions to herself, Brandi reassured him: "Fine, but you don't have to worry about him."

"Good. Hope it stays that way."

The following week Dr. Moore, the English lit department head, called Tim into his office. He held the fifteen passing compositions for Tim review for the hands-on trip the following weekend. "I've picked the best three from each of your four classes, some from Dr. Graham's, and some from Elliot Dumay's classes. I've decided to select the reserves from Alan Ford's freshman class. I figured you'd appreciate seeing the list, since most of them are your students. From your Tuesday and Thursday classes I've picked Joan Dorsey, Tiffany Jackson, Ronald Lawson, Jean Dunlop and Brandi Miles . . ."

"Brandi Miles? Really? Her paper was that good?"

Dr. Moore raised his brow. "Yes, Miss Miles passed quite well, in fact. Why?"

"Nothing, really; she had some problems with her focus at first. That's all."

"Are you sure that's all, Tim?"

"Yes, why?"

"She's a very lovely young woman; no man can deny that, including you. I have seen how you brighten up when her name is mentioned. What's going on?"

"Nothing. Yes, she's gorgeous, but . . ."

"I didn't say 'gorgeous'. I said she was lovely." He put his pen down, and came around to Tim's side of the desk. "I'm having a problem with your reaction to her. The car wash, for example, was a dead giveaway. You tried to hide it, but it didn't work, not with me. You could barely take your eyes off her."

"What are you getting at?"

"I'm not 'getting at' anything. You need to calm down, because we don't need a scandal here, Tim."

"I know this already, and there will be no problems. I value my job here. Look, you've known me for years, long enough to know that I would never cause any trouble for the school."

"I know that. You're a good man. I just don't want you in any trouble. I know your life has been hectic— those attacks, your divorce and . . ."

"Charlotte is not the reason for anything I may be going through now, Derrick. I would rather keep her where she is, out of my life."

"Just make sure Miss Miles stays out of it, too." He pulled out her essay. "This A+ puts her at the top. Were you concerned she couldn't do it?"

"No, she catches on fast." Tim tiptoed around his next words. "You know a lot of the students will be at the hands-on with me, including her, and I want to you reassure you . . ."

"I don't think you'll have to worry about her. She knows she needs to do well to keep that scholarship. I also know she'll want to be there because of you and your class. She seems to like you a lot and trusts you. Just stay on your toes, Tim. I trust you to do the right thing for yourself and this university. Now go on and have a ball at the hands-on in Albany. And another thing you need to do . . ."

"What?"

"Lighten up. You worry too much!"

Good advice, but Tim was used to worrying; that was what he did best from the day he was born.

CHAPTER 11

The very idea of spending the weekend in Albany with Mr. Untouchable was driving Brandi crazy. She didn't know how she would be able to stand it, but knew ultimately she had to make the best of it. The hands-on was important and she had to qualify for the next phase, the writers retreat in Niagara Falls. But the idea of the entire trip was making her anxious, and she looked forward to having it all behind her.

As if she didn't have enough to worry about, her car was refusing to start. She gave it the gas, praying it would crank, because the bus to the Albany Convention Center would leave by noon. She pressed down on the pedal, waited, tried it again—still nothing. It was 40 minutes to get to the bus.

Both of her parents had gone to Brian's hockey game and it would be after 12:00 before they returned. There was only one move to make: try and catch up with Tiffany. Then she remembered Tiffany was hitching a ride with her brother, who volunteered to drive her there on the way to his friend's house. Brandi hadn't asked early enough to ride with them, so they left. Her only other option was to page Tim, and pray he could pick her up. Either that or call Eric and ask him to take her up there. She killed that idea, because no way in hell was she going to ride that distance and have to endure him and hear his mouth. That left Tim!

After paging Tim, she waited for him to ring back. She looked up at the darkening sky. A big storm was headed their way. Everyone wanted to get to Albany ahead of it.

The phone started ringing and she answered without looking at the display. "Tim, thank God you called back."

"Brandi. Why aren't you at the bus?"

"My car won't start. Can you pick me up? We should still have enough time."

"Are you at home?"

"Yes, I'm ten minutes away from Madison."

"Okay, but we will really have to hurry, because the bus will take off without us. Be ready to hop in when I drive up."

"I'm sorry, Tim. Thanks a bunch."

Fifteen minutes later, Tim pulled up and honked. He liked her outfit: an ice-pink, velvety jogging outfit that hugged her curvy, yet slender frame in all the perfect places. He knew he had to get his mind out of the gutter, because it was going to be a long trip up to Albany. Sweating over her would only make it longer.

Brandi hopped, in bouncing to whatever was playing on her headset, and smiled at him. "Thanks, Tim. I don't know what I would have done without you."

He spoke louder so she could hear him over the music. "It's okay. I'm just glad you caught me. I was at the bus doing the head count and didn't see you. That made me . . ."

She snatched the headphones off. "Okay, I can hear you better."

"I didn't see your car in the lot, nor you on the bus. I got a little worried. Then I got your call." He checked his watch. "I told them to take off at 12 whether we were there or not."

"Why? Don't you want us to be there?"

"Of course I want us to be there, Brandi. I know the way. In case we had problems, I didn't want the others to miss out on the presentations." He pulled into gear and headed west on the expressway.

"I hope you didn't mind me paging you?"

"I gave you the number in case you needed me, and you did, so don't sweat it."

A CD case rested on her lap. "What are you listening to?"

She teased. "Something you wouldn't know about."

"Really wise, Brandi. I did manage to crawl out of the caves of Europe to learn music."

"Just kidding. I'm sorry if that bothered you."

"Nothing Brandi Elaine Miles does bothers me. So, what is it?"

"*Unwrapped* volume two. It's good, so is volume three."

"Isn't Jeff Lorber on parts of one of them?"

"You do know a lot to be a cave dweller. Yeah, you want to listen? We can put it on yours."

"We'll be at Madison shortly, so keep listening. Enjoy yourself."

They arrived at the school by 12:16, and the bus was gone. That unnerved him to no end. "Damn it!"

"I'm really sorry, Tim. I went to the university bookstore and picked up my paycheck, thinking I had enough time to go back home for some things. This is all my fault."

The only thing on his mind was deciding what route to take. Seeing her brood over the situation made him feel bad. He turned her face to his, feeling baby soft skin barely kissed by pink blush. Her skin was so warm and tantalizing. "Come on. It's not the end of the world. I know the way up there. We can take the same route the bus took."

"We should be on that bus. I went back home to get music that I could have lived without until after the trip."

"Brandi, don't worry about it. I'll gas up, and we can get started. The storm is not supposed to hit until later in the day, anyway. We have plenty of time. Take out 'Hidden Beach' and let's hear it."

"Really?"

"Yeah, it's going to be a long trip, so we'd better listen to something on the way up there. What do you have?"

"Everyone." She flipped open her leather case full of CDs and showed it to him.

Erykah Badu was the first thing he saw. "Let's hear her."

"You like Erykah?"

"Darn right I do. Anything smooth and mellow gets my attention."

Around 1:00, they had to pull over to the side of the road. The wind gusts were practically pushing the car. The rain was blowing so hard the wiper blades couldn't keep pace. He wished the truck had been out of the shop; it could take this kind of weather better than his Mercedes Coupe.

They sat by the side of the road under an underpass and talked. "Brandi, take that disc out so we can hear the weather reports."

The radio repeated that the storm was ahead of schedule, and that flooding was expected. Tim had never seen rain like this in his thirty years of living. He was concerned, because he knew they would never make it on time to the convention center. What also worried him was the people on the bus. He didn't let on to Brandi just how concerned he was, because she looked concerned enough herself.

2:30. The seminar had started. They were not going to make it in time for the main event. He hoped Monica and Daniel Lang had made it. They were his back up, had an extra set of his notes, and knew the program well. Some of the students had taken their own cars, and he wondered if they were able to make it.

Finally, there was a break in the weather and they pulled off in the direction of Albany. They had gotten a good start, but the main road to the convention center was flooded. Tim stared straight ahead. "Christ!"

Brandi had dozed off but was awakened by his sharp tone. "What's wrong?"

"The main road is flooded, and the rain is picking up again." He looked around. "Where's the bus? It couldn't have gotten through this." He turned the radio up and heard the announcer forecasting tornado watches everywhere. "We'd better back out of here and try another route."

"Is there another one?"

"Yes, but I don't know where. Maybe the bus driver found it."

They drove another half-hour, and could feel tornado weather approaching. Tim looked up at the dark sky. "We had better find somewhere to stay until this blows over. We can't even make it back home in this weather."

"I just wish I hadn't gone back home."

"This is not your fault, Brandi. We missed the bus by minutes at the most. I doubt if they even made it up there." He tried calling Monica and a few of the students, but the reception was lousy.

"What are we going to do?"

"I don't know. Let's back out of here and hit another main road. Hopefully, it won't be flooded. Maybe we can find a restaurant. You hungry?"

"Not really. You?"

"I'm okay—for now."

He slowly backed up and made it to the road. They drove on looking for lodging as the storm grew worse. Finally, they saw a motel sign. Tim smiled. "We can get something to eat in there, hopefully."

Tim pulled into the motel. Moments later, he was back, soaked to the bone. "There's no restaurant, just snack machines. They do have a room that we can stay in until the storm passes."

A motel room was the last place she had wanted to be with him. "Do they have two rooms?"

"I already asked, and they only have one room left. Other travelers booked the rest at the last minute due to the storm. Should we take it or stay in here?"

"You'll catch pneumonia if you stay in those clothes."

"My pants aren't too wet because I ran, but this shirt. . . ."

"Come on, let's get the room." That was not her preferred choice, but there wasn't another one available. Her only salvation would be to sit on the bed, eat whatever candy they could get, and play her music. Ignoring him would be hard, but she had to do it. Looking at Tim without a shirt on in a room with a bed in it could drive her completely crazy.

They went over to the desk clerk, and Tim put his credit card on the counter. "We'll take the room."

The woman blurted out: "It's taken."

Tim could see her eyes shifting from Brandi, then back to him; he knew what the deal was immediately. "How can it be taken? I was just in here, and you said there was one room available. I want the room, now where's the key?"

"Sir, the room is taken. A couple came in after you."

"No one walked into this place after me. The driveway is empty except for my car. What did they do, walk here in the rain? Where's the key?"

Brandi tugged on his wet sleeve. "Tim, we can stay in the car and let the shirt dry."

"I'm not staying in any car when I know a room is available. This is ridiculous! I want a manager out here immediately or I cause trouble. Will that be necessary?"

The woman glared at him then reached under the desk. "We only have the honeymoon suite available, and housekeeping hasn't gotten to it yet."

"I don't care at this point." He slid the card over to her and waited for his receipt. Once he signed it he shoved the receipt into his pocket, stared at the clerk with contempt then took Brandi's wet arm. "Come on."

It was disturbing seeing Tim that mad, but he had good reason. She hated when people looked at her that way.

They walked up the second-level steps, and Tim opened the door to the luxury suite. He checked the place before letting her enter, just incase something shady was going on. "It's clean already. I knew she was lying just to get us out of here. Backwards bit . . ."

"Tim, don't say it. She's not worth it."

"I have to get this off my chest somehow."

"Not like that."

"Whatever. Go on and get settled."

"Don't let her upset you like that, Tim. It's over now, so let's just deal with what we have. It is not over. We're trapped in this place and can do nothing about it."

She wasn't exactly crazy about sharing a room with him either, knowing how they would have to fight to stay away from each other. She walked into the honeymoon suite with pink-and-plum accents.

The large bed was in the middle of the sunken room. "Pretty."

"Should be for what it cost, and the bull we had to take at the counter." The look on her face made him regret getting so mad. "I'm sorry, Brandi. It's just that . . ."

"I know. Things haven't worked out the way you wanted them to. I feel bad about that."

"Don't. It's not your fault, and I'm sorry if I made it seem that way."

"I know your heart, and you'd never do that. Go on, get out of those wet clothes. "

"Thanks for understanding." He went into the bathroom to hang his wet shirt over the shower railing and wash up.

Brandi lay across the bed listening to her music, trying to ignore this other side of him, though it was rather sexy. She pulled the covers over her head, not wanting to think about being in a honeymoon suite with him. She could still hear him splashing about in the bathroom, probably nude by now. Turning her CD player up and drowning in his Drifters CD did not calm her. Nothing worked. Her mind was in overdrive from want of him.

Tim walked out tying a terrycloth robe around his waist. He threw a matching one on the bed. "They left us these."

Thank God. She tossed him a candy bar and returned to her music. "That's your lunch. Enjoy."

Unable to reach anyone by cell phone, he assumed they had made it to the conference. He started riffling through the material in his briefcase.

By evening, they were tired of watching television and touring the small pool area and vending machines, so Brandi returned to the room and decided to call home to tell everyone she was safe. She neglected to tell her parents she was in a motel room with Timothy Polaris. Hearing their mouth about that would be the last straw; she was in no mood to explain herself.

The rain was still heavy and the tornado, though still a distance away, was expected to hit neighboring communities. New York City was already a washout, as were the surrounding areas. She and Tim stared through the picture window in the front of the building and saw nothing but darkness and sheets of rain.

Brandi ate the last of her chips and yawned. "Why am I so tired? It's only 8 o'clock."

"It's been a long day, Brandi. I'm tired myself. Why don't you get some sleep?"

"I have never gone to bed this early; not to sleep, anyway."

Hearing that comment wasn't helping him, though he knew she hadn't meant to frustrate him that way. He ate his last chip and tossed the empty bag away. "I might grab a beer at the bar."

"I'll call home again to see if everyone's okay. Hopefully I can get through this time."

"Don't count on it. You were lucky before. You didn't tell them I . . ."

"Of course not. I told them I drove up with Joan."

"Good. All I need is Dr. Moore about this."

"Why are you so scared of him?"

"I'm not scared of him; we're friends. The problem, we're such close friends that he knows without my having said anything that I have the hots for you."

"You still like me that way after all the trouble I've put you through?"

"How can I not? Look at you, gorgeous beyond reason, a good head on your shoulders, and you're sincere. I see why Eric is so crazy about you. Brains and beauty are a lethal combination. I'm hating this motel more and more because you're here and I can't do a thing. I can barely look at that bed without thinking of you."

"I know the feeling, believe me. As far as Eric is concerned, my brain was the last thing he considered. He didn't think I would catch on to him and my best friend getting it on."

"He's a twit. Forget about him. We have to forget about each other, too, so long as we're in this room together."

"What do we do?"

"What can we do? Nothing! Not a darn thing!"

Tim was alone in the meager motel bar, nursing a scotch and soda. He spent the entire evening looking down into some drink, and pretending the woman upstairs really wasn't there. But she was there, and that's what he was truly afraid of. How could he sleep in the same room with her and not touch her? Then he thought about what had received several days ago—a letter from Columbia welcoming him to the staff. Suddenly, he couldn't wait to get away from Madison. Madison had been his favorite place to be—then Brandi Miles stepped into the picture. The farther he was from her by day, the better he thought he would be. The thought made him smile. As quickly as it had come, the smile disappeared. The idea of another relationship still scared him. He had decided that he didn't know how to hold one together, but he wanted to try with Brandi.

The letter from Columbia stayed on his mind, but he had yet to tell Brandi about it. He knew he had to tell her sooner or later, but not that night. No, his agenda for the rest of the evening was getting to the bottom of his drink, and then watching Brandi sleep, dying to be sleeping with her.

Tim returned to the room and found Brandi asleep on one end of the bed. The first and last thing he had wanted to do was to get on that bed with her. They would end up accidentally touching one another, then it would cease to be by accident. Before long they would be out of control and making love. As she slept with just the terry cloth robe on, he could hear her even breathing. A slight moan escaped her lips.

He slumped into the chair at the foot of the bed and watched her sleeping. Twenty minutes of daydreaming about being on that bed made him mad—mad at himself for wanting what he couldn't have, mad at her for being so beautiful and untouchable, mad at the crappy weather for throwing them together. He slammed his newspaper down, removed his shirt, put on his terry-cloth robe and tried relaxing in the chair. He drifted to sleep but was soon jolted. The flashing red numbers on the digital clock told him he had been asleep only a few minutes. He was awakened by the rain pellets slamming hard against the window, plus the ache in his back from the chair. The rain wasn't letting up, and the wind was blowing with hurricane force. He *had* to stay there. They both had to stay there.

A TASTE OF TEMPTATION

The bed looked so comfortable, and Brandi lying across it made it look all the more inviting. All he wanted was a part of the bed now. He was tried, angry; all that could go away if only he was in a warm bed. Brandi left an entire side for him, but he just couldn't trust himself to be even that close to her. Tim got up and sat on the edge of the bed staring down at her. Her robe had come undone, and the sheet was barely covering her. Even in the dim light he could still see her partly exposed breasts, her nipple barely covered by the sheet and robe. His eyes moved down to her stomach, the band of bikini panties hovering just above her pubic line. God, how he wanted to touch her. He slowly removed the earphones and put them on to see what she had been listening to. Nothing could pacify him but touching her, but all he did was look.

CHAPTER 12

The roar of distant thunder awakened Brandi with a jolt. One arm was wrapped around Tim tenderly stroking his upper back as he lay across her. Realizing what was happening, she jumped up, forcing him to his side. Her hands covered her mouth. "God, no. What have we done?"

The sudden movement awakened him. He sat up on the bed, and saw the scared look on her face. "What's wrong?"

She held her hands tightly together; her lips parted but no words came out.

"Brandi, are you okay?"

"Tim, what did we do? What did we do here last night to mess up our lives?"

"Brandi, calm down. We didn't do anything."

"Why did I wake up with you in my arms? Why were my hands on you? Why was your skin on mine?"

"We didn't do anything. I slept in the chair for most of the night. You would have remembered had we done anything. I definitely would have. I got tired of the chair, and I sat on the edge of the bed. I guess I fell asleep. I'm sorry if I scared you."

"You didn't scare me. I scared myself thinking we had made love and not having any memory of it. That's not the real issue here, though. I . . . I was afraid it would get out, that you would lose your job, that . . ."

"How would it have gotten out? Besides, I would never let anything like that happen to us." He thought about the letter from Columbia, and figured now was definitely the time to tell her. He still couldn't touch her until he was away from Madison—away from Brandi.

He leaned back on the headboard. "I received a letter from Columbia."

"Columbia? What about?"

"I . . . uh—"

"You're leaving, aren't you?"

"Yeah. It's hard telling you this."

"Just answer this, when?"

"The end of the semester,. Dr. Moore knows, and is already searching for my replacement."

Tim's replacement. Sounded so awful. No one could truly replace him. Everyone at Madison would hate her if they found out she could be the reason he was leaving. "What about the trip to Niagara Falls? If you're not at Madison . . ."

"That's still on; both schools are going."

"That's good, at least. What about this hands-on we were headed for? Is it cancelled?"

"For now it is. I spoke with Dr. Moore about that last night too, once the phone lines cleared. He's going to reschedule it for the week before the semester ends."

"That's good. What about the bus?"

"The bus parked, and everyone slept on it. They are en route back to New York."

"I'm glad they're okay. So, is this what you want, moving to another university?"

"It's what I need."

"You *are* doing this for me, then."

He didn't quite know how to answer her. If he said yes, he ran the risk of taking the easy way out for them. If he said no, her feelings would be hurt. He was fleeing, not *from* love but maybe *for* love. "I'm doing this for many reasons. Columbia is a great school, and I'm lucky to get on its staff. I've always liked Columbia, but Madison took me first, and I gladly went. It's actually harder to get a teaching position at Madison than it is at Columbia."

"Level with me. I know you love Madison. I see your enthusiasm when you're in front of us, teaching your guts out. Every other word out of your mouth is about Madison. Now, are you leaving because of me? Tell me."

A heavy sigh escaped him. "Yes."

"I didn't want that to happen."

"I'll love Columbia just as much. I'm in my element wherever I teach. It could be Princeton or Yale, just as long as I'm teaching. Besides, I'm connected to Columbia in a way after all."

"How?"

"Every other semester, I give a speech on the life of literacy program. I encourage reading and writing programs at both schools. I gave one at Madison last summer. Next month, it'll be at Columbia. But, Brandi, I want to be with you. I can't do that at Madison, and I can't expect you to leave there. You have more at stake than I do with the Seymour scholarship, and I can't let you put that at risk when I could make the change."

"You really did it for me, huh?"

"First time I've ever really wanted to do something for a woman other than take her to bed."

"When do you leave?"

"The end of the semester. December eleventh is my last day."

"The minute you can, will you call me?"

"That's my plan."

"Good. I have something to look forward to. I'm flattered that you would do this for me, and maybe a little—in love."

"Don't fall for me so soon. I don't know about relationships, Brandi. You know they've never . . ."

"I know, never worked for you. One will, and I hope it's with me."

"Just hang in there with me. We only have a few more weeks before the end of the class and I promise to call you."

"I can't wait."

Brandi passed Tim's final exam with flying colors and turned in an excellent paper on Nathaniel Hawthorne, but one thing almost clouded her happiness about her grade—Tim's leaving. In a much bigger way, however, she was happy about his move. It would allow them to be together, spend some much needed time in one another's arms. Yes, that was the spark that put an instant smile on her face. She would be able to see him more than just in lecture. She could see him in life and love.

Two days after the final exam in Tim's class, Tiffany visited Brandi. The first thing she said: "Have you visited your dear Timothy Polaris over there at Columbia yet? He's there setting up his office before the Christmas break."

"How do you know? Oops, sorry, you are the voice of New York. Of course you know where he is."

"I did go by and say good-bye to him, since I was absent his last day of lecture. I gave him a really big hug, one big enough to melt a hole right through me, and it felt so damn good."

"Did it make your day?"

"Sarcasm is hideous on you and you know it, especially with those shoes."

Brandi looked down at her beige pumps. "What are you talking about?"

"It was a joke, girl! The point is, Brandi, you need to go see him."

"Tiffany, I'm sure the man has been busy getting his classes arranged and adjusting to a new environment. Besides, I've been busy myself."

"I thought by now you would have sprouted wings and flown over there."

"I don't want to seem pushy. I may just go over and say hi."

"Just hi? You can do more than that now, he's not your professor anymore."

"I know that." Brandi had wondered why Tim hadn't called her since leaving Madison. She wanted to believe he was too busy settling in, but something told her it might be a little more than that.

"I know a way you can see him."

"Give it a rest, Tiff."

"No, I'm serious. You haven't had the courage to see him, but I sure have. He's giving that speech on the literacy programs before Columbia closes for the break. Wanna go?"

"I know he'll be there. He told me about the program a few weeks ago. I have to go, anyway. I tutor adults one night a week in reading, my boss thinks it'll be good for me to go."

"Cool, we can go and see Timothy. Maybe after the lecture, he'll take us to dinner—or to bed. The bed thing sounds enticing."

Brandi laughed at her friend's sly suggestion. "Where do you get these ideas, your older brother?"

"Who better? He's been around; that's for sure."

"Tiffany, Tim is more to me than just someone who's great in bed. He's a sweet guy, smart, and the fact that he loves helping people makes him that much more attractive."

"I know this already. I just love to fantasize about him."

Brandi and Tiffany sat in the back of one of Columbia's lecture halls watching Tim speak on the importance of adult literacy programs. Brandi missed him so much; he looked great up there speaking to a large crowd. He seemed relaxed, happy. But Brandi was lonely for him, needing contact with him—any contact. She was determined to see him at the end of the session, to find out what was up with him, what was up with *them.*

Tiffany followed her to the podium at the end of his speech. They waited for the crowd to thin out before squeezing in.

Tim had spotted them at the back of the crowd and could barely keep his eyes off Brandi. He knew why they had waited in the back to get the chance to speak with him alone, and he was glad. He had missed Brandi terribly, but time hadn't been his of late. Getting settled at Columbia was more involved than he had anticipated, but he was still happy with his decision.

Tim shook hands with the last of the attendees, then turned to Brandi and Tiffany. "Funny seeing you two here; how are things?"

Tiffany spoke up first. "Not too well without you. You really had to leave us, huh?"

"I have more flexibility here." His eyes met Brandi's. "How are you doing, Brandi?"

"Good."

"I'm glad. You look well."

Tiffany noted the awkward exchange and decided to come to the rescue. "Brandi, I want to look at some materials on the back table. Take your time; I'm in no hurry. Dr. Polaris, it's really great seeing you. We'll miss you at Madison. I'll pay you if you come back."

"Can't do it, Miss Jackson; Columbia is it for now. I'm glad you came tonight."

Brandi waited for her friend to be a good distance away. "Are you going to be happy here?"

"Yes, very happy. I miss Madison, but I expect to love my new classes." He moved closer, lowering his voice. "I haven't had the chance to call . . ."

"It's okay Tim. You must be very busy."

"I've been under pressure to get set up. It's been hectic, leaving Madison and rushing over here to get my office together all before the break. There hasn't been any time in between to do anything other than fall into bed when I get home. I hope you understand."

"No need to explain. I know you will call me when you can."

"I've missed you more than I had imagined possible, but I will call. You know that."

"Is it okay if I call you?"

"Sure. I'm hardly ever home, though."

"I'll take my chances. Just relax. We can take it slowly, work ourselves into a relationship . . . if you still want one."

"I do."

"Then go easy on yourself. I wanted to see you, Tim. That's the main reason I'm here, that and my adult tutoring job."

He was close enough to smell her perfume, something floral and sensual, and she looked so sensational in her designer baby pink and silver suit. He suppressed the urge to take her into his arms right then and there. "God, I've missed you, Brandi."

Security walked in before she could respond. "It's late, Tim and I need to get going."

He caressed her baby-soft skin on the back of her hand. "Give me a few days."

"I've waited this long. What's a few more days?"

They slowly parted, hands lightly touching. He watched as Brandi joined Tiffany. He had been so glad to see her he could barely think straight enough to pack up his briefcase. No woman before had excited him quite the same way. He would not rest well until he made that call to her.

Tiffany could hardly wait to get the low-down on Brandi and the professor. "So, what did you two talk about for so long?"

"I wasn't up there that long. I wanted to know if he liked Columbia."

"Hell, you could have asked him that with me standing there."

"Then why did you leave?"

"Brandi, I know that look in your eyes. You love the guy, so admit it. I think he feels the same way."

"Maybe."

"No maybe. Look, it's okay now. He is not your professor anymore. Don't you know what that means?"

"Why not enlighten me, Tiff?"

"Act snotty all you want, but it means you can get into that bed with him, girl! You can get down and dirty with the one man women on both campuses are drooling over."

"Both campuses?"

"Yeah, dummy! Didn't you see how he captivated the women at the lecture?"

"He was interesting. The men enjoyed it, too."

"But for different reasons. The women were checking out his fly butt!"

"I know."

"All I'm saying is that the man makes your head swim. Go with the flow of the tide, girl!"

"We'll see." She hoped he would call; prayed he would call.

Tiffany sat on Brandi's bed and watched her finish dressing. "I'm glad you decided to go skating with me. You need to do something to get out of this funk you've been in for the past few days. What's wrong with you, anyway? You haven't done a thing during Christmas break. All you do is go to that part-time job then come back home. What's the deal?"

"I can't deal with this weather. It was too hot for too long, then the storm, now this snow."

"It *is* the middle of December! There should be snow in New York by now."

"I know that, Tiff. I'm sick of the changing weather." She took her ice skates from the closet and slung them across her shoulders.

"That's a cop-out, Brandi. Something else is wrong, and you're not telling me. Come on, I'm your best friend. You can tell me."

"I can't talk about it right now. I will soon."

"Must be bad. You're not sick, are you?"

"I'm not sick."

"Then what?"

"I can't talk about it now, okay? Let's go. The rink at Rockefeller Plaza gets crowded fast."

"Yeah, with dudes."

"Yeah . . . dudes."

Tiffany stopped in her tracks. "Why did you say it like that?"

"No particular reason."

"I know what's wrong with you. You've been in this depression since you saw Dr. Polaris at Columbia."

"Will you drop it? I don't want to talk about him, either. Now come on, before the rink fills up."

"Wait one damn minute! Did I hear you say you didn't want to talk about Tim?"

"Yeah, so?"

"Yeah, so? Girl, what's really going on here? Have you two fallen out?"

"How can you fall-out with someone who hasn't spoken to you or called you like he said he would?"

"He hasn't called?"

"No."

"Have you called him?"

"He said he would call, Tiffany, and I don't want to seem needy."

"The hell with that. Call him and find out what the deal is."

"That might be the only solution. But suppose he doesn't care anymore?"

They continued walking away. "How can you say that? You know he cares. Maybe he's just been busy Christmas shopping and getting adjusted to his new job. Besides, how will you know anything if you don't call him?"

"Naturally, you're right. Maybe I'll call him tonight when we get back." Brandi saw the red BMW parked across the street. "That darn thing's been here off and on for days. I think it's Eric trying to get into my business again, and I'm tired of it. I need to tell Dad. He'll make him buzz off."

Later that night before drifting off to sleep, Brandi awaited Tiffany's late-night chat. This was a nightly ritual for them.

As she waited, her mind went back to that weekend she and Tim were stuck in the motel together . . . but not really together. He never touched her. She smiled as her hand traveled beneath the sheets, stroking her thighs and inching up to where she was most potent. Thoughts of him crowded her mind. She soon climaxed at the very thought of him being inside of her.

She picked up the phone after one ring, knowing it was Tiffany. "I can't talk right now, Tiff. I want to call Tim before it's . . ."

"I don't think you have to call now; you're speaking to him."

She sat up quickly. "Tim?"

"Who else?"

"I was just thinking about you."

"Really? What kind of mind-blowing things were we doing in that imagination of yours?"

"You really want to know?"

"Sure."

"I was imagining you in my arms, and that's all you get for the night."

"Poor me; I guess I just have to suffer for a little while longer."

"What took you so long to call me?"

"Lack of nerve. You know how I am."

"I'm so glad you finally called. I miss you so much."

"I miss you, too. I was thinking . . . maybe I had better take you out before I lose my mind from not seeing you."

"A real date?"

"A real date, not a hot night at some club."

"You have to admit that was a cool night."

"I beg your pardon, it was a *HOT* night. Seriously, though, I would like to take you out, treat you like a real woman—now that I can do that. I won't have Derrick Moore breathing fire down my back."

"I can't believe how much I've missed you. When can I see you?"

"How about tomorrow night? It's Saturday evening, and we won't have to be home early."

"Are you suggesting we really spend some time together?"

"Brandi, I think we should just make it a date, not rush anything."

She lay back on her pillow. "I think you're right. You want to pick me up here?"

"Don't you want to decide where to go first?"

"I don't care, as long as I'm with you. Dinner would be nice."

"Great. I know an incredible seafood place. I remember you saying how much you love seafood."

"You remembered that?"

"I remember everything about you. I remember looking out at my class at Madison and seeing you, wishing I could be right next to you."

"Now you can. Tomorrow night. I know something else we can do after dinner, but it's a surprise."

"I love surprises; your surprises; like the one you gave me the night we met."

"Really? What was that?"

"You went home with me."

"What woman in her right mind wouldn't have?"

"I can't wait to see you. Is 7:00 okay?"

"It's perfect, Tim." They said their good-byes, and she fell asleep that evening hugging her pillow, savoring the thought of finally being in his arms—again.

"Is my hair okay, Mom?"

Mrs. Miles studied Brandi's image in the mirror. "You look beautiful. He's a lucky man."

"What about my make-up and this dress? Do you think . . ."

"Brandi, one look and he'll drop to his knees."

"I sure hope so. It seems as if I've waited a lifetime for this night."

Mrs. Miles adjusted the strap on Brandi's shoulder. "Tim is very important to you, isn't he?"

Brandi dabbed at her lipstick. "More than you know. When I first met him, I didn't know that he was a professor at Madison—my instructor. You remember me mentioning someone that I wanted a relationship with, but couldn't because he was scared of them?"

"Yes. Is he the same Tim? I thought you were over him in nothing flat!"

"Nope! We just couldn't be together because of Madison. Now is different. Imagine the look on my face when he strode into lecture."

"I can't imagine that. He must really think a lot of you to transfer to another university to be with you."

"He's always liked Columbia. I was the push he needed. At least that's what he told me."

"Good for you, but do you think he's really ready now?"

"Mom!"

"Brandi, I just want you to be sure. Your father and I don't want to see you hurt over an man who has had bad relationships in the past."

"The only way to get over bad ones is to get into a better one and nourish it, help it grow. I know he can do it."

"I sure hope so for your sake. Just take things slowly with him. Talk to one another, get to know who each other is before you get too deep into anything."

"Mom. Come on. I am twenty years old." She couldn't find her watch. "Mom, what time is it?"

"Almost 7:00, and again, you're perfect, so stop fretting."

"God, I'm so nervous. I can't believe I actually have a date with the legend. Wait until I tell Tiffany. She'll freak!"

"The legend? What are you talking about?"

"That's what he's called at Madison. The girls will miss him like crazy."

"He is pretty. Don't tell your father I said that again."

She kissed her mother's cheek. "Your secret's safe with me. Where's the jacket to my dress?"

"It's downstairs. I ironed it for you."

"Good. I'll get it. If he comes before I get back, tell him to . . ."

"I know what to do. My mother did the same things for Theresa and me. Although she did it way more times for Theresa. Besides, it's good to let him wait for a minute. It builds a man's anticipation."

"What about mine?"

"You're anxious enough! Go and get the rest of that dress."

Tim rang the doorbell at 7:05. Brandi remembered what her mother said, and waited upstairs in her room. Mrs. Miles let him inside, taking him by the hand. "Dr. Polaris; how nice to see you again. I take it these flowers are not for me."

He smiled embarrassed. "Sorry, maybe next time."

"I'm only kidding, but I do love lilies." She watched as he casually looked around for Brandi.

"I'm probably the last guy you expected to see picking up your daughter. Surely she has talked about me since I last saw you."

"You're all she talks about lately."

"I'm not there anymore."

"Brandi told me."

Mr. Miles came in from the den. Seeing Timothy Polaris there to take his daughter out wasn't sitting well with him, but he said nothing other than calling Brandi down.

At the top of the balcony stood a very nervous, very beautiful young woman going on the date of her lifetime. Nothing else existed but the young man standing next to her mother—the man in the khaki pants, navy shirt and black peacoat. She watched as his honey colored eyes sparkled after seeing her. She carefully descended the staircase toward him. "I hope I'm not over-dressed."

He could hardly speak. "You look beautiful."

Mrs. Miles interrupted sounding nervous. "Brandi, he brought flowers."

She took the bouquet from her mother. "They smell so wonderful. Thank you."

Mr. Miles eyed them until his wife spoke up. "Jeff, Brandi's coat is on the chair. Will you hand it to her? I'll put the flowers in a vase."

"I'll get her coat, Mr. Miles." Tim took the coat from the chair and held it open for Brandi. "Button up; it's getting cold out there."

She did what he said, and picked up her bag. "Northern Lakes Seafood, right?"

"Anything you want. This is your night." He looked at her parents: her mother was smiling broadly; her father was trying not to have a coronary. "Nice seeing you both again. Ready, Brandi?"

More than you know. "See you two later." She took Tim's hand and they left.

The minute the door closed, Mr. Miles's snide comments started. "She's not supposed to be dating her professor."

"He left Madison, Jeff. We told you that."

"It's still . . ."

"Jeff, Brandi is insane over him, and there's nothing you or I can do about it. She's grown."

"He's a criminal. I finally remember where I saw him. He was a little punk who was tossed into my precinct more than a few times when he was a teen."

"That was then. He apparently got his life together. He's a sweetheart, now drop it."

Before Tim opened the passenger-side door, he took her into his arms. He could barely control himself as he pressed her back against the truck, kissing her as if he had just come from the wild. His arms wrapped her tightly as he pressed his body hard against hers. His mouth gently pulled and sucked hers, barely able to catch his breath. She felt warm against him despite the cold. And she felt utterly fantastic.

Brandi held on to him for dear life, not remembering if ever she had felt that wonderful before. Her kisses were as feverish as his, matching him tempo for tempo. Having him so close to her ignited memories of their first night together. She slowly broke the kiss and stared into his flushed face and listened to his heavy breathing. "I can't believe I'm in your arms again."

"I can't believe I kissed you out here. I couldn't wait for us to get inside the truck. I hope your parents didn't see us."

"Mom understands. Dad seems to have forgotten what passion is, except when it comes to my mother." Her hand grazed his cheek. "It feels like a lifetime ago since I've touched you."

His hands moved up and down the sleeves of her coat. "Let's get you inside. I can't have my lady freezing out here."

His lady. That was exactly what she had wanted to hear. *Tiffany will die when I tell her about this tomorrow.* She breathed a heavy sigh of relief. *Thank God this man is finally here with me.*

Sitting across from Tim seemed almost surreal to her. He looked different somehow, different from Tim the professor. His almost perfect features, deep-set hazel eyes took her back to The Entrapment. He was, once again, Jacob Anthony Wells. "I almost don't know what to say to you?"

"Why is that?"

"It's as if I start talking to you, my dream will end, and you'll go back to being my professor at Madison."

"It won't happen. I'm at Columbia to stay."

"I'm just relieved you're happy there. I can now get off my guilt trip."

"I'm happy here. I was so nervous turning into your street, that my hands began perspiring. That's some feat, since its twenty-five-degrees outside."

"I can't imagine you nervous over anyone."

"Well, I am sometimes."

"We're all like that sometimes, even the famous Timothy Polaris. Anyway, remember I told you I had something special for you?"

"It doesn't get any more special than what I'm looking at right now, Miss Miles."

She leaned over the table and gently kissed him. "I really do have something for you, but not what I originally planned. I tried to get tickets to Jeff Lorber. He's at the Garden tonight, but it was sold out by the time I called."

"You were going to do that for me?"

"I know you like him."

"Yes, very much, but I'm having more fun where I am right now."

"You're so sweet, but I did get something else—movie tickets. We both like horror films, so I got tickets to *The Demon Dead.*"

"Another movie where some maniac is running around town slicing up young virgins?"

"That's it. I know it's silly, but that's what makes them fun."

"Cool. We can sit in the back and make out."

"Exactly my plan. How did you get to be so special? Someone did a good job raising you."

"Not really. I told you I was a troubled teen."

"Yes. I remember, but you still turned out perfect."

"I did manage to get an education. I'm not perfect, though. That's what saved me from the streets."

"I know you were at Huntington College before Madison."

"Yes, for two years."

"That's a good college—hard to get into."

"That's the one."

"No wonder they had you teaching there. You have to have brains on top of brains to get in there."

"I'm not as smart as I should be."

"The smartest man I know. How many of your female students were checking you out? I know they were, so don't deny it."

He lowered his eyes, smiling faintly. "I used to get pinched in the halls. I never actually caught anyone doing it because the halls were so crowded. I suppose I had a fan club of sorts. It was rather annoying, to tell you the truth."

"Then you shouldn't be so damn gorgeous."

"I don't see it."

"Of course you don't."

"I moved to Bronx College, same thing over there. I made the girls keep their distance. They were not there to drool over me, but to learn, and they did. I had the top honor classes."

"Good for you because you have a lot to offer students. I should know because I got an A from you. It wasn't easy, though."

"You had the brains. All I gave you was the motivation. You're a smart young woman, Brandi, and I feel so lucky to be in your presence." He took her hand, kissing it. "I get to taste you—tasting temptation; sounds like a romance novel."

"Maybe it can be, Tim."

"There is no maybe. You're smart, beautiful and everything I've ever wanted."

He saw a glimmer in her eyes, one that she couldn't control. He commented, "What has got those wheels turning around in your brain now?"

"My other surprise."

"Two surprises?" His eyes leered into hers. "What have you done?"

She pulled a book from her duffle bag. "I also remember you telling me about your high school days."

"Really? When?"

"Conversation during one of my tutoring sessions."

"Right. Those were some tough years."

"I found your year book." She opened the book to his graduation picture. "You were the cutest damn guy in the school. Look at you."

"I was a mess back then." He briefly stared at the picture before returning it to her. "What would make you dig up that thing?"

"I wanted to see what you were like in school. You look the same . . . you looked smart."

"That's the only thing I had going for me at Lawrence Denby High. Despite my past school records, they took a chance on me." He gave an embarrassing smile. "Maybe I should have attended Al Capone High, or John Dillinger High."

"That's another thing, you make me laugh; something hard to do since I'm so serious."

"I love making you smile. It really does something to me, Brandi."

"I'm glad because I really want to please you, you know, do the right things now that I have a second chance with you. What more could a woman want in a man?"

"One without issues."

"Everyone has those."

"Not everyone has Greg for a brother and the parents I had."

"Tell me about him."

"Nothing really to tell. He and I are as far apart from one another that I think I would barely know him now."

"That's so sad. My brother is a pain in the rear but I love him nonetheless. I wish it were different for you."

"Me, too, but I don't want to be sad tonight. We can discuss Greg another time. Tonight is for you, only you. Order anything your heart desires."

She stared into his eyes. "I already have that."

Brandi finished a plate of lake perch with lemon sauce; Tim had the oysters in Almondine sauce with potato. Neither wanted dessert, but Tim had the waiter bring a box of chocolate hearts from the gourmet candy counter. They both had a piece; it was like a toast to a new relationship . . . a new love.

At the theater, they sat in the last row. There was one other couple in the same row but further down. Having Tim sitting that close to her made her whole body tingle. Her hand rested on his upper thigh, and she could feel the heat emitting through the fabric of his pants. His hand covered hers, moving it higher until the tenting between his thigh pressed against her palm. She massaged him, feeling his strength, his power, his hunger.

Tim moaned low to her advances, letting her take her liberties with him. He put his arm around her, holding her close, inhaling the sweet scent of her hair and body. His hand cupped her breast, tenderly massaging the puckered tip to an exquisite hardness, wanting to taste it, but settled for giving her tolerable pleasure. His lips sucked and caressed each tiny little finger.

Watching Tim stroke her fingers with gentle tongue swirls made her ache for him, saturating her panties. They kissed throughout the rest of the movie, and sat there after it ended just staring at each other in wonder that of actually being together.

They pulled in front of Brandi's house and 1:30 in the morning. Tim asked: "Did you have a good time?"

"It was incredible."

"I hope you weren't disappointed that we didn't go back to my house. I just want to go as slowly as possible."

"I'm not disappointed. I had a wonderful evening with a man I have been dreaming about practically every night. We have time."

"I hope not to give you nightmares."

She kissed his cheek. "No silly. Every time I think of you, I get flushed. It feels so good."

"You're so beautiful; I don't know how long I'll be able to hold off. You're special to me, Brandi, unlike any other woman who's been in my life." He kissed her lips once more. "I had better get you inside."

He walked her to the door, and waited until she was safely inside. Concern soon clouded the good vibrations he had felt all evening. Could he keep her happy, or would his past life intrude, and make her run from him?

CHAPTER 13

Sunshine peeking through the blinds roused Brandi, and a smile instantly appeared. Remembering the wonderful evening she had spent with a man who made her world turn was the perfect way to awaken. Then her smile suddenly faded. *Was it a dream? Did I simply dream that Timothy Polaris kissed me last night, that we made out in the movie theater?* She sat up in bed, mumbling, "He had to be real. I can still smell his aftershave on my skin." She looked at her nightstand and saw the box of half-eaten chocolate hearts. He was no dream; his arms had been around her and she still burned from his kisses.

Like a giddy schoolgirl, she grabbed the cordless and punched in Tiffany's number, hardly able to wait telling her about her date with Tim. It rang three times before Tiffany's sleepy voice came on. "Who is it?"

"Tiff, guess what?"

"Brandi? What could you possibly have to tell me at 8:30 on a Sunday morning?"

"Well, this might just wake you up. Tim took me out last night."

"What?

"Tim! We went out last night."

"Have mercy! You and pretty Timmy had a date? It's about time."

"Yes, it is."

"You lucky broad. Where did you go?"

"We went to Northern Lakes Seafood. He brought me flowers, Tiff. Eric never gave me flowers."

"Surely you knew about this date before last night. Why didn't you tell me before now?"

"Because I wanted to keep my expectations low in case he cancelled."

"He would never cancel on you. Hell, he left a university for you."

"I know, but until things are set in stone, I won't go overboard. You know that."

"You said he took you where?"

"Northern Lakes."

"That's an expensive joint, girl. He must really care. None of my dates would have dared take me there. They couldn't have afforded it because you know me, its got to be shrimp, lobster, crab, and a side helping of, yes, more shrimp! Tell me you had the oysters."

"No, but he had them, and he was live last night, girlfriend."

"Really? Did he throw down on you?"

"He was an absolute gentleman. He bought me candy, took me to the . . ."

"Can all that! Did you tongue dance with him or what?"

"Tiff! Well, yeah. What woman with common sense wouldn't have kissed him? We made out in the movie theater. And that's all you get."

"Well, goodnight, Irene! Check you out, making it with the white Superfly of the entire city. He is jammin', girl. You sure you didn't do more than kiss him? I would have slammed him down on that car seat, and . . ."

"I get it! I know what you would have done to him and I don't think he would have survived. For us, though, It was sweet and innocent."

"Darn right! See, you don't know how to take advantage of an opportunity."

"With him I do. I want it to last, Tiffany. It was so magical last night; he looked so different, not like a professor, but like a regular guy."

"Timothy Polaris ain't no regular dude, girl! Sorry to burst your bubble."

"I don't mean that. It was like he was—Jacob Anthony Wells."

"Who?"

"The name he gave me the first night I met him."

"Yeah, I remember. Girl, you got a lot in store for yourself. Do everything this man tells you to do. If you don't, I will. Get me?"

"He and I are going to my cousin Verdeen's wedding next weekend, so eat your heart out."

"Right, rub it in, why don't you."

"Shut up and get dressed. Aren't we still going to the mall?"

"Yeah, catch you in a half-hour, and be ready, Brandi. My dad only lets me have the Hummer for two hours. He probably thinks I'll sell it."

"You've done worse."

Both she and Tim were tired from dancing at Verdeen's reception. They were quiet on the way back. Tim stared straight ahead. He looked so good in his tuxedo; his after-shave was so husky and manly, making her want him more and more. They had decided to put that part of life on hold until they both ready to go deeper into their physical relationship again. She pulled at his sleeve. "Did you have a good time at the wedding?"

"It was a lot of fun."

"You sure? At times you looked bored."

"Who could be bored with you around? I just didn't know anyone there. You know how it is. Besides, weddings make me nervous."

"Why?"

"My mother remarried, and that relationship was a disaster for my brother and me. The guy treated us exactly like what we were to him, *stepchildren*. There was no love between us at all. Then there was my marriage to Charlotte, another disaster."

"I'm really sorry. Had I known, I wouldn't have suggested the wedding. We could have done something else tomorrow."

"No way. I wanted to be with you. It was your cousin's wedding, and you couldn't miss that." He parked and faced her. "I'll do anything to be with you."

"We have worked pretty darn hard to be together, haven't we?"

"Yeah, I'm in the game now; no sitting on the bench for me."

"If this is any consolation, Verdeen told me that you were 'hot-t-t.' She said it just like that."

"No one cared that I was the only white guy there?"

"Everyone thought you were great. Were you uncomfortable?"

"I had you there to keep my mind active, too active. You look, well, that dress you're wearing is enough to make me lose it."

"That's why I wore it, and I caught the bridal bouquet, too. What do you think about that?"

"Good catch. One day you'll be tossing it."

"At our wedding?"

"Stranger things have happened."

"I hope Tiffany catches it. She'll need to be off the market, if she doesn't marry before I do. Actually, she needs to be in an asylum for the sexually insane. You know, I had to peel her off me at the mall last weekend. She wanted every detail of our date. She's got it bad for you."

"Do you have it bad for me?"

She leaned over and kissed him. Her tongue danced with his briefly before pulling away. "Does that answer your question?"

"Yes, but I have more questions."

"Walk me inside and you'll get your answers. Mom and Dad haven't left the reception yet."

"What about Brian?"

"Staying the night with a friend." She winked at him. "Let's go."

Once inside, he helped her out of her coat and then embraced her. "We'd better get in some really good kissing before your parents return."

"My thoughts exactly." Her arms wrapped tightly around his shoulders, caressing his silk shirt, feeling his muscles flex as though they were rods of lightening—hot, wild, and dangerous. She ruled his every move, edging him on, feeling him pressing hard against her stomach.

Tim loosened his tie, then lifted her dress to finger the band of her panties. His fingers tickled her stomach as she responded to his advances. His hand slid inside the silk panties, stroking her skin, inching towards her core. "Keep doing that. Your hands are so strong." She was moist for him, and he took advantage, dipping inside, feeling her throb against his fingers, slow, rhythmic movements in and out of her body.

He moaned, "I want you, Brandi. I know what we agreed on but . . ."

"I know, but not here." The ringing phone startled them. He whispered in her ear. "Let it ring."

Brandi pressed against him, not wanting him to stop. She ached for him as they kissed. Her body soon shuddered against his, holding on to him, clawing at his back as a rush filled her mind and body, *I love you, Tim.* She slowly broke from him, staring at him in awe. "You really are incredible."

He kissed her shaking hands. "No, but you are. That was a heck of a good-night kiss, darling."

"Sure was." She re-buttoned his first two buttons, looking into his eyes. "I really think I'm falling hard for you, Timothy Edward. You're the only man my eyes can see."

Minutes later, they heard keys turning the lock on the front door. Mr. and Mrs. Miles stepped inside. Her mother smiled at the couple still standing in the middle of the floor. "I see you two beat us back."

An embarrassed smile crossed Brandi's face. "By seconds only." It was definitely time for Tim to go before their faces gave them away. "Here's your coat, Tim. Call me tonight. I've got practice early tomorrow for the championship game between Madison and East Pointe U."

"You'll do well. I'll be there, too."

She smiled and lowered her voice; her father was still standing within earshot. "Good, I can see you after the game."

All he could do was smile. "Walk me to the door." He looked at Mr. Miles, who was pretending to fix a crooked picture—with his coat still on. "It's getting late, and we both have to get up early."

Mr. Miles watched Brandi kiss Tim good night and waited until the door was closed before confronting her. "Brandi, about this Timothy guy. There are things about him that you should . . ."

"Yeah, isn't he great? I'm crazy about him." She started to run up the steps but her father stopped her again.

"Brandi. You and I need to talk about Timothy Polaris."

"What is there to say about him other than he is all I've ever wanted?"

"You don't know this guy the way you should."

Brandi slowly walked back down the steps and looked her father square in the eyes. "Dad, I know you don't want me dating white men, but this isn't your decision. Tim and I are a couple now, and that's all there is to it."

"He has a past, honey, and . . ."

"He told me about his being arrested as a teen. We all have problems, and apparently he has worked through his. I don't want to discuss this anymore, Dad."

Mrs. Miles entered the room again as Brandi left. She stared at her husband with an *I can't believe you approached her about him* kind of look. "You don't need to talk to Brandi about Tim, Jeff."

"She needs to know about him."

"He will tell her, not you. If you keep hounding her, you will drive a wedge between you and your daughter. Don't you know I would have left my parents' house in a heartbeat had they said anything negative about you? She will, too. You don't want your daughter to leave, do you?"

"No, that I don't want. But she just doesn't understand about him."

"You need to drop this, Jeff. You run old issues into the ground. You always have."

"Fine, it's dropped. I just don't want her hurt."

"He won't hurt her."

He shoved his hands into his pockets and shrugged his shoulders. "Can you make me some coffee? Add some scotch to it; I think I'll need it."

After the loss to East Pointe U, Brandi took an unusually long shower after everyone else left the locker room. Her Aunt Theresa drove her to the game and was waiting for her in the stands. Brandi needed to think about things. Everything seemed to be on her mind that night; the game, her life with Tim, even Eric's juvenile actions were still on her mind. Eric had denied responsibility for the tire tracks across Tim's lawn. But she wondered if he was behind that. He was always wrongfully accused—in his mind. He never faced things. But

Tim was first and foremost on her mind that night, and every night. He was the reason she wanted everyone gone so she could walk from the dressing rooms with him and steal a juicy kiss. Theresa would just have to wait an extra five minutes to take her home.

When she stepped out of the shower, all activity had ceased, letting her know the place was still empty. She put on her stockings, bra and skirt. Before she could finish with the buttons on her blouse, the power went off—then the lights. Not being able to find her way in the darkness, she anxiously called out. "Hello, is anyone here? Is there someone in here?" When she didn't get a response, her fear intensified. She began to feel her way around the walls until she got to the light switch. It immediately came on time enough to see a figure duck around the corner. "Hello?" Nothing. "Who is out there? I'm not kidding. I'll get security. Eric, is that you?"

Tim stepped from the corner laughing. "If you get security, then the kiss is off."

"Tim, you animal! What are you doing here? I thought you left home in tears like the rest of Madison's crowd."

"I was in the mood for one of my swims, since it was such a tough loss. Besides, I wanted to stay behind and see you."

She ran into his arms, kissing him. He backed her against the wall moving his mouth up and down her neck. His hands did double duty trying to find a way around her bra. He slid the straps from her shoulders and fondled her breasts, making her call to him more and more.

Brandi could taste the perspiration on his skin. That excited her and made him feel and smell more primitive than he wanted to be. Her legs parted for him and his hands quickly moved between them, pressing her deeper into his erection. She pulled the T-shirt over his head and caressed each caramel-hued nipple then kissed his lips. Her words sounded choked as she tried kissing and talking at the same time. "God! I thought you would never get in here, and then scaring me to death with that little stunt of yours. You're so bad."

"I *am* bad; bad enough to scare the panties right off you. Speaking of panties, where's those cool red and white ones that makes me crazy every time I see them?"

"Part of a uniform . . . had to take them off. You can pull these off instead." She moved his hand to her panty line, feeling his fingers enter her. Her voice lowered. "God! Don't ever stop doing that to me."

Suddenly, pleasing her became a second thought. He had to tell her, talk to her about what had happened earlier that evening, but he didn't want to scare her. He also didn't want her dead, so there was no backing out of what he had to say. His words might ruin their relationship, but she would be saved in the process—if they were lucky!

His mouth left hers. "Brandi, you know how I feel about you, don't you? I mean . . . no woman's ever made me feel the way you do."

She saw worry in his eyes. "Yes, I know how you feel. I know how we both feel." Her nose brushed his playfully. "Why are you so serious all of a sudden?"

"Nothing's wrong, well . . . not exactly."

Her fingers brushed his still-damp sideburns. "Not exactly?"

This was so hard for him to say; having to take Brandi out all the time instead of them being alone in his house for once. Everything seemed to be falling apart for him, just when his life was at its best. Getting over Charlotte, which Claire helped him do, would be a breeze compared with making it difficult for him and Brandi to be together.

She brought his face back to hers. "You left me, Tim. Where were you?"

"A world away."

"Can I be in that world with you?"

"There are a lot of complicated things going on in my life now, and I just don't want anything to happen to you because of them."

"What could happen? Whatever it is, we can deal with it together. Right?"

She didn't get it, and he didn't know how to make her get it unless he was bold and up front with her. "What I'm trying to say is that maybe we should continue to go other places instead of to my house like I promised. I mean . . ."

"What brought this on? I want to be alone with you, Tim. I think we can handle that now."

"I know we can, but things are happening lately. The truck incident, me being attacked, the trashcan in my living room—something could happen to you."

Something else was going on, but making him admit it was difficult. "What else aren't you telling me, Tim?"

"Brandi, I . . ."

"There is something. What else happened?"

She was too smart for her own good, and he knew she could read him, so he came out with it. "There is something else. Racial slurs were spray painted across the back of my house. The first thing I thought about was your being in there and getting attacked."

"Are you okay? You weren't attacked, were you?"

"I'm fine, but my house is trashed."

"When did this happen?"

"Before the game; that's why I can't take you there yet. I don't mean for long, just until I find out who is doing these things."

"How long are we talking?"

"Not long. I swear."

"Tim, I don't think anything will happen."

"I don't want to take that chance. If you were to get hurt, it would kill me. I really wish you would do this for me, just for a while. We can still be together."

She moved into his arms again. "I know, but I want to be alone with you. I don't want you handling this thing alone. I'll help you."

He had to smile. "You really care about me, don't you?"

"You know this already."

His lips engulfed hers tenderly; he could hardly believe a woman could care for him that much. "You're right, we can handle this together. I just don't want you hurt."

"I won't be. Now kiss me again before I pass out."

"Whatever Brandi wants, Brandi gets." His mouth covered hers in relentless passion, barely able to break from her long enough to breathe.

Moments into their kiss, they heard a voice coming from the hallway; startling them. "Brandi? Where the heck are you?"

CHAPTER 14

Brandi broke the kiss. "Oh, my God; it's my Aunt Theresa! I forgot about her. I don't want her catching you back here with me."

"She knows about us, doesn't she?"

"Yes, but . . ."

"You think she would rat on me being in here with you?"

"No, but she has loose lips. You being back here with me may get out accidentally. I just don't want you in any trouble, Tim. You understand, don't you?"

"Don't panic. Everything will be fine. I'll hide behind the lockers until she's gone. Hurry and button your blouse before she gets here." He gave her a quick kiss before ducking behind the last row of lockers near the mirror. His back pressed firmly against the wall just before Theresa opened the swinging doors. Perspiration dripped from his wet hair. With no towel in sight, he reached for the hem of his t-shirt. Having forgotten he'd taken it off, he cursed under his breath, realizing he'd left it on the floor.

Brandi saw the shirt on the floor and quickly stuffed it into her duffle bag as Theresa entered the dressing area. She smiled as if nothing was wrong, patting her half-buttoned blouse. "Wow, sorry I'm so late. I didn't realize the time. These showers were acting funny; first, cold water, then all hot; hard to do anything without the right temperature." She knew her temperature was on fire due to Tim making advances on her body—and mind. "I'm almost ready. Have a seat on the bench while I finish."

"Just slow down; we have time, although I have been waiting over a half hour for you. I haven't gotten in a word edgewise since walking in here; and you know that's unusual for me."

"Sorry. I'm just so rushed."

"I've noticed. What's got you in a tizzy all of a sudden?"

"Excitement from the game?"

"Maybe it's excitement of Dr. Timothy Polaris."

"What? No, it's not that. Yes, he is a cutie, but I've got other things on my mind."

"Who could have other things on her mind when she's dating Timothy Polaris?"

"True." Brandi was sick of the small talk. Her concern was Tim sitting in that cramped corner, aching to get the heck out of there. "Look, I just need to check my hair, then, we can go."

"Mirror big enough for two?"

"Sorry, it's a small one." *Is she deliberately trying to destroy me, or what?*

"Odd for a lady's locker room."

"Give me a second." Brandi hurried to the mirror, looked around it and saw Tim in a huddle, practically sweating bullets. She whispered. "Tim, I'm so sorry about this. I know you're dying back there."

"It's hot in here. You two hurry up."

"I found your shirt on the floor and picked it up before she saw anything."

"Don't sweat it. It was all bunched up; could belong to anyone as far as she's concerned."

"You don't know my Aunt Theresa. She scopes anything she thinks belongs to a man, especially you."

He pulled her into him and kissed her warm lips. "Go on and get out of here before your aunt figures out something."

Brandi returned to Theresa and picked up her duffle bag, "Okay, let's roll."

Theresa eyes her. "Not just yet."

Oh, my God! "Why? What's up?"

"Don't play with me, girl. You know I can't leave yet."

"Is something wrong, Aunt Theresa?"

"Sure is." She walked towards the mirror and stopped in front of it. She patted her French roll and makeup. "Girl, you know I can't walk out of here without making sure my hair is on-jam. Your boy Timothy could see me. I can't be looking bad in front of his fine self. As I suspected, there is room enough in this mirror for two. I swear, you are so dramatic, Brandi Elaine Miles."

"Can we go now?"

"Yep. Good as new now."

"Wait! Let me see if the shower is completely turned off." It was a ploy to see if Tim had been able to duck around to the other side. The stall was empty, so she knew he had made it out.

Hearing the women's locker room door slam, Tim let out a sigh of relief. *I can't risk getting caught like this again. This is too much for me.* He looked at his watch and realized the building would be closing soon. He looked out to see if anyone was in the vicinity. All clear. He washed up and left, his mind on Brandi, remembering how wonderful it was to have her in his arms.

After approaching his truck thirty minutes later, he was surprised that no one had done anything to it. He thought that maybe the heat was finally off him after he had contacted the police. Then he remembered that a patrol car constantly circled the campus at night.

That night, Brandi ran from the bathroom to catch her ringing cell phone. "Hello?"

"Hello yourself, sexy queen of my dreams."

"Tim. I was just thinking about you. I wish you had been in that shower with me tonight."

"I was near it."

"Yeah, after the scare you gave me."

"You recovered quite nicely."

"You did, too. I see you made it back to the men's side without running into trouble. That was a quick move."

"I'm a quick guy, which brings me to why I'm calling. I can't stand being without you now that I can actually date you. Let's do something tonight."

"You *are* quick. I can't, though. I have some on-line work to do for my literacy group."

"This is Friday night. You have the weekend."

"I promised them I would get it done."

"Enough said. Do your work but be ready for me tomorrow night, okay?"

"Yes, sir. Can't wait to see you. Where are we going? Back to your house?"

"Brandi."

"I'm just checking, Tim, although I doubt anything will happen to me."

"I'll make it up to you, and I'll be creative. I'll give you an evening you will never in your life forget."

"I have that every time I look at you."

"The compliments! You make my life. The very idea of you refutes every negative thought I have ever had about relationships."

"That's quite a compliment."

"I mean it. Dream of me tonight, and wait for me tomorrow night."

Shivers ran up and down her spine when she thought about being with him the next night—in his bed if he would just give in to going to his house. That would be a perfect ending to a perfect night.

Brandi saw his truck pull up in front of her house. "Mom, he's here."

"Good. Invite him in."

The look on her father's face normally would have upset her. Instead, she warned. "Dad, whatever you think Tim did in the past, that was a long time ago. He's a man now, and I'm asking you to be civil, because I plan to have him around for a long time."

"Did I say anything?"

"No, thank God!" Before opening the door, she looked at her father. "I mean it; don't ruin this for me."

"I will never ruin my baby girl's love life."

"Good." When she opened the door and saw Tim's face, a feeling of unease gripped her. "Tim? Are you okay?"

"Yes. Why?"

"You look sad."

He greeted her parents and then helped Brandi with her coat. "I'm fine, really. It's been a long day. Let's just go."

Once inside of his truck, she turned to him. "Okay, what's really wrong? You're being very quiet and you barely spoke to my parents."

"I just didn't have a lot to say."

"You're usually a chatterbox, especially with my mother."

"There's a lot on my mind today."

"Such as . . . ?"

His visit with Claire earlier that day hadn't gone as smoothly as in the past. The visit, for once, wasn't about Brandi, but about his brother. Tim wasn't in the mood for talking about Claire or his brother, so he tiptoed around the subject. "I miss Madison already. This time of year is really hard on a person who is not around family."

"You have me. You can come over here for the holidays."

"Come on, Brandi. Your Dad and I exchanging gifts and sharing a brandy by the fireplace isn't exactly going to happen. As you probably know by now, he knows my past. I remember him being the arresting officer way back when."

"What did you do to get arrested?"

"Fights mostly."

"Like plenty of other youths. It's common for people that age—sometimes." She noticed the persistent sadness on his face and decided not to harp on the topic. Her voice softened. "I *could* come to your house."

"That's not going to happen either; not right now."

The sad look on his face made her heart ache for him. There would be no one for him to be with for Christmas. They always had to go out in order to be together. That wasn't exactly the happiest way to spend the best holiday of the year. She took his hand in hers. "You want to go somewhere and talk about it?"

"Not really. It won't solve anything." He leaned across and kissed her cheek. "I've got a better idea. Let's get something to eat, then maybe take in a game of bowling or pool. Have you ever gone bowling?"

"I rolled a forty-five one time. Is that good?"

"It stinks! Let's do the pool hall. You'll like it."

"Cool, so long as a big strong man shows me how to play."

"I've got your back . . . and everything else if you'll let me."

"I'll let you, all right."

They pulled into the parking lot of Mason's pool hall. Brandi looked around at the surroundings. "This area doesn't look like one you would frequent."

"I know it looks a little rough around here, but I grew up on the streets. My brother and I, well, let's just say me for the time being. I had a ball playing pool."

"That's good. Let's go inside."

The minute he and Brandi walked into the hall, all eyes were on them. Men stared at Brandi and women smiled at Tim as if wanting to reach out touch him.

Tim paid for a table in the corner and escorted her over to it. Men at a table next to them leered at Brandi's tight jeans and midriff sweater. She overheard their comments and began to feel a little self-conscious. Tim saw her expression. "They're okay, honey. Ignore them." He handed her a stick. "Know how to work this?" handing her a pool cue.

"Are you kidding?"

"It's easy. All you do is hold the stick and *poke*. Get my meaning?"

That got her attention. "I know how to hold *your* stick, if that counts for anything."

"It counts for a lot, and from what I remember, you held it quite well."

"We could recapture the moment at your house tonight."

"Don't get me started with you. We may have to put on a little display here tonight if you keep egging me on."

"Wouldn't those chumps like that?"

"Yeah, a live display; that would get the joint rolling, wouldn't it?"

"You are such a nut, Tim."

He handed her the stick and leaned in behind her. "Now, just relax and let the stick slide across the green."

The thought of his erection pressing against her mid back made her ache for the seclusion of his house. She loved the feeling, wanting to be with him more than ever.

After two miserable games of pool, Tim went to pay for another game and brought her a soda and a stein of beer for himself. While he was gone, the taller man wearing a leather jacket and torn jeans put his pool cue down and approached Brandi. He sat on the edge of the table, taking her by surprise. The very idea of him leering at her made her mad. "Can I help you, sir?" She knew that he wasn't there to offer her pool advice.

"You certainly can help me, young lady. I'm Ike, and you're putting some moves on my libido."

"Sorry. It was purely unintentional."

"I think it wasn't. I saw you looking at me."

"You saw wrong, now if you don't mind, Tim, *my man,* will be back shortly. I don't think he'll think kindly of your being here."

"So what? Tim, huh? Now I know the wimp's name. He looks like a sissy twitching around in them tight jeans."

"But you thought enough of him yourself to watch how he looks in those jeans. Go back to your little table with the rest of the boys. You can all check out Tim's tight jeans together."

"Trying to say something?" His arms wrapped around her hips.

"Get off me, and I'm not *trying* to say anything." She looked over his shoulder and signaled Tim.

Within seconds, Tim came back, staring at the stranger. "Why's he here?"

"He won't leave me alone."

Tim faced him. "Take a hike."

"I will, but with your girl on my arm. She's a little confused about something."

"I don't think so, but you are."

Brandi pulled at Tim's sleeve. "Let's just leave. Don't fight with this crack head."

"Don't worry. I would need an actual opponent to have a fight. Get lost."

"Your girl has a color problem, and only a real man can help her overcome that." His buddies egged him on.

Tim was in the mood for a fight, having been upset about practically everything that day. But he didn't want Brandi seeing that side of him. "My girl already has a man, now if you don't mind." He put the cue stick back into Brandi's hand and helped her aim.

A cue stick crashed across Tim's back, forcing him and Brandi onto the table. He stood, pushed Brandi aside and picked up his stick.

"Tim, let's just go. He's an idiot."

Ignoring Brandi's plea, he pulled away and faced off with the man. "You want to fight? Fine, let's do it. That's the only thing I seem to be able to do well."

"He's not worth it, Tim. Let's go."

"You're right." He laid the stick down and followed behind Brandi. Midway through the pool hall, the man followed them, plunging a fist in the middle of Tim's back. Tim turned and landed a left hook across the man's face, dropping him to the floor, where he passed out immediately. Tim sank to the floor in pain.

Brandi screamed. "Tim, what's wrong? What is it?"

A large crowd was forming around them as the manager approached, holding the rest of the men at bay. "Sir, are you okay?"

"I think I broke my hand."

Brandi helped him to his feet; tears rolling down her cheeks. "Let's go. We need to get to emergency. That hand is swelling."

Once outside, Tim reached into his pocket for the keys and Brandi automatically took them. "You can't drive like this."

"I'll be fine. Give me the keys back."

"No way; you driving like that could get us killed. You're in too much pain to drive anywhere."

"Stop playing around, Brandi. I'm fine."

She pushed the alarm key and it didn't go off. "What's wrong with your alarm?"

"Someone jimmied it."

Not letting that stop her, she unlocked the door manually, pulled up the hood and disconnected the alarm. "We can drive it now. Get into the back seat."

She drove as fast as she could while eyeing Tim in the rearview mirror. Her tears returned. "Had it not been for me being such a big shot with that nut, none of this would have happened."

"Don't be silly. This is not your fault."

In no time, they were in front of Mt. Sinai Hospital.

Brandi slowly slipped his jacket and shirt over his bandaged left hand. She handed him the bottle of painkillers from the pharmacy and a glass of water, then helped him get into his bed. "Take one of these and lie back."

"No, we need to get you home."

"I'm staying here until you're better."

"You know I don't want you here as long as things are happening to me and my house."

"Has anything else happened?"

"No. That's only because I have a sensor camera in the garage now. Whoever the nut is, he's scared of cameras."

"Then lie back and let me do my thing."

"Your thing? What thing is that?" he said with a smile.

"Comfort you; make sure you have everything you need."

"I do. You're all I need."

Her head rested on his bare chest while her fingernails delicately stroked his muscles. "This wasn't one of your best evenings, was it?"

"Aside from being with you, the entire day was a washout."

"What happened?"

He did not want to discuss Claire or his brother. "Among other things, I learned that I may have to escort students to the writing clinics at Niagara University; that is, if one of my co-workers can't reschedule his surgery. Also, the cops gave me hell about having a camera installed in my garage."

"Why?"

"I purchased one that links my house to the cameras in the precinct. It cost a bundle, and they're giving me the runaround, claiming that they may be too busy to respond to every incident. What did I buy the darn thing for if they won't respond?"

"I think something else is wrong tonight."

"Yeah, like my busted fist."

"No. Something's on your mind, and I think it's your brother. Tell me about him."

"What made you decide that?"

"I see how you stare off into space when I'm horsing around with Brian. You always seem to go to another place. There are things I need to understand about you, like what happened with Greg."

"You will never know what that was like, so trying to explain it would be useless."

"Can't you try?"

"Look, Brandi, you have a loving relationship with your brother, even though you think you hate him at times, so let's not get into something you can't fathom."

"I want to know everything about you."

"You would run like crazy."

"I'm not that demented, despite what Tiffany says about me. Come on, trust me. I want to know what it was like for you in that troubled childhood. Maybe I can make the second half of your life a happy one."

"You are doing that already. It's clear that you won't let up until you hear all the dirt. So here goes. I grew up on the streets, as I told you. I was arrested all the time, and was in and out of foster care more times than I can count."

"What happened to your parents?"

"Nothing! Dad was too drunk to give a damn about us, and eventually left when I was eleven years old."

"He just left you and your brother?"

"And my mother, who then blamed Greg and me for him having left—me more than anyone else."

"Why would she do that?"

"I was more trouble, always harder to understand, tougher to get along with. I danced to my own music and never followed anyone except for my brother. That was a big damn mistake."

"You just needed more love than what you were getting."

"I didn't know what love was until I heard my baby's heart beat for the first time. And now with you, I really know what love is. I just hope I can give you what you need."

"You've doing it already. That's why I want us to get to know one another. Tell me more about you and Greg."

"I don't know anything about him, really. I haven't seen him in years. I went to his place to see his new baby, my niece, Destiny. She's eleven years old now. My daughter would have been about ten years old. Her name was Dorian."

"I love that name."

"That's our story. We had a big falling out years ago, way before Destiny was born. He blamed me for something that wasn't my fault."

"What?"

He hadn't meant to let that slip. "I don't want to bring that up. It's involved and sordid, horrible."

His speech beginning to slur; the pills were taking effect. "Okay, sleepy-time, Tim. I'll be here with you, so don't worry about anything."

"I need to take you home. . . ."

She sat up, stared at his relaxed face, the face of an angel—maybe hell's angel, but an angel nonetheless, and she loved him. She once again rested her head on his heaving stomach, needing to be near him, wanting so badly to explore lovemaking with him. Her hand traveled to his zipper, tracing the thick metal, wanting to play inside, but not wanting to awaken him. Instead, she settled for massaging his thighs. When he became fidgety, she stopped.

His groggy voice urged her on: "Why did you stop? That felt great."

"I can play later. You need to go back to sleep." His eyes slowly closed and he drifted into a deep sleep. Brandi held him close. She felt closeness was what a marriage was about, love and closeness. She loved being close to this man, and wanted to wake up and lie down with him for the rest of her life.

The flashing lights from Tim's alarm clock awakened her. She sat up, looked at him zapped of all energy, and decided it was time for her own bed. She called a cab, fixed her hair and took his keys from the dresser to lock up. Sitting on his dresser was a letter addressed to Mr. Gregory Polaris at an address in Schenectady, NY. She quickly wrote down the address, hoping for a chance to get Tim and his brother back together. But she wondered if contacting him would make matters worse. Not knowing what she would eventually do, she shoved the scrap of paper into her purse and waited out front for the cab.

She saw the cab approaching and waved it down so the driver wouldn't honk, possibly awakening Tim. On the ride down Tim's street, she saw that familiar red car again. She asked the driver to stop so she could get the plate number, but as she approached the car, it took off and sped down the street. She stared until it was out of sight, wondering if it could be Eric.

CHAPTER 15

Tim woke with a start and looked to the side. No Brandi. He reached for the phone and called her. His hand was still throbbing badly, but nothing could stop him from seeing if she had made it home safely. It was 9:30; surely, she was awake by now. He could hardly wait to hear her sexy voice again.

Brandi caught the phone on the second ring, seeing 'Polaris' on the display. "Just the man I was thinking of. How are you this morning?"

"Great, now that I know you made it home okay. Why didn't you wake me before you left?"

"Because you were sleeping so soundly. That painkillers knocked you straight out."

"I think it was the beer from the pool hall."

"How's the hand?"

"It hurts, still a bit swollen."

"You hit that guy really hard. It was kind of exciting watching you nail him."

"I didn't think my girl was the fighting type."

"There's still a lot about me you have to find out about. I like romantic things like having my man cook for me. Are we still on for that tonight, or does your hand hurt too much?"

"Nothing will keep me from cooking for you."

"Will this cooking be in or out of bed?"

"Maybe both, but let's not rush things."

"Never heard a man say that. Men are usually the ones rearing to go."

"I don't want to rush with you. I want everything to be perfect. I want what we build to last a lifetime." He put the phone on speaker and re-bandaged his hand while they talked. "Everything will be as you like it tonight. Oh, that reminds me. I got tickets for Shakespeare's *As You Like It*, for tomorrow night. You said you wanted to see it."

"I do. Thanks. So, what are we having tonight?"

"I still have to go to the market, but I was thinking of rack of lamb, mashed potatoes and chef salad, and key lime pie for dessert."

"I didn't know you could cook. That's so exciting."

"I learned early on, since I was on my own."

"I'm sure everything will be wonderful, Mr. Timothy. That would be a good name if you ever get your own cooking show."

"It'll never happen. I like teaching too much."

"What time should I come over?"

"That's not going to happen, either. I will be your personal chauffeur. I'll be uneasy about you coming here as long as the person behind the attacks on me and my property is roaming free."

"You have had some trouble because of me, haven't you?"

"Don't feel bad about it. Nothing has been your fault."

"Have you thought about moving?"

"There are nuts everywhere, Brandi. I can't start running from them. Besides, I like my house, and my neighbors. We all watch out for one another." He checked the time. "Hey, if I'm going to cook tonight, I'd better get to the market. I'll be there around six. Is that good for you?"

"It's perfect."

A short while later, Tim discovered a hateful threat spray painted across his truck's windshield: "She was lucky—this time! Next time will be different!"

He backed away from the truck and looked for the camera attached to his garage. It appeared intact. He removed it and took it straight to the police station to have the footage checked.

That evening, Tim pulled in front of Brandi's house, and watched as she ran out and hopped inside, giving him a quick kiss. "So, what did my personal chef make me for dinner?"

"Brandi, about dinner, well, I didn't make it."

"You didn't? Why? Was your hand hurting too much?"

"It wasn't that . . ."

"Its okay, Tim, we can go somewhere else."

"I think we will have to. We have to talk, Brandi."

He looked bewildered and frustrated. "Tim, what's wrong?"

"A lot." He started the car. "I'll tell you after we get something to eat."

"I think I need to know now, because this is sounding really bad. You're scaring me. Is it something that concerns me?'

"Ultimately."

"Ultimately? I don't understand."

Tim soon turned into Tasty's Burgers. "Let's go in and order something. Then we can talk."

"I'm going to have an anxiety attack. Can't we just talk now?"

He got out and opened her door. "I'm sorry about this, but I couldn't take you back to my house for dinner."

"Okay, this is becoming maddening. What happened?"

He escorted her to a table and sat across from her. "Brandi, the truck was trashed again. Someone spray-painted the windshield."

"My God! Were you hurt?"

"I'm fine—now."

"I did see that red car again. I tried getting the plate number, but they sped off. What was spray painted?"

Their waitress took their order and left. He took Brandi's hand. "Something to the effect you were lucky to have gotten away with your life last night."

"You're kidding!"

"I'm definitely not kidding, Brandi."

"Did you go back to the police station?"

"Yeah. I took the surveillance camera with me. There was motion on it, but not enough to make out any real detail. Everything was fuzzy because of the darkness. Whoever it was made sure to stay on the other side of the truck, but I don't know how anyone could have seen the camera. It was hidden by shingles. You have to get pretty close to the area to see it. It would have nailed them, and someone knew that."

Their food arrived and they waited for the waitress to leave. "What did the cops say?"

"All they can do is continue to patrol the area and decipher what they can from the tape."

"Maybe Dad can help with this."

"What can he do, Brandi? He doesn't want me near you in the first place. Now with this stuff happening, I'm sure he would rather you not be around me."

"All Dad is trying to do is keep us apart because of this stupid race thing he has going on."

"It's more than that, Brandi. Your life is in danger, so is mine."

"Then what do you suggest we do about being together?"

"I do have an idea, but you won't like it. I don't even like it."

"Maybe I won't, so just tell me."

He fumbled for words, trying to find a simple, calm way to present his idea, but he couldn't come up with anything but the truth. "Brandi, as I said, your father doesn't want you at my house anymore; neither do I, until these attacks blow over."

"Tim, do you want me to be with you?"

"Sure."

"Then what's the problem?"

"Brandi, I don't want you hurt. Being with me could be dangerous for you. If something were to happen to you, I would die."

"Are you suggesting we not be together at all? I know we aren't safe in your house, but there are other places we can go, Tim."

"You're not understanding me, Brandi. Someone has something against me, and will apparently do anything to get to me. I don't know if it's a race thing, or something else."

"What do you mean something else? Did you do something to someone?"

"No! I can't remember every single thing that I may have done in the past, but I can't remember hurting anyone. I don't know why I've been targeted, Brandi."

"Look, Tim. Other mixed couples have this problem. Someone doesn't like them, but they still stay together. Nothing is going to happen to me while I'm with you. Don't you want to be with me?"

"You know I do, Brandi, and this isn't a black and white issue. Someone has it out for me, and I don't know why. The best thing right now is to cool it until I can find out who is doing this. This is hard for me, too, you know."

"We can work this out. We don't have to be apart because of Dad's stupid issues."

"Can't you understand? It's more than his dislike of me. He's a cop, Brandi. He knows what he's talking about, and I think he's right."

"We don't have to split up."

"We're not splitting up. We are just going to be separated for a little while."

"How long?"

"Baby, I don't know how long, but I promise you that I want you with me. That's why I'm trying to find out what's going on. Do you think I can stand going to your funeral?"

"You're taking things out of proportion. We just started dating, and now I can't have you. This is ridiculous, and too quick for us not to be together."

"It won't be long; just long enough to get a handle on everything."

She pushed her plate aside. "Suddenly, I'm not hungry anymore."

"Brandi, don't do this. I know you're upset."

"Upset! That's an understatement. We can still see one another through this. That's what loving couples do, Tim. I think other things are going on with you."

"Like what?"

"You're letting things scare you, like my Dad. He's finally getting to you. I think this entire race thing is getting to you."

He stared for seconds. "Cool it with that, will you? The last thing I'm scared of is your father. You have to believe that."

"I don't know what to believe anymore. All I know is that the only man that I've ever cared about is using excuses to get away from me. Tim, don't do this. Let me stay with you and work this out together."

"I wish things were that simple."

They ate the rest of their dinner in silence, neither one willing to back down. Once in the car, Tim took her hand. "Brandi, please, don't read anything into this. I just want you to be safe."

"It doesn't have to be this way."

"Brandi, don't cry. Look at your beautiful face all stained with tears." He kissed her trembling lips, feeling her inner heat and needing her close to him, but afraid to risk it. "I'd better take you home. It was a risk just bringing you out. I had to see you, though."

He pulled alongside the curb and held her before she got out. "Brandi, I know you're mad at me, but don't be."

"We didn't have enough time together. I waited for you to leave Madison, and it was a long wait, believe me. Now that I have the chance to be with you someone ruins it. I still think this could be done another way."

"What way? I'm doing the best thing for us. I couldn't stand it if you were mad at me. This won't take forever, I promise."

"It's going to feel like it. Dad and I need to talk, because I still think part of this is his idea, and he's scaring you."

"Don't confront him. This is about you and me." He brought her lips to his, kissing her as though it would be the last time.

She suddenly pulled away. "I can't do this, not with a man who may not be mine anymore."

"You will always be mine, Brandi. This is temporary."

"Are you sure about that?"

"More sure than anything else in my life. I want you, Brandi, but I want you safe first and foremost."

"Will you call me?"

"Every chance I get."

He walked her to the door, not venturing any further. Brandi saw his reaction. "Aren't you coming in?"

"Not for a while. Besides, your Dad might have something to say to me about even being out with you after warning me not to. I don't want to make things any harder than they already are. You understand, don't you?"

"I don't understand anything anymore, but I know you have to do this."

Their lips met once again before he left her at the door.

Her father met her at the door. "For Christ's sake; you were out with him, weren't you?"

"Yes. You know I love him, Dad, so why would you even say that to me?"

"The guy is dangerous, Brandi."

"I think this is about your funny racial issues and nothing more. The thing is, whatever you said to him worked. He doesn't want me around, either. Thanks a lot." She ran upstairs and slammed her bedroom door, wondering if she would ever see him again; wondered if he would call like he said he would.

Tim called her off and on but was unable to reach her. Each time he called the house phone, her father would hang up on him. On Tim's sixth try, Mr. Miles answered the phone again. "Is this that crazy ex-boyfriend, Tim, again?"

"Yes, so you might as well call her to the phone because I'm not going to stop calling."

"She doesn't want you calling here anymore."

"Did *she* tell you that or did you come up with this on your own?"

"I don't have time for conversations with men who ditch my daughter."

"I thought you would be glad we're not together."

"Frankly, I am, but it hurts me to see Brandi crying over a criminal like you."

"Whatever. Where is she?"

"Out with a friend; a male friend."

"She's home, so just let me speak to her for a minute, then I'll be out of your life—but not hers."

"My daughter has been crying for two days now. She tried hiding her emotions but her mother got it out of her finally. What did you do to Brandi?"

"Nothing. I'm trying to protect her."

"Right. I believe that about as much as I believe trees can fly. I told her you would be trouble, and since you are, if I see you on my display again, I'll find you."

The phone practically shook in Tim's hand from anger. "Find me, then. I'm on Lakewood, third house from the corner. I'll leave the porch light on." Tim thought about his words and realized that was no way to get back in Brandi's good graces. "Look, man, I love her and that's why we are apart for a while. I would never do anything to hurt her. Please, let me talk to her."

Click!

Tim stood in the middle of his living room holding a dead phone. His heart bled, but what was more important than his own bleeding heart was finding out if his Brandi was okay. He would think of nothing but her that night, and would cuss the insensitive monster making his life hell.

On Christmas Eve, Tim went back to work because he had forgotten his Palm Pilot. Brandi had not turned her cell phone on, and he thinks it was on purpose. He had blown it with her, and he knew it. All he had wanted to do was try and explain his actions again and hope she would finally understand. Her father warned him about calling the house, so he didn't. But that wasn't enough to keep him from her. The day before, he went shopping and bought her a present. He, at least, wanted her to have it under her tree. That way, she would be forced to recognize something from him.

He packed the gift into his briefcase, retrieved the Palm Pilot and left. Seemingly within minutes, he had pulled up in front of Brandi's house. The Miles house was beautifully decorated for Christmas, reminding him of a Christmas palace—something he had never had in his own childhood. Brian was outside shoveling the snow that had fallen the night before. He was torn about going in, not wanting to further hurt Brandi by showing up and not taking her into his life again. A face-off with her father certainly wouldn't have helped the situation. At that point, the last thing he cared about was Mr. Miles. He wanted to mend Brandi's heart and tell her they would be together soon. He decided to go in and take his chances.

He tooted the horn to get Brian's attention. The boy trotted over as Tim rolled down the window. Brian smiled. "Hey, aren't you the guy at the basketball games?'

"One and the same. Are your parents home? I would like to ask your father if I can speak to Brandi."

"They're out shopping."

Even better. "Then is Brandi home?"

"Yeah, she's in her room trying to drown out her tears by playing the stereo on sonic sound."

"Is she okay?"

"She cries all the time. No one tells me anything. I actually feel sorry for her—almost." He added with a smile.

"You're some kid, Brian."

"You think I can still play ball with Madison?"

"Maybe one day." He scanned the front of the house. "I would really like to see Brandi."

"Come in with me. If she'll turn down that ghetto music, as Dad calls it, maybe she can hear me."

Amused, Tim shook his head and followed the boy into the house. Tim stood in the middle of the living room as Brian went for Brandi. The inside decorations were as pretty as the ones outside. He looked at the pictures on the table. One was of a baby in a yellow gown; had to be Brian. Another was of a baby girl, maybe three months old. She was wearing a frilly, pink dress. Dimples were on either side of the baby's beautiful brown face. Brandi's face. He picked up the picture, gently touching the infant's smiling face. He loved her so much, and hurting her the way she thought he had was killing him; no one had given him the chance to explain anything.

Moments later, Brian bounced down the stairs, still tracking wet snow on the plush carpeting. "She'll be down." He ran off with some video game in his hand. Tim stood waiting for Brandi. She appeared at the top of the steps wearing something pink; it was her signature color, and it looked great on her. Her lovely brown legs looked as tempting as ever. All he wanted to do was slide his hands up and down them, kissing her, making everything bad go away.

Brandi came down the steps, looking at him as if she couldn't believe he had the nerve to show up at her house after what he had done to her. Tim started to speak, but she broke in. "Why are you here?"

"I had to see you, Brandi."

"All of a sudden, after ditching me, you have to see me."

"Brandi, please let me explain this again."

She faced him point blank. "Are you seeing someone else?"

"I don't want anyone but you."

"You have a funny way of showing me. You don't call in two days even to see how I'm doing. I see how Miss Shang looks at you. Maybe you're seeing her."

"Don't be silly, Brandi."

"Who's being silly? You break us up and blame it on someone trying to get to me through you."

"I never said that. They're after me, and will get you if you're in the way. Why can't you believe that?"

"Maybe it would be believable if everything else wasn't true."

"Like?"

"My father scaring you. He knows I'm mad at him."

"So am I." He stared into her eyes. "Are you okay?"

"Do I look okay? Look, make this quick because Dad will be home soon, and I don't want to hear his mouth. I don't want to hear yours as well, trying to explain to me why we can't be together. Nothing would have happened to me. You just got spooked."

"Brandi, that's so untrue. Someone doesn't want us together and I . . ."

"I think that's you and Dad. So, why are you here?"

"If I was scared of being with you for whatever reason, would I have moved to Columbia just so we could be together?"

Made sense, but she was mad. She lowered her eyes to the floor. "Maybe it's that fear of relationships thing haunting you again. I don't know what it is, but what do you want?"

"Just to see if you're okay. I'm concerned about you, and I'm sorry things have happened this way."

"So am I." Tears started welling in her eyes. "Can you please leave, since you're not interested in working things out."

"There's nothing to work out. All we have to do is wait."

"How long? We've had this conversation before. It wasn't convincing then, and it still isn't."

"Please, just trust me."

"I trusted Eric, and look what it got me."

"I'm not Eric, and I just need a little time."

Tiring of the conversation, she walked to the front door and opened it. "What do you really want, Tim?"

The opened door meant that things were over between them. He had forgotten the gift was in his briefcase. When he remembered, he opened it, placing the small package in her hand. "I just want you to have your gift."

"I don't want it. Take it back."

"It's yours, keep it."

"Look, all I want is for you to leave, and take this gift with you. You left me cold, now want to warm up all of a sudden. You're nuts."

"You and I are not over, whether I'm nuts or not. Please, can't we go somewhere and talk?"

"Wouldn't that be dangerous for us? Now, do I need to call the police to get you out of my house?'

His eyes bore into hers. "You would do that?"

Tears uncontrollably rolled down her cheeks over the sound of his voice. "Tim, just leave. If you love me like you say you do, you'll leave me alone. This on and off thing is terrible."

"I can't believe this."

She pushed the door further open, and he moved to the screen door. Before he stepped out, he tried one more plea but she stopped him. "Just leave!" Her words choked through the tears, rolling down her face.

He put her gift into his pocket and watched as she slowly closed the door. Through the closed door, he could hear her crying, and hated himself for somehow letting her down.

Tim woke to the sound of his doorbell ringing. He peered through his curtains and saw his co-worker, Dean Mori, at his door. Tim cursed under his breath. *What the hell is it now?* He opened the door. "Dean. What's going on? I thought you were preparing for surgery?"

"Something last minute came up. My doctor wants me to have the surgery earlier than April, and I won't be able to go back to work so soon after that. Colletti can't do it because of midterms, so Mr. Moore told me to talk to you and get you signed up immediately. I have the paperwork."

"Do we have to do this now?"

"Afraid so. The new school year starts soon, and they need the paperwork as of last week. After all, this is your project. You're second in charge after Colletti. They wanted me to have it first, since you were new to the school and still getting used to being there. This is really important, Tim."

"I know, Dean, but April is when my class will have their midterms as well."

"Adams will take care of that. Besides, Niagara Falls in April is beautiful; wish I could go."

Thoughts of Brandi entered his mind. *She and I will be there together, in a motel. No problem, she hates me anyway, so how could anything happen?* "Dean, this is just a little much on me right now. I don't think I'll do it justice with all that's going on with me."

"What's going on?"

"Too much to talk about in one night."

"Are you going to be okay over the holiday? Seems like there's some heavy stuff going on with you."

"I'll be okay."

"You should be with your family on the holiday."

"I should have a family worth being with."

That took the man by surprise. "Well, you could come over. Sasha and I are having a few friends over. You're always welcome."

"Maybe. Thanks for the invite."

"So, pal, will you do Niagara?'

"Do I have a choice?"

"Not this time, guy. You will do a good job." He looked at his watch. "Gotta go. I'm on my way to the airport to pick up my youngest son, Jeremy. Think about the invite."

"I will."

Tim walked him to the door. After he was gone, Tim looked at the bottle of liquor on the table, and it was looking better and better by the minute.

The day after Christmas, Tiffany slowly opened Brandi's bedroom door; she was lying across her bed whimpering. She walked in and sat next to her friend. "Brandi, your mother called me."

Brandi took a tissue, patting her eyes dry. "Why?"

"Why do you think? You cried all day Christmas day and now. Is it still about Tim?"

"You really are a smart one, aren't you?"

"Brandi, this is serious."

"It is serious. Tim and I are through. He was looking for a way out because of my father and society's views on interracial relationships."

"Don't blame it on that."

"*I'm* not. He is."

"And you know this for sure? He told you this."

"Not in so many words."

"Then ask him, Brandi. Get to the real dirt and ask him. Stop being so stupid. The man has a good reason. Someone's been attacking him. I think that you wanted him so much that the least little mishap has clouded your mind. Brandi, listen to reason. The man is crazy about you and you're messing it up. I sure wish I were in your shoes. A good man is hard to find."

Brandi wiped her eyes. "I . . . I know. I've been thinking about that all day and last night. I tried calling him, but couldn't reach him."

"Did you go to his house?"

"Although he told me not to, yes, I did, but he wasn't home, Tiffany. He, he wasn't home."

She started crying and Tiffany took her into her arms, trying to console her. "Brandi? Brandi. Call him now. He may be home, since his favorite movie is on television."

"*Animal House*? He must be home."

"Then call."

Brandi reached for the tiny cell phone, stared at it for a while, and then punched in Tim's number. They held their breath as the phone rang . . . and rang. Then his recording came on: "You have reached Timothy Polaris. I can't take your call now. Leave me a message at the beep."

Brandi's voice shook as she spoke. "Tim, please pick up. I really need to talk to you. I'm really, really sorry for doubting you, and I need to tell you this face to face."

She started crying again and Tiffany quickly took the phone, trying to console her. The crying continued as Tiffany held her tight. "He'll call you back. I know he will."

On his end, Tim heard Brandi crying. He lay on the couch, replaying the message over and over in his mind. He felt awful for Brandi, but felt she was right about him not being secure with relationships. But he loved her beyond reality, and in such a short amount of time. The last thing he had wanted to do was hurt her. Yes, staying apart would definitely be best. She would get over him—but would he get over her was the question?

He picked up his glass of wine and continued watching *Animal House*, but not even it could take his mind from the only woman he knew he had ever loved. His phone rang again. He quickly answered it, thinking it was Brandi. His spirits dropped when he heard Monica Shang on the other end. "Yes, Monica, what is it?"

"I have an extra ticket all of a sudden for Breck's Dinner Theater. My wonderful boyfriend was called out of town for his job. Would you like to go with me?"

"When is it?"

"The thirtieth of this month."

He shrugged his shoulders. "Sure. I'm not doing anything else. I'll be back in town by that time."

"Where are you going?"

"Maybe to find my brother, or go to my cabin up north. I could use some family right now; even the worst family is better than nothing."

"Has something happened?"

"A lot, but I don't want to get into it."

CHAPTER 16

Brandi listened to the exchange between Eric and her father. They were still a little strained around each other because of what went on between her and Eric, but Mr. Miles tried to be tolerant because of his friendship with Mr. Fontaine. Eric would have been her father's top pick if he had kept his hands off other women. She knew Eric still wanted to try again, but her heart wasn't having any part of Eric romantically. They were friends; they had agreed on that, and there was no slipping back. She watched her father being friendly with Eric, wishing he could be that way with Tim. Her dad still had a color problem, though ultimately the problem was hers, because Tim was nowhere around. That was why Mr. Miles was smiling like a Cheshire cat. He said it was the Christmas holidays, but Brandi knew better.

It was time to leave for the show, so she took Eric's hand, pulling him away from her father. "Come on, it starts in about an hour."

"We have time. The place is only a half-hour away. What's your hurry?"

"I just want to be there for the start of it. Is that so bad?"

Before he could answer, his phone rang. Brandi listened in on the conversation, getting what little she could. He flipped the phone down and turned to Brandi. "Dad has an emergency at the office to take care of before leaving town. He can't sit with my grandmother until I get back from Breck's."

"Well, what do we do? We have these tickets. Can't your mom do it?"

"She's already in Nevada waiting for Dad. I'm really sorry about this."

Mr. Miles spoke up. "Brandi, see if Tiffany or one of your other friends can go. If not, I'll go with you."

"Thanks, Dad, but I know you and Mom were planning on . . ."

"Don't worry about that. Eric, you better get going."

Eric kissed Brandi's cheek then took off. She looked at the tickets with disgust. "I'll call Tiffany and see if she can make it at the last minute." She called Tiffany's cell and waited for her to answer.

"Tiffany, I've got an emergency."

"What?"

"Eric can't make it to Breck's. He has to sit with his grandmother. Can you go?"

"Thanks for saving this for the last minute, Brandi."

"It wasn't my fault. This just happened."

"I have plans with Stuart around ten."

"It ends at nine. Please go with me; save me from having to go with my dad."

"Wanda or Brina can't go?"

"I tried you first. Come on, Tiff, you're my best friend."

She waited as Tiffany hemmed and hawed, finally saying, "Okay, I'll go, but we have to be back by ten because he's giving me one of my gifts tonight. Know what I mean?"

"Knowing you, I do. Tell him to keep it on ice. Be there in a half-hour?"

"Okay, but how do I dress?"

"A nice dress or pants suit."

"Cool, I'll be ready. You owe me, Brandi; you owe me big time."

Brandi was amazed when they walked into Breck's. The place had been newly remodeled: all-wood floors, mahogany paneling, nice dinner tables with a rose on each table. The place had a Da Vinci appeal. "This place is gorgeous. I haven't been in here in almost five years. I was here for a school luncheon in high school."

Tiffany nodded in agreement. "Lots of things have changed. It was totally renovated about two years ago. Why not? The place makes money hand over foot. Tonight is the best night to be here, apparently."

"The murder mystery?"

"Yes, but I think Eric bought these tickets tonight because its also the grand opening for the remodeling."

They walked to their table, which was dead center; where they could see everything. Brandi handed Tiffany the menu. "With the price he paid for these tickets, we can order anything. I hear the lobster bisque is fantastic. I know how you like it. Maybe we can have that for the appetizer."

As Tiffany looked though the menu, she noticed a woman across the isle walking to a table. It was Miss Shang. Tiffany looked again to see if what she saw was right. She touched Brandi's arm. "Isn't that Miss Shang?"

Brandi looked where Tiffany was pointing. "Yes, that's her. Why is she here alone?"

"Maybe she isn't alone. She could be waiting for her date."

"Maybe. Let's go over and say hello."

"Can't we order first? I'm starving."

"The waiter won't be over for a while." Brandi laid her napkin down. "Tell you what. If I'm not back, which I should be, place my order." Brandi briefly scanned the menu. "I'll have the turtle soup appetizer with Italian crackers. For the entrée, I'll have the baked Alaska whitefish with brown rice and a salad."

Tiffany sneered at her. "Are you sure that covers it?"

"Oh, for dessert . . .

"Just cool it and hurry back."

"Why not go with me?"

"Because she gave me a B- on a paper that should have been an A. Dr. Polaris would have given me that A."

"Right. I guess your world is coming to an end."

"Oh, buzz off. You want a Coke or something with it?"

"Sure."

Brandi walked across the room and held her hand out to Monica. "Miss Shang. What a surprise seeing you here tonight."

Monica stood. "Brandi. Good seeing you. Are you here for the grand opening?"

"That and the murder mystery."

"It is supposed to be very good."

Brandi looked around as if to find Monica's date. "You aren't here alone, are you?"

"No, my date is meeting me here."

"Oh, yes. Aren't you getting married soon?"

Monica swallowed hard and stumbled over her words. "We . . . we're postponing it until the summer."

"He will be here with you tonight, won't he? It's a very romantic-looking place. I was supposed to be here with Eric Fontaine, but he had to cancel at the last minute." She pointed to Tiffany. "My best friend offered to go in his place. You remember Tiffany Jackson, don't you?"

"Sure. She's a smart young lady."

"Yes, with a very smart mouth. I love her to death, though. Anyway, that's why I'm here."

"I'm not here with my fiancée, Brandi. Timothy Polaris is meeting me here." Monica knew those words would hit Brandi like a ton of bricks. She had known about the brief romance, since Tim had spoken of it to her after he left Madison. A curt smile appeared. "He's such a wonderful man, and he was so excited about coming here tonight. He should be here soon."

Brandi had to remember she was an adult and not a baby, though she wanted to throw a tantrum in the middle of the floor. She also stumbled for words. "Really? Timothy Polaris? I wasn't aware that he liked murder mysteries."

"He loves them."

He apparently loves other things. Brandi was beginning to let her emotions run away with her. There had to be an explanation as to why he wasn't returning her calls and why he was attending this affair with Monica. Her eyes briefly glanced around the room, panic-stricken. Her heart was suddenly racing, hands nervous, words barely able to pass through her now dry mouth. Yes, blowing Tim off on Christmas Eve had been a big mistake, and she knew she had blown everything out of proportion, as usual. It took her good friend to help her see reason, but it had been too late. Tears slowly welled in the corner of her eyes, though she tried to hide it. A strained smile came across her face. "Well, Miss Shang. I hope you enjoy the evening. I should go back to Tiffany."

"When Tim comes, why don't you stop by and say hello to him."

"I might."

Monica saw the look on Brandi's face, and had wanted to smile, but she decided not to rub more salt into the wound. "Are you okay, Brandi?"

"Sure. Just a little tired. Good to see you again."

"Likewise."

Brandi hurried back to her table and took her purse. "Tiffany, lets get out of here."

"Out of here? Why? We just got here, and didn't Eric pay a small mint for these tickets?"

"I don't care about the tickets, Tiff."

Tiffany stood, seeing the hurt look on Brandi's face. "What's wrong?"

"Can we just go?"

"What did Miss Shang say to you?"

Brandi faced her friend, tears suddenly streaming down her face. "She said Tim was her date tonight. He will be here with her, and he hasn't even called me. Maybe I really did ruin everything. I just wish I were dead." Brandi walked from the table, and Tiffany quickly followed behind her.

Inside Tiffany's car, she listened as Brandi practically sobbed on her shoulder. "Do you want to go back home?"

"That's the last place I want to be."

"I can break my date tonight and we can buy some burgers, sit back and watch monsters hack up stupid bitches."

That made her smile. "Sounds tempting, but Stuart wants you to meet his family tonight."

"I can meet them another time. You need to be with someone other than your parents."

"I . . . I know, but I want you to have fun tonight. You already took too much of your time to come with me tonight."

"Brandi, I think it's more to it than that. I think he's friends with her."

"She is awfully pretty and smart."

"So are you. He doesn't want Monica Shang, trust me."

"Why are you so sure of that?"

"I see how he looks at you. He doesn't want anyone but you."

"Then where is he—other than at Breck's Dinner Theater with Monica?"

"Come on. Let's get those DVDs and some burgers and hang out tonight. You can call him later and see what's going on."

"If he answers."

"I think he will."

CHAPTER 17

New Year's Eve night was killing him. Brandi called again during the day and the night before. It took all of his willpower to not call her. But after her last call, his defenses began to break down. Her sweet, sexy voice was stirring his emotions. He loved her so very much, and the idea of not being with her was maddening, especially on this particular night—the night for lovers.

An hour later, he found himself parked in front of Brandi's house looking up at her window. He could see her shadow moving along the window. Even her shadow electrified him, and he began to hate himself for not returning her calls. He still thought he wasn't worthy of her, but having her at his side clouded out any and all emotions other than being together. His cell phone shook in his hand. He debated whether to call her or go up to the house. Knowing her father, Tim knew he could get killed on the spot if he entered the house. After all, wasn't he the *monster* who tore poor Brandi's heart to shreds? That would be his mark for life, at least in the Miles household.

He looked at the phone again. If he did call, he didn't know what to say to her, or how to say it. How would he explain not calling her back? He had no answers, but one thing was for sure, he needed to be with her that night, despite how he felt about himself.

He pressed the speed dial and her phone rang. Anticipation built as he awaited her voice. He almost disconnected the call, not knowing what response he could get, but he kept clutching the phone. Finally, her perfect voice. "Tiff, is this you? My caller ID is still screwed. Anyway, I think I'll just stay home tonight. I don't want to be the third wheel with you and Stuart . . ."

"Brandi. It's me."

Silence.

"Brandi, talk to me. It's Tim."

"Oh, my God! Tim, is it really you?"

"I got your calls, baby, and I'm so sorry." He could hear her crying. "Baby, don't cry . . ."

"Tim! Are you actually calling me, or am I crazy?"

"I'm here, Brandi. I'm parked in front of your house. I got all your messages and I was a fool not to . . ."

"Stop! I was the fool, Tim. I was so stupid to let you go. I knew for sure that you'd never want to see me again." She looked from her window and the flashing lights. "I'm coming down. I have to see you, Tim. I miss you so much. Please, say that I can see you tonight."

"I'm in front of your house. Of course you can see me. What about your dad, though?"

"I don't care what he says. I'm coming down to be with you." She laughed, "Besides, he's probably snoring with a box of Cheese Puffs in his hand. You stay right there, Tim. I'll be out in a few minutes."

"I'll be here, and I can't wait to see you. I love you so much, girl."

"I thought I'd never hear you say that to me again."

Tim's hands were still shaking. He anxiously awaited Brandi, stepping outside the truck as cold as it was, just to see her run to him.

Moments later, Brandi ran across the snow towards his truck. They both stopped just inches away from one another and stared, stared as if they had just seen the most miraculous thing on the planet. Tim spoke first. "Are you real? Are you actually here with me?" He took her frosty hands in his, bringing her fingertips to his lips kissing them. He then wrapped his arms around her. Their lips met, and it was like electricity charging through them both.

Brandi cried against his warm flesh. "I love you so much, Tim."

He broke their kiss, opened his passenger door and helped her inside. Before she could breathe, he was in the driver's seat, pulling her into his lap. They kissed again and again, hating that they had been apart. He stared into her eyes in the darkness. "I've darn near gone crazy without you, Brandi."

"Same here. I was a mess until you called a minute ago. Tiffany and my mother tried consoling me, but nothing worked . . . until tonight."

She handed him his gifts. "I've wanted to give you these since the afternoon you left me, but I was so bull-headed that day. I didn't even think about the gifts until you left."

"Gifts were the last thing I was concerned about." He looked at the gifts Brandi placed in his lap. "These are the only ones I've gotten, well, other than this truck."

"I've noticed. What is it?"

"An F-150." He slowly opened the smaller package and took out a silver and crystal pie key chain. The back was inscribed, "Two halves always make a better whole."

"Do you like it?"

"I love it. I have one for you; the same one from the other day." He reached in back and retrieved a small silver and red box. "Here, open this."

"What is it?"

"Open it and see."

She kissed his cheek then tore off the silver wrapping. She lifted the lid and saw a platinum tennis bracelet.

"I know how you love playing tennis, and I . . ."

"I love it, and I'm wearing it tonight. I can't believe you've spent this kind of money on a crazy girl like me."

"Crazy is a matter of opinion."

"So you say. Open your other gift."

"I will, but later. Tonight is New Year's Eve. Big C and the gang have invited me to an all night bowl-a-thon; want to go with me?"

"Who the heck is Big C?"

"A college buddy of mine who weighs about 250 pounds."

"I can imagine the power he has behind one of those bowling balls."

He kissed her cheek. "He's a great bowler, but not as good as me."

"I know your power . . . and I miss it."

"I'll take care of that after we leave Lightening Lanes. How 'bout it? Will you go with me?"

"I'll go anywhere with you, but I can't bowl."

"You don't have to. All I want is the kiss at midnight."

"That's a given."

"Let's go somewhere else first. I know of a little jazz club that has the best slow music slow enough to make out to in a tucked away corner."

"Sounds juicy; let's go."

They entered a darkened little 1940s-style jazz club and sat at a table in the back. The nightclub had great ambiance, with many pictures of all the jazz greats on the walls. He ordered a Black Russian for himself and a non-alcoholic drink for her to toast their reunion.

Brandi saw the pictures on the back wall. "I'm sure you know who all these musicians are."

"Every single one. We have Tommy and Jimmy Dorsey, Sarah Vaughn, Miles Davis. My personal favorite is the one to the far left."

"Billie Holiday?"

"Good girl. You remembered."

"How can I not? I want to remember everything that makes my man happy."

"You make me happy. That's all I need in life, Brandi. I'm so tired of doubting myself."

"Then don't do it anymore. You have me, Tim. That's all that matters."

The background music changed to one of his favorites, bringing a smile to his face. "You've got to be kidding me. I haven't heard this in years, though I have it at home."

"What is it?"

"The one and only Quincy Jones; this track is 'Walking in Space.'" His eyes closed to the melody, his senses taking in each note. "Listen to the way Hubert Laws plays the sax."

She watched as Tim relaxed to the song; drinking in everything it offered. The sound was smooth, mellow and exciting at the same time. Her hand covered his. "You look so damn sexy when you're like this, Tim."

"Just when I listen to Quincy Jones?"

"You know what I mean."

"Tell me again. I can't hear enough of your sweet voice."

She moved in closer to him, whispering in his ear. "Every time I look at you, I get chills. You sitting in here in this darkened room listening to exactly what excites you, well, there are no words for it, other than saying you that I can't wait to make love to you." Her hand slipped under the covered table, massaging his inner thigh, working her way up to everything she had dreamed about.

"You keep that up, darling, and I won't be able to give a damn whether Eric Gale is playing the heck out of that electric guitar of his or not."

"That's exactly my plan, Dr. Polaris."

"I may have to skip Big C's party on account of you."

"Another one of my plans." Her lips met his again, taking everything she could from him. "I can't imagine a night any more perfect than this one. I'm with the love of my life . . . nothing else matters."

"I know exactly what will make it more perfect." He excused himself and approached the band getting ready to play and whispered something to the lead musician. He ducked back into the corner with Brandi.

"What did you tell that guy?"

"I requested something . . . another song that drives me crazy; it reminds me of you."

"What is it?"

"'Satin Doll' by Art Blakey."

"I'm hardly a satin doll."

"When you're in my arms, satin is all I think about, that and other things."

"You're too much, Tim, and I love every inch of you."

They listened to the piano intro, getting a feel and flavor for the smooth sound. Tim took her hand. "Dance with me?"

"We'll be the only ones on the floor."

"So what? It will inspire others. I want you as near to me as possible in this place."

They walked hand in hand to the middle of the floor, embracing one another as if they had been lovers for years. She delicately wrapped around his neck, fingering the feather-light hair on his neck. Her body moved into his, feeling his manhood pressing against her tight slacks. "You feel so good to me. I could just move right through you."

His arms tightened around her slender hips and waistline. "If you keep making these delicious dance moves against me, we may not make it anywhere else but back to my place."

"You know that's what I'm aching for."

"Naah, C will kill me if I don't show. He knows I've been a wreck lately."

"Not anymore."

He nibbled her earlobe. "No, not anymore. I do want to show you off; make all those ladies jealous."

"Screw them for now. Move closer me, make me beg for you. You know I like torture."

His lips met hers once again, not letting go until after the music had stopped.

They pulled up to his house around one in the morning; Tim put the truck in park and leaned into Brandi, taking her hand. "I hope you had a good time tonight."

"I did. Your friends are really cool, especially Big C."

"Casey told me to deliver you a message once we were away from the bowling alley."

"What's that?"

"He told me to tell you that you were hot. I licked my lips and told him I knew that already."

"You were on fire tonight yourself. You really slammed that ball down the lane. It was like you owned the joint; you were so fast and smooth. The pins just burst into the air after you rolled. You won all three games against everyone."

"Were you impressed?"

"Extremely, but it made my lousy forty-five points look ridiculous."

"That's okay. You looked really hot rolling those gutter balls, baby."

"You're about to get hot as well, the minute we step through that door, Dr. Polaris. Don't tell Big C that—it's our little secret."

"I won't tell. Casey's a cool dude; gotten me out of a lot of jams."

"Got you out of a lot of jams, did he? That Donielle would love to get into a jam with you, as would a lot of women. Stay away from her."

"She saw how I kissed you at midnight, and knows she hasn't a snowball's chance in hell with me."

"Speaking of kisses, why don't we go inside and finish saluting the New Year."

"Best damn plan I've heard all night. You know, the last time I touched you the way I'm going to tonight was last summer after we left The Entrapment."

"I know, and I've been on fire ever since."

The minute they entered the house, they were all over each another. Tim felt so good in her arms, something she had missed desperately. He nourished her with every touch, taking in and giving back in return.

Coats fell to the floor. Her fingers feverishly unbuttoned his shirt, then traveled to his muscles, contours, and every part of him that intensified her senses.

Tim watched her eagerly descend to his zipper; arching his back to her advances. He savored her expertise: taking him between her lips, stroking, fondling until he almost crashed. He took her face between his palms, pulling her away from him temporarily. "The bedroom or the fireplace; your choice."

"Why not both? We can christen one room at a time."

"I'll get the champagne. When I return, you had better be ready, willing . . . and nude."

"I have that down to a science already."

He made a quick fire and put on a Quincy Jones CD, *Walking in Space*. When he left the room, she walked over to the fire; feeling its gentle heat warmed her face and hands. She removed her blouse and jeans and let the fire warm other parts of her. Her hands moved to her juncture, spreading the lace panties aside, envisioning Tim taking her, stoking her fire. She lay against the carpeting, giving into the pleasures her mind allowed. Sweet nectar saturated her fingers as she shuddered from her own pleasure.

Tim came back in time to catch her show. "My God, girl! What are you trying to do? Drive me completely out of my mind?"

She looked up, startled. "Tim, I . . ."

"Don't stop the show on my account; watching a beautiful woman do that is a guy's dream come true." He sat the champagne goblets on the table. "The only thing missing is me." He unzipped his pants again, motioning her to help him slide the elastic around his erection. She took him in her palms, squeezing, stroking until they could barely stand it.

After having clad himself with proper protection, he moved the lacy red bra straps down from her shoulders. He loved how the lace felt between his fingers. "Where in the world did you get this lingerie?"

"Believe it or not, Eric gave it to me. I think it came from Frederick's of Hollywood. That's where his mind usually spends the night."

"I'll give it to him; he has damn good taste. The sight of you in lace does things to me."

A smile lit her face. "I can tell. Now, show me exactly what this red lace does to you."

He pulled his undershirt over his head, dropping it to the floor, and met her face to face. "I've been dying for you, Brandi. I could scarcely look at you in class at Madison without picturing this moment." He leaned her back against the shag carpeting, her thick, dark hair flowing freely across its thickness. He marveled at how gorgeous she was; she looked even sexier than he remembered. He slid her bra down he torso before unhooking it. His fingers slid the hooks as his tongue made a trail between her breasts.

Her back arched with pleasure, bringing her breasts closer to him. Her mind danced as his tongue circled her nipples, sucking each with equal velocity, as she cupped his scrotum, matching his tempo stroke for stroke. Each tender nipple heightened to peak perfection as his lips devoured them.

He released himself from her clutches, kissing his way down to her stomach, dipping and poking into her navel. Her cries of desire burned inside him, propelling him forward. Removing her panties, he dipped into her moist valley with swift tongue swirls. Every inch of her tasted sweet, like heaven itself, and all he wanted to do at that point was die, and go straight to Brandi's heaven. Every move he made stirred memories of that incredible evening he had spent with a supremely intoxicating female.

Her folds shivered against his lips, aching as he dipped deeper and deeper into her. Tears rolled down her cheeks as she received his pleasure. When he stopped, her eyes opened wide. "Tim?"

No answer as he was hurriedly removing the jeans trapping his ankles. He hovered over her, their eyes locking. *Thank God! Thank God for this night.* He slowly bent to her, tasting her warm lips. He straddled her, placing her legs above his shoulders. The minute his flesh met her opening, he wanted to give into release. No, his point was to satisfy her—over and over and over. . . .

His pressure ignited her, and she pulled at the plush carpeting as she readied herself for the ride she had lived for. She felt his rod deeply implanted into her, rocking her, becoming frenzied, practically moving her across the carpeting. Her screams became deadly powerful as he rocked her. Her desire for him was electric. She could hardly believe she was looking up at him, finally; the most magnificent being she had ever seen; he was beautiful, perfect. Her eyes steadily bore into his as she massaged his well-toned muscles. They would break to kiss—long, lavish kisses that made them even hungrier for each another.

Their tempos matched, moving in rhythm against one another for what seemed to be hours. Their desires erupted in duo screams, and moans. They had conquered every part of the living room, making love in every position imaginable.

When they were done, Tim lay across her, totally spent, totally satisfied . . . completely in love.

By the time they had finished, Quincy Jones's "Love and Peace" was playing . . . again. They had made love through the entire CD.

They lay side-by-side, talking, listening and learning about one another again. Tim brought their entwined fingers to his lips, kissing her fingers, feeling the tennis bracelet against his chin. He vowed, that night never to keep anything from her again, though his life would be a hard thing to explain to anyone. He didn't know if she would stay or eventually run if she knew all the wrenching details of his life, but he had to take the chance.

But first, he had to know about Eric. His words came slowly. "Brandi, I know this is personal and you don't have to tell me this, but, did you sleep with Eric?"

"With Eric? God no, not after he was with Stacey. He and I don't have that kind of relationship anymore. He never even asked. He knows I love you, Tim, and that there could never be anything between him and me again."

"Good. I know men, Brandi, and had you slept with him, he would take it to mean you are his no matter what. I know that's what I would think."

"You should, because I do belong to you. He was actually kind to me, almost too kind. I could barely believe it was the same guy."

"Maybe he's finally growing up."

"No, I think my father told him he'd tear his heart out if he did anything to me again."

"He still has cell deficiencies, so be careful around him."

"I will, just for you. Besides, who would sleep with him after having the likes of Timothy Edward Polaris?"

"You're making me out to be something I'm not."

"Wrong. One thing though, we have to be honest and straight about everything, Tim. Can you promise me that?"

"I'll say yes to anything when it comes to you."

She rolled over on her back pulling him along with her. "Then shut-up and make love to me again . . . Dr. Polaris."

"No way; it's almost four in the morning. I had better get you home before the old man, along with Eric, has the entire NYPD on my trail."

"Eric and my father are the last things on my mind."

"I know, but I had better get you dressed and home anyway."

Her arms encircled him. "Sure you want to do that? I can make getting dressed awfully difficult."

"Brandi . . . !"

They left the house an hour later. She proved to him just how hard getting dressed could be.

She watched from the screen door as Tim drove off. Her parents' comfortable old house was still in the quietness of dawn. She was sure her father was snoring away; however as sound a sleeper she knew her father to be, he could still hear a floorboard crack in the basement. Brandi knew she would be in for it because she had failed to tell anyone where she was going that night. She could have used her cell, but she was having so much fun with Tim and his friends, she simply forgot. It was nice to see Tim having so much fun, and knowing she brought out that side of him made her happy.

Not being quite in the mood for reprimand from her father, she stepped back into the cool night air. A light snowfall had covered the lawns, making everything seem new and clear. That was what her relationship with Tim was now, new and clear—a time for complete honesty and love. She loved the idea that she would have him as a whole, not bits an pieces.

Out of nowhere, she heard her name being called; she reached for the screen door. It was Eric standing in front of his car across the street. She met him halfway. "Eric, what are you doing here at five-thirty in the morning?"

"I should be asking you the same thing. I called last night to see if you were doing anything, but no one could find you. They said you were probably out with Tiffany."

"I did go out, but not with Tiffany."

"Then who were you with?"

"A friend."

"Really? Just a friend?"

"Look, Eric, had I known you wanted to do something, we could have made plans. Why did you wait until the last minute to call me?"

"I had things to do, and I figured . . ."

"You figured me to be home anyway, right? People make plans in advance on New Years Eve. Don't assume I'll be home waiting for you. Someone called before you did, so I took advantage of the offer."

"You didn't answer me. Who were you with?"

She shook her head, realizing the old Eric was back, and uglier than ever. "I was out, plain and simple. Satisfied?"

"Were you with *him*?"

"Maybe I was, maybe I wasn't. Who's to say? Who are you anyway, the next Jeffrey Miles? Funny, you don't look like him."

"Don't be cute, Brandi."

"Look, Eric, it's too cold and dark out here to be arguing with you about what I do with my time. If I needed a lecture from my father, I'd go inside and get one. You are not my father or my man any more, so lay off."

He took her hand, rubbing her chilled fingertips. "Baby, now don't get defensive. I care about you; I want you to be safe. I know I should have called you earlier, but you know how I am. I'm a last minute kind of guy."

She withdrew her hand. "I'm not a last minute kind of girl. I like notice. You didn't give me any, so I left with the first, and best, I might add—invitation."

"Meaning what?"

"Figure it out, smart boy."

He smiled a snarky smile. "You know who you're sounding like?"

"No, but I'm sure you'll tell me."

"I will tell you. You're sounding like that silly chick who was dating her college professor. Are you her again?"

"I didn't date him while he was at Madison, Eric."

"I think I see where this is going, and it's about to stop. You are my girl. Remember that."

"Buzz off, Eric. I'm tired."

She turned to leave, but he grabbed her hand.

"Let me go."

"No! Where was he when you needed a man, huh? I was around when he dumped you, and now you're about to leave me because Joe White Boy is back in the picture. No way!"

She jerked away. "You son of a bitch! Do you think you own me? This conversation is so finished." She tried opening the screen door but he pushed it shut. At that moment she knew Tim had been right about Eric. Her voice remained calm. "Eric, I am tired and want to go to bed."

"We need to talk."

"It's too late for talk; now move so I can go inside."

"Not until you hear me out. Take a drive with me. We can go and get pancakes, your favorite."

"Do I need to call Dad out here?" She held up her cell phone, but he knocked it from her hand. "Are you nuts or something?"

He picked up the phone. "Maybe I'll call him and tell him who you were with. Wouldn't that be a cool idea?" He started dialing the number.

"Eric, stop!"

He handed her the phone and called to her father at the top of his voice.

Neighborhood porch lights started coming on, hers being one of them. Her only recourse was to run to her car and lock all the doors until she could find her ignition key and start the car.

More lights came on. She finally found the key. As she drove away, she could see Eric racing to his car to follow her.

It seemed as though she had been driving for hours before she pulled into Tim's circular driveway. When she came to a stop, she looked around to see if Eric had followed. He hadn't—not yet. She sat there looking at Tim's house, all dark and quiet. Not even Myrrh was in his heated doghouse in the back. She knew Tim was fast asleep, and hated to disturb him. But she had little choice in the matter. It was only a matter of time before Eric came around, causing trouble for Tim to finish, and he would finish it!

She pressed hard on his buzzer. It felt like forever before he answered it. When he came to the door, she ran into his arms, barely able to speak. "Can I stay the rest of the morning with you? Eric is after me."

"He's what?" He flung the door wide open, but saw nothing but Brandi's car tracks across part of his lawn. "What happened?"

"Eric was waiting for me when I got home."

"You were inside when I left you."

"I went back out, trying to think of an excuse to tell my father about where I was."

"An excuse." He locked the door and led her into the living room. "Why do you need an excuse? Tell him the truth, that you were with me."

"You know how my father is. Besides, he'll get on me more over not calling, as opposed to being with you. Eric wouldn't let me in the house. He blocked my way and started waking up the neighborhood. I didn't know where else to go, Tim."

He wrapped his arms around her. "You're safe here, and no one will hurt you. Come on, let me warm you up and get you into bed. You're tired and cold."

He helped her undress, giving her an old pajama top to sleep in. He buttoned it and kissed her neck. "You still smell so good—like you've just made love to your man."

"Gee, where could that scent have come from? I could tell you, but I'd rather show."

"No. Sleep is on the menu now." He pulled the covers back on the bed. "Slide in and get cozy."

Before he returned to bed, he walked into the living room, and peeked through the curtains, but saw no sign of Eric. Moments later, he snuggled next to her, feeling her back pressed firmly against his stomach. His arms encircled her. "Nothing will hurt you, I promise." For the first time since his marriage ended, he wanted a woman to share his bed with him the entire night.

For Brandi, nothing existed in the world other than the man at her side. Tim's calm breathing soothed her, the feel of his body next to hers relaxed her; it was like being married, it was so familiar, so sensual. "I love you, Timothy Edward."

His body pressed closer to her. "I love you, too." He smoothed the blanket across her frame, falling asleep with her wrapped around him.

Eric pulled in front of Tim's house and saw Brandi's car in the driveway. Skid marks left in the snow testified that she had been on the run from something—from him. What angered him was the overwhelming feeling that Tim had won the battle. He smiled, thinking that the war had not yet been won.

CHAPTER 18

Tiffany walked in with the last of the decorations, dropping them into Brandi's lap. "It was real clever of your mother and her sister to plan a Valentine's Day party, then skip out on decorating this joint."

"Why should they do that when they have us? Besides, my parents married on Valentine's Day. They plan to be together before the party, shopping or something. I think it's very romantic that they're still hot for one another."

"Yeah, yeah, whatever; I still don't want to decorate this house. This is a big house, Brandi!"

"I know, but there are a lot of people coming over, and mom wants the house to look great! Come on, help me with this stuff before Tim comes over. I don't want him to have to decorate Dad's house, knowing they're still not on the best of terms. They're getting there, though."

"What? Tim's coming over?"

"Yeah. Why?"

"I hope tonight will be one of their better ones; if not, prepare to clean up after the fight."

"They've been alone together. Tim has had dinner here before, and he and Dad have actually had a beer together while watching the Knicks. I had to actually pull Tim away so we could go back to his place."

"I guess your father figured he'd better get along with Tim or lose his daughter."

"You got it, because Tim is a permanent fixture in my life. Also, I don't want Tim having to do anything, because this is also partly a belated birthday surprise for him. He was at a conference on his birthday in January."

"I bet your aunt can't wait to get over here to see him."

"She's sweating me big time about him, asking if we've done it yet."

"I know you have, and I'm sick over it."

"Why?"

"Because I can just imagine how on-jam he is in bed, girl, and that he's not with me doing it!"

"You're so silly. I will not say a word about what Tim and I do together."

"You don't have to; your blushing cheeks say it all."

"Enough; help me with these balloons."

"How's it going with what you want to present at Niagara, Brandi?"

"Good, I guess, Tim. I still won't concentrate on winning. It's early though; only March. Besides, that would take me too far away from you."

"This could be a good opportunity for you."

"You're a good opportunity for me, now cut the crap and finish that steak before I finish it for you."

His cell pulsed and he looked at the display; it showed Dr. Drexler's number. "I'd better take this. It's my doctor."

"Anything wrong?"

"Not to my knowledge." He excused himself and walked into the lobby of the restaurant.

He returned with a somber expression on his face.

"Tim, what's wrong?"

"Nothing; she's just checking on me."

"Why? Nothing's going on with you for someone to check."

"It's nothing."

Brandi knew it was something, but couldn't pin him down. "Are we still going bowling?"

He looked around at the crowded restaurant, then back to her. "Sure, we should get there before the crowd takes the lanes."

On the way to the alley, Tim was silent, turning to her favorite radio station to keep her occupied while he tried to sort out the news brought to him by the phone call back at the restaurant.

Brandi bowled her two games and became tired of bowling a score of less than 65. She watched Tim continue practicing. Yes, something was definitely on his mind. He threw the ball down the alley with such ferocity it made her think he was trying to destroy the lane. It was as if he was in a trance, picking the ball up almost robotically, not thinking, just rolling. He beat his own record, but Brandi was concerned about his actions. She met him at the ball return, stopping his hand before he could retrieve the ball. "Tim, what was that call really about?"

"Brandi, why are you down here? This is dangerous."

He moved her aside and rolled the ball with lightening speed.

"Tim, what's wrong? Can't you tell me?"

"Nothing is wrong, Brandi."

"Ever since you got that call, you have been preoccupied."

"I'm just tired."

"Then let's go, because you and that damn ball are scaring me. I've never seen anyone throw a bowling ball that hard. You're rolling strikes without even trying."

"Isn't that the point?"

"Don't be cute, Tim. There's anger behind that ball. Come on, let's go so we can talk."

He refused to talk about the phone call; instead, he rested next to Brandi as they watched movies well into the night. His mind was not on *House on Haunted Hill,* or any other movie he and Brandi had rented. It stayed on that phone call off and on until they were ready to leave for Niagara University.

Brandi and her fellow classmates sat behind the first-class curtains laughing, singing and enjoying the flight. Tim heard her laugh, her voice, and wanted to be out there with her, but he was worried now, and he had a feeling Eric was the cause of the worry. His concentration level dropped to its lowest point and he fell asleep in his seat. He woke as the plane taxied into Niagara Falls International Airport.

They arrived at Niagara University on a blustery evening in early April. The weekend had been reserved for Madison's retreat, so there was hardly any student activity that weekend, and an entire dorm building had been reserved for them. Tim immediately gave out the dorm assignments so he could pass out in his own bed, but he still had Brandi and Tiffany's assignments. He spied Brandi in a corner alone, and called to her. She lugged her suitcase over to him. "Brandi, where were you? I've been looking for you for over ten minutes to give you and Tiffany these room assignments."

"Take it easy, Tim; I was just down the hall getting a Coke. Are you okay?"

"Sure, I'm just tired I guess."

"You've been tired a lot lately. Is it me?"

"Don't start that again."

"I'm serious. Ever since that call a couple of weeks ago, you've been in the twilight zone."

"I'm sorry about that, but everything's fine."

She was not convinced. "Yeah, sure; anyway, I waited for the crowd to disperse. Those women standing around gawking at you were making me sick."

He looked into her face. "Are you okay?"

"Just tired and ready to go to bed—with you."

"Umm, Brandi, don't go there. You know we can't share rooms here." He handed her the room assignment. "I put you with Tiffany."

She looked down at the room number. "Where's yours?"

"The floor above; I'm not telling you which room."

"Spoilsport. I'll figure it out." She dragged her suitcase over to Tiffany, and they got on the elevator. She blew him a kiss.

The doors closed on her lovely face. He wondered how on earth he was going to survive in that hotel for six days without making love to her. And he wondered how he was going to cope with the intrusion of Eric Fontaine in their lives. He slowly rolled his own luggage to the opposite elevator, and rode up to room 712.

Tim walked into the banquet room for the start off meeting and found himself sitting next to Brandi. Earlier that morning he had seen her and other class members setting the room up and placing papers, handouts and menus. Did she have anything to do with switching her seat with Frank's? He slid into his chair, and in a low voice asked her: "What have you done? Frank was supposed to be seated next to me."

"You checked the seating arrangements?"

"I check everything; now, what did you do?"

"I switched with him. He didn't care."

"Fine, Brandi." He shook his head at her audacity as the rest of the staff filed in. During the first speech, he glanced at Brandi and caught her seductively nibbling a sausage link. He tried to ignore her, but he could still see her out of the corner of his eye. She was sliding the sausage between her lips. He felt an instant erection and slid further into the chair so no one would notice. The room buzzed with conversation, making it possible to speak to Brandi without being overheard. "You are a devil."

"And a good one at that."

"Whatever!"

Wasting no time, her hand moved under the table, resting on his lap briefly before unzipping his pants. Her antics took him by surprise, making him sit up straight. She wasn't going to stop her little games, so he relaxed. He was embarrassed and excited at the same time and he struggled to hide his emotions.

Brandi was relentless: fondling, stroking, massaging his scrotum. Trying to stem the rising tide of passion, he grasped her hand. Too late. Seconds later, heat waves flashed through his body, and his pants became soaked with his own moisture. He glared at Brandi, who was pretending to listen to Mr. Tobias's boring speech.

For once, he was not grateful for that fabulous release, because standing to deliver his speech was now impossible. He had to get out of there; he tipped over his glass of juice, letting it land in his lap. Anything to get out of there and change his pants.

The breakfast meeting adjourned. Tim hated that he had been scheduled to speak last anyway. He wanted it over so he could retreat to his room, allowing Brandi no latitude. He told everyone to meet him back there for lunch for the last of the speeches. When the last person left, he went to Brandi pointing to his wet pants. "That was so wrong, Brandi."

She dabbed at his wet pants, but he pulled back. "Why did you do that to me?"

"Because you need some levity in your life. You've been moping around for weeks now. I thought it would help."

"It didn't!"

She heard anger in his voice. "I'm sorry. I just wanted to take your mind off whatever has been consuming you."

"During a speech I was supposed to be making? Brandi, I don't even know what to say to you now."

She moved closer to him, making sure the door was completely closed. "Did you enjoy it, though?"

"That's not the point."

"You did, didn't you?"

"No . . . yes, but, Brandi . . ."

She pressed her hand hard against his lasting erection. "Good thing your pants are dark. Here, cover up with this." She handed him a large napkin. "I would go with you to help you change, but I've got work to do. Sorry you're so mad at me."

"Just go and get your work done." He held the door open for her. Monica met him at the entrance, smiling as she looked at him. "How did you manage to spill that juice all over yourself?"

"It just happened is all." He walked past her to the bank of elevators.

After the luncheon meeting, Tim was too tired to attend the festival at the park that evening. Brandi would be there, and he didn't want to be tempted by her again, not after her little stunt at the breakfast meeting. Then he thought about it, hating himself for being mad at her. She had only been trying to help, as she had been ever since he had gotten that call from Claire.

That afternoon, he walked to the gift shops on the waterfront near Niagara Falls, looking for something nice for her to make up for his temper. In the distance, he could hear the festival music playing reggae, Carlos Santana, and Sergio Mendez. He loved the Latin sounds almost as much as he loved American jazz. Music always reminded him of Brandi dancing against him. He saw the time and realized he needed to get back to work, reviewing the papers to be presented at the end of the retreat.

But the music still playing in his ears made it hard to go back to work. Instead, after reaching the waterfront near the dorm rooms, he leaned over the railing facing the falls. The falls were breathtaking, a wondrous beauty and a magnificent place for lovers. Too bad he and Brandi couldn't share a room or that experience. They did not need more havoc in their lives. No, he had to leave Brandi alone until the trip was over.

A gentle breeze gently blew droplets of water onto his face, causing him to think of Brandi's tender caresses. She was never far from his thoughts. He hated that he hurt her feelings earlier that day. Still, he ached for her. He missed her nearness above all else; he had never experienced loving a woman the way he loved her.

From a distance, Brandi watched him. She wanted him in her arms, but was fearful that he was still angry with her. She didn't know whether to leave him alone with his reverie or talk to him and apologize again for making his life hell that day. She had never seen him so upset over something that was not life threatening. Something was behind it, and she knew it.

She came over and stood next to him, letting the same cool mist dampen her skin as well. They enjoyed the water in silence until she broke the mood. "I thought you would have been at the festival tonight; God knows you need to have some fun."

"Wasn't really in a dancing mood tonight."

She moved closer to him. "I'm really sorry about today, Tim. I never meant to hurt you. I hope you realize that."

He took a deep breath, and then turned to her. "It was never really you that I was angry with. I just needed someone to blame it on. I'm sorry for being so mean lately."

"You haven't been mean, but I know something is going on. Is it the fact that Eric is being so disagreeable?"

"I don't care about Eric; you know that. He can jump into the falls as far as I'm concerned. No, there have been other things."

She put her arms through his. "Maybe one day you'll tell me."

"I guess that time is tonight. I've kept you in the dark long enough. Remember that call I took in the restaurant some time ago?"

"Sure."

"Brandi, someone broke into my doctor's office and made off with my files."

"Really? Why didn't you tell me this before?"

"I didn't want to upset you. It was made to look like a break-in, but only my files were stolen."

"Why would someone want your files?"

"I have no idea. All I know is that those files had things about my life in them; my life as a child, everything. Everything I told you about my past is in there. The last thing I need is someone having access to that."

"Is Claire okay?"

"She's fine, but the cops still have no lead. I don't know why someone is so intent on making my life a living hell."

"You don't think Eric had anything to do with this, do you?"

"I don't know what to think anymore." He looked at his watch again. "It's getting late and I have work to do; so do you."

"I left Tiffany at the park after seeing you here. I'd better tell her I'm calling it a night; you know, get some of that work done."

"No, you have time. Go and enjoy your night out."

She watched him walk towards the dorm rooms with a cloud of doom overshadowing his good looks. She wished that she could join him in his room and make life a little better for him, but knew he would never say yes to that.

CHAPTER 19

A refreshing shower always relaxed Tim. He dashed on Polo body splash; hoping, probably in vain, to stimulate his seemingly dead senses. He put on his jeans and a white shirt, leaving his underwear in a pile on the floor. He raked his hands through his still damp hair, and then turned to concentrate on the stack of papers waiting for him near the bed.

Before starting on the papers, he gazed through the picture window at the night sky. The festival was still going on in the park. Where was Brandi in that crowd? Probably dancing her delicious butt off somewhere. He had forgotten to give her the present he had bought, a silver heart pendant to put on the chain he had given her for Valentine's Day.

His stomach began to churn; he hadn't had dinner. Tim checked the local restaurant's take-out menu and ordered a Ruben sandwich and a drink. His mind drifted back to his missing case files. He knew he couldn't worry over that all night, he got busy on the stack of rough drafts.

A half-hour later, delivery was at the door. He opened up with a generous tip in hand and stared into Brandi's face. She was holding his food order.

A smile hovered briefly on his lips, then faded. He should have known she would find his room. "I don't know whether or not you deserve this tip."

She gave him the bag and took the ten from his hand. "If anyone deserves this tip, it's me. How do you like my new job?"

"How did you finagle this?"

"I was sitting at the bar in the restaurant when your call came in. I tipped the waiter a ten to let me bring the order to you. I told him you were my professor."

"And he believed you?"

"Charm and a pretty smile can fool any man."

"It sure fooled me. Keep the ten; you deserve it." He sat the bag on the table. "You can't stay here, Brandi."

"Sure I can; no one saw me." She took his drink from the foam bag and began sipping it. "This is great! What is it?"

"Something you have no business with; give me that. Now, you have to leave, Brandi."

"No. I'm worried about you, Tim. That's why I was at the restaurant. I wasn't in the mood to party after seeing you so depressed. I had to find a way to see you again."

"But not here."

She moved into his arms, inhaling his aftershave. "Umm, you smell so damn good."

"Brandi, you have to leave. We can't make love here, and you know it. Besides, the walls are thin. Someone could hear us."

She paid no attention and lay across his bed. "I'll be quiet."

"You're never quiet."

"Then you shouldn't be such a good lover."

"Please, Brandi."

"No. I'm here to comfort you tonight. I don't have to have sex with you to do that."

"You know we end up doing that, anyway." He leaned over her, barely inches from her lips. "I'm serious. You've got to get out of here."

She unbuttoned her pink chiffon midriff and slipped out of her matching skirt. He sat on the bed next to her. "I am serious about this. We could get caught."

She moved in behind him, whispering in his ear. "It's just us in here, Tim."

The feel of her thighs against his damp skin made him move closer to her. His muscles relaxed under her gentle massaging fingers. He put his drink aside. "Fine, I give up."

"What are you talking about?"

"You heard; I give up fighting you about this sleeping together thing on this campus. I have no more energy for it."

"I'm not trying to fight you, Tim; I just want to love you."

He stood, removing his pants and shirt. "I've been holding off for weeks now because my mind has been so occupied, but the fact is, I've missed you way more than imaginable." He returned to the bed, wrapping her within his warmth. "I've really missed you, my angel."

She squirmed in his arms, forcing her breasts deeper against him, forcing him to hunger for them. The moment his lips met her taut nipples, rockets shot off in her head. "Make love to me, Tim, please."

He reached for his pants and took the condom from his wallet, handing it to her. "Do it, Brandi. I know how you love putting it on me."

"It's a bona fide gas doing this to you. I know that sounds so seventies, but that's how I feel when I'm with you, like nothing is more important."

"How did I get to be this lucky?"

She fit the elastic around his maleness and smiled into his face. "I don't know; kismet maybe?"

He moved her to her side, swirling his tongue across every part of her, from her breasts to her navel. His fingers filled her core, rocking, pumping her slowly—the way she liked it. That wasn't enough for him, though. He had to taste his angel, get his fill of her before taking them both to heaven. He took her from behind, kissing and stroking her tender folds, lapping his way into her body—draining her. He felt his own pressure becoming intolerable; he knew he couldn't last much longer without being inside of her.

Knowing what he needed, she lay on her back, awaiting his pressure . . . his pleasure. He poked creamy wet folds, pushing harder with each stroke until he was deeply implanted in her. He heard her low screams and reveled in them. They were nourishment for his soul.

He collapsed on top of her, staring blankly at the red flashing numbers on his alarm clock. It was nearing 3:00. He smiled at Brandi resting in his arms. No woman had ever satisfied him both mentally and physically the way Brandi had.

For her, the only thing that mattered in the world was the man behind her. She was committed to spending the rest of her life making sure he was pleased in every possible way. She kissed his hand. "I love you so much, Timothy Edward. Thanks for giving me a life."

He was awakened by phone hours later. "Yes, what is it?"

"I'm sorry to have to disturb you, Dr. Polaris, but I have a student down here, a Miss Tiffany Jackson. She's concerned that one of her suite mates hasn't returned from the festival. She wanted me to call you."

He knew it was about Brandi. Not wanting to discuss anything with Tiffany, he roused Brandi. "Honey, wake up; I need you to talk to Tiffany."

"What? What's she doing calling here?" She took the receiver, waiting for the attendant to put Tiffany on. "Tiff, everything is okay."

"Oops, sorry, but I didn't know where you were."

"Now you know, so go back to the room."

"Are you having fun?"

"Tiff, I will talk to you later, okay? Not a word to anyone."

"I swear."

"You'd better."

She handed him the phone. "I'm sorry, Tim."

"Not as sorry as I am." His head rested the pillow, his mind racing. *Now the whole damn world will know Brandi was with me.*

Several students had already presented their papers on 18th-century authors. The heads of Niagara University were very impressed by how diligently the students had worked at the retreat. They had always been impressed with presentations from Madison and Columbia.

Brandi was set to present her paper on Thomas Paine in the next half-hour. However, when Tim looked in Brandi's face, he knew something was wrong and took her behind the stage. "Brandi, what's wrong? Why have you been crying?"

Her panicky voice rushed through. "Something is really wrong, Tim. My paper is gone."

"What do you mean, gone?"

"Just gone! I didn't want to tell you until I absolutely had to. I tried to access my files from the computer to print the paper again, but it wouldn't give me access. The paper on my file at home is unedited. Nothing came up but the old paper that didn't have an ending."

"I thought you had the paper in your book bag. You carry that everywhere you go."

"I went to buy a soda from the machine and left the bag on the table with the other student papers. When I came back, Dana told me somehow my paper was gone. I had her go back and get it for me while I swallowed the last of my drink. I checked again myself, and Dana was right. It was gone."

"You will present, Brandi. I'll get the converted disc from . . ."

"We looked for the disc, and that's gone, too."

"Miss Shang has one."

"She doesn't; we already asked. She said it was erased by mistake and that other class papers are now on it. She also looked on her hard drive; everyone did. The papers are just not around."

Brandi was not able to present. The university could not extend the retreat for another day due to classes starting. Tim and Monica sat in the conference room discussing what had happened with the papers. They were glad at least that four students had been awarded the grants—two from each university, with Tiffany getting the highest grant amount. Tim felt bad for Brandi not having a chance to compete after he persuaded her to try for it, anyway. He felt that he had let her down and, no matter how Monica tried consoling him, he was sick about it.

Brandi walked in the minute Monica left. "Tim, are you okay? I know you took that pretty hard."

"Am I okay? I should be asking you that." He shut the conference room door and took her into his arms. "I'm so sorry about everything."

"I feel better now. I really didn't want to leave you and come all the way up here for school, anyway. I just didn't want my chances taken away."

He kissed her forehead. "You should be at the restaurant celebrating Tiffany's and the other students' accomplishments."

"I couldn't leave you in here alone when you were so worried."

"After everything that's happened to you, you still thought of me?"

"I can work on another grant another time, but I can't get another Timothy Polaris. I saw you becoming unglued trying to explain everything to the judges. It hurt me to see you like that."

"I love you for thinking about me, Brandi. I love everything about you."

Brandi saw the faraway look in Tim's eyes. "You think you know who did this, don't you?"

"I have my suspicions."

"It wasn't Eric. He's a snake in the grass, but he would want me to win. He would want me to be away from you."

"You have a point. I guess that takes me back to square one."

As Tim reached for his scotch glass, someone knocked on his door. He had left explicit instructions with the front desk that he needed alone time, at least for a couple of hours. They were leaving the next morning, and he had to work through his emotions before returning to Columbia to explain everything to his dean.

He opened the door to see Brandi smiling at him. "Are you feeling better? I was told you had a headache."

"Who let you up here?"

"You know I sneak around, go anywhere I want to. Don't worry, no one saw me come up here."

She walked to the bed and sat, patting it for him to join her. "Come on, I've got something to make you feel better."

"No way. We shouldn't do that again until we're back in New York."

"I don't mean that, Tim. I just want to give you a massage, work out those kinks, help you relax."

"The scotch can do that."

"I can do it better. Come on; it's just a little massage. Take your shirt off and lie on your stomach."

He removed the shirt and did as instructed. He loved how her fingers slowly massaged his upper chest, squeezing, stroking his pecs. He tried not to enjoy the massage but, she was working magic on him. He loosened up and all thoughts of the missing papers disappeared, at least temporarily.

He turned over, facing her as she made him feel like a new man. Her hands moved to the ripples on his stomach and sides, gliding across them vigorously, working him into a gentle moan. "Feels great, huh?"

"Fantastic."

Brandi gave him a kiss that was hard to break. Their lips parted and she looked down on a man she loved to the ends of the earth; not a perfect man, far from it. That was what she loved about him. He wasn't common, or easy to figure out, but he had a solid heart. He saw her as a person, a loving young woman, not a color. She needed that.

As for Tim, he didn't see the perfection others claimed to see when he looked in the mirror, just a bunch of mixed-up nerves in a tired body with many insecurities. He knew Brandi loved him, and that was all he needed to get him through any and all things, including how society viewed them as a couple.

Before long, he was breathing unevenly against his pillow. She watched him sleep, thinking how he looked like a big baby lying there so helpless. Awake, he was a force to be reckoned with, a man who would fight tooth and nail with no thought of being defeated—except by his family. She thought about that envelope with Gregory Polaris's name on it, wondering what he looked like, wondering what kind of a man would avoid his brother. No answers, and Tim wasn't ready to provide any.

She pulled the covers over him and walked out.

The trip back to New York was terrible; no buzz about how great the trip had been, no laughs and hand-slaps from instructors congratulating one another for being masters of the universe. But it hadn't been a total wash; several of the students were all set with grants. Theirs were the only voices heard on the plane.

It was hard for Brandi to be excited, even though her best friend's paper had won the top grant. Tiffany tried making her feel better. After a while, though, even Tiffany ran out of words of encouragement. She watched as Brandi sat there fumbling with the silver heart pendant Tim bought her at Niagara Falls.

"When did Tim give you that?"

"This morning before we boarded the plane; he forgot to last night what with all the confusion."

"Is he okay?"

"Not really. Someone took the discs, and he feels responsible; all the professors feel that there must have been something they could have done."

"Like what?"

"Who knows? Tim thinks he's Superman and can see everything in the nick of time. He can't, though. He's only human, and I wish he'd remember that."

"He will; give him time."

They landed in LaGuardia Airport an hour later. Brandi and Tim stole a few minutes in a corner to say good-bye without having to endure snickers or comments from students or her father. Although her father and Tim were on much better terms, he still couldn't accept the idea that Brandi was going to date whomever she wanted to, whatever his race. She was too tired and too upset to hear Mr. Miles' views on her relationship.

That night after getting Tim's goodnight call, her mind returned to her missing paper, and the fact that she wasn't curled up in Tim's bed. She knew it would be days before she saw him again. She knew him well; he would hibernate and punish himself for not being on top of things at Niagara Falls. She hoped nothing would push her to the back of his mind.

CHAPTER 20

Brandi's twenty-first birthday was proving to be a drag. Tiffany, a few other friends, and her parents were having dinner at the Excelsior. There were presents, balloons, her favorite food, shrimp—everything that should have made a birthday great. But one thing was missing—Tim.

Her mind stayed on him until the waitress approached her with a big bouquet of pink peonies. She didn't know what to think and looked around as the chatter stopped. Tiffany was the first one to break the sudden silence. "Well?"

"I don't know who sent them yet, Tiffany, so hold your horses."

"You know who they're from, just read the note."

Brandi pulled the note from the middle of the bouquet and read silently: *You've made me want to live again . . . a hard thing for a mere mortal to do. Then again, you're not mortal, you're my favorite fairy tale. All my love, Tim. Hope to see you tomorrow night? I have plans for you.*

Again, Tiffany was the first to speak. "Are they from Tim or not?"

"Of course they are."

Her mother reached for the bouquet. "Umm, these smell so wonderful. He must love you to send this big a bouquet." He eyed her husband. "Size does matter, despite what anyone thinks."

"I get your hint, honey. Your bouquet will be larger next time, I promise."

Brandi smiled. Tim was fine, and she would be in his arms soon.

Brandi wanted to thank Tim over and over for the flowers. Of all of the gifts she had received last night at her party, his flowers meant the most!

He picked her up that evening for dinner. They then went to the place where he had begun to fall in love for the first time, The Entrapment.

They reached his house at 12:30. He took her inside and sat her down on his bed. She smiled, knowing he was trying to make everything perfect. He put on a jazz CD, poured her a glass of wine, then came to her with his hands behind his back. "Tim, what are you doing?"

"Making everything perfect."

"Everything is already perfect. Come and join me on the bed so I can make everything incredibly perfect."

"Not yet, I have something else to do. May second is a special day, Brandi. It's the day the Lord sent you to me. True, I was only nine years old when you were born, but you were destined to be mine. Don't you agree?"

"Sure, but where is all this going?"

He knelt between her thighs and handed her a small silver box with a white bow attached.

"Is this what I think it is?"

"Depends on what you think it is?"

She quickly opened the box and saw a platinum wedding band with diamonds. "You've got to be kidding me."

"I'm not kidding. Here, let me slip it on you."

She watched as he slid the band on her waiting finger; she stared at it, barely able to speak. "Tim . . . this . . . this is the second most beautiful thing I've ever seen."

"The second? What was the first?"

She leaned over and kissed him. "You. The minute I saw you, I had to have you, Tim."

"I've only done this once before, and I pretty much botched it up. It's different this time because I feel this in my heart, Brandi. I know this is right. Okay, here goes; I . . . I want you to be my wife. Will you? Please save me, save my life, and become half of it."

She had waited to hear him say those words for what seemed like an eternity. "Yes, God yes, I'll be your wife."

"You will? You don't want to think about it?"

"What's there to think about? I'm miserable without you."

"Me, too, but you know that I'm not the proverbial man next door with an apple tree in his yard. I fight, drink, I . . ."

"I'm in love with you, Tim. I know you're not perfect. Maybe that's why I love you. You're different, exciting, everything I want and need."

He didn't say a word, just kissed her as if the world were about to end.

She soon broke the kiss. "When?"

"You decide."

"Tonight?"

"Brandi!"

"I'm just kidding. I have always wanted to be a June bride, and it's only a month away."

"That's perfect!"

Later that evening, Brandi pressed her ear against her parent's bedroom door. Hearing her father's snore, she quietly pushed open the door and went to their bed and shook her mother's shoulder. "Mom, wake up, I've got to tell you something."

A sleepy Mrs. Miles rolled over and looked at the clock. "Brandi, it's 3:30 in the morning. Can't this wait?"

"No. I can't hold it in any longer. Look." She held her ringed finger in front of her mother's face. "Tim gave this to me. We're getting married."

Mrs. Miles immediately sat up. "What did you say?"

"I said Tim and I are getting married. Look at my ring."

Her mother stared at the ring; tears filled her eyes. "Tim proposed to you?"

"Yeah, we're getting married in June."

"Jeff, wake up. Our baby is getting married." She looked at the ring again as Jeff stirred awake. "This is gorgeous, Brandi. When did this happen?"

"A couple of hours ago." Mr. Miles sat up in the bed. "Dad, Tim and I are getting married."

He shook his head until he was fully awake. "This must be some kind of a nightmare. I thought you said you were getting married."

"Dad! I am getting married. Look at the ring Tim gave me."

He took her hand and stared at the sparkling ring. "Brandi, isn't this a little soon? Shouldn't you think about it?"

Before Brandi could answer her mother cut in. "Jeff, she's in love. Did anyone tell you to think about it?"

"No, but. . . ."

Her mother squealed, returning to Brandi. "My baby is getting married." She and Brandi hugged as her father pretended to be happy.

A fidgety and nervous Brandi could hardly sleep that night.

The next week she, Tiffany, Mrs. Miles, and, at times, Tim, made arrangements for a June wedding. Tim left the planning and decorations to his soon-to-be-wife, and gave her all the money she needed to take care of everything. He booked the honeymoon, though.

Brandi had no classes on Monday, it was her only day to sleep in, but the doorbell woke her. It rang three times before she realized her parents had gone to work. She looked from her window and saw the FedEx truck, and she knew that the wedding dress she had ordered had arrived. With just a robe on, she ran to the door.

She opened the door and smiled at the face of the courier standing there with the box. "You have a delivery for me?"

The driver quickly scanned the FedEx letter. "Are you Brandi E. Miles?"

"Yes."

She signed the ledger and he handed her the item.

She looked down at it, disappointed. "Is this it?"

"Yes, ma'am."

"You don't have a bigger one in your truck for this address?"

"Sorry, this is it."

After she dressed, Brandi sat on the bed staring at the box. She picked it up then out it down; picked it up again, put it down. Finally, she tore the side off and pulled out a stack of folders. "What the hell is this stuff?"

The first manila file had a note attached to it: *This is the real deal on your boy wonder, Brandi. You'd better read this before you get too happy about that diamond sitting on your pretty finger. Happy reading!*

She looked at the outer package again. "Who is this? No one knows I'm engaged to him, other than my family and a few friends. They wouldn't send me anything like this." She read the contents of the first folder. *November. The minor Timothy Edward Polaris Jr. was placed into Chandler Home for Boys for excessive fighting and aggression towards classmates. Lagging grades despite his exceptional ability. Returned home five months later. December of the following year, the above mentioned minor ran away from home and broke into Fitzers Party Store a week later; returned to Chandler for a period of 6 months—returned home in July.*

Brandi looked up from the file. "What is going on here? This is not Tim. Someone's making up lies." She stopped reading, but felt compelled to continue. Her first thought was of Eric, who had been acting like a total ass of late. Then she remembered Tim saying someone had broken into his doctor's office. Even Eric wouldn't do that.

She dismissed the files. His youthful escapades were not news to her. Tim had told her about them. He and his brother had a terrible childhood, but he had come clean about that, so why was someone sending her crap she already knew? They were about to be married; she trusted everything he said and did.

Still, the file beckoned her, she began reading page after page, describing altercations Tim had been involved in since he was nine years old. She hadn't know there were so many. He had mentioned several things, but nothing as extensive as what was in the files. Her first instinct was not to believe any of it, but the documents didn't seem to be bogus. "What is going on here? What else is this nut trying to pin on Tim?"

Finally, the last file. *Timothy Edward Polaris Jr. returned to Chandler for aggravated assault on his brother . . . killed another youth in an altercation.* She threw the folder down. "Oh, my God; no way! No way did he do these things. He would have told me." Then she thought about it; why would he tell her? If true, he would never admit it; it would have been too hard to admit to. She jammed everything back into the envelope. Tim was the only one who could make sense of this crap.

She was up to 85 mph before she realized she was speeding. Nothing in that envelope was worth getting a ticket, or worse, killing someone, so she slowed down. She was on the Long Island Expressway, wondering how Tim would react to this, if he would try to find out who had sent the files to her. She didn't know anything, but she did know that Tim would get to the bottom of it. So these were the files that had caused him to flipped out after the break-in at Claire's office. Still, nothing made sense; Tim was not a murderer.

Tim had back-to-back classes that day, but she had to show him what was going on.

His freshman comp class was just letting out, and she sat outside of his door impatiently waiting for his last student to leave.

Tim smiled at her as she rushed in. "I was just thinking about you. Come in and lock the door. I've got about twenty minutes before I have to be across campus."

She closed the door but didn't lock it. "I was thinking about you, too. I really do have to talk to you."

"Let's go in back, where it's more private."

"Maybe we had better." She followed him and waited until the back door was closed. His lips met hers; he felt warm and exciting. She hated disturbing the moment, but she had no choice. She ended the kiss.

"Come on, you know I don't have much time today."

"You and I need to talk."

"Sure, but later." He tried moving back into her arms but she sidestepped him.

"Tim, stop. I'm serious. Something has come up, and you need to know what it is before everything gets blown out of proportion."

"Is it something about the wedding?"

"I wish."

His eyes searched hers. "What's going on?"

She held up the folder. "This, this is what's going on. Someone FedExed this thing to me this morning." She placed it in his hands.

He could feel his body heat rising, feel the anxiety stirring in the pit of his stomach. "I knew it would show up soon."

"*What is that crap*, Tim? Help me understand."

"These are the files that were taken from Claire's office. Did you read any of this?"

"Yes. That's why I'm here. Tim, I know you and Greg had a terrible life as kids, but there are things in there that don't make sense."

He leaned against the wall. "Then you know about the number of foster homes I was in?"

"Yes, but that's not the problem. You told me about those, although I had no idea there had been so many. Look, Tim, I know things were bad for you, and that there are things that you haven't told me. I understand. Who would want to talk about such things? But you could have tried trusting me."

"What do you know that I didn't tell you, other than that petty robbery rap?"

"Maybe you should tell me."

"I don't know what to say, Brandi! Things happened! My life was not a smooth road. I was a kid when everything happened. I hope you realize that."

"I know one thing that happened. I was hoping you'd admit it now that everything is in the open, but I suppose you won't . . . can't."

"I know what you're getting at. Paul died of a blow to the head. I did it. Is that what you're searching for?"

"That's the one!"

"I didn't know how to tell you. I didn't know if you . . . well, if you would walk away from me. Brandi, Paul used me as his whipping boy. He and Greg were best friends. He knew I was part of the reason Greg's life was hell. I couldn't get this boy off my back. Every chance he got, he was nailing me. I got tired of it one day and hit back! He died, and my brother has hated me ever since."

"Why would your brother take his side against yours? You were his brother, not Paul."

"He was reaching for straws as I was, Brandi. He was a kid, a hurting, mixed-up kid. What do you expect?"

"I expected you to tell me about this before I found out from anonymous troublemakers. You've known me long enough. You could have come to me about this. I understand how kids are, Tim. What I don't understand is why you didn't trust me enough to let me into your life; even the ugly stuff, Tim. Everyone has some."

"Didn't I just say I didn't know how to tell you?"

"What else don't you know to tell me? What else are you possibly hiding from me?"

"Nothing!"

"Tim, you and I are to be married soon! You can't trust me, and you're about to marry me? Haven't I had enough of men holding back on me? Look at what Eric did to me."

"I'm not Eric."

"Then who are you, because I don't think that I know anymore."

"You can't be serious, Brandi."

"I am serious. You withheld information about your life the entire time we've been dating. I have told you everything about me: embarrassing stuff, all the things that hurt me. I even told you about a man sleeping around on me. If that's not embarrassing or humiliating enough, then I don't know what is."

"Brandi, just listen to me."

"Why couldn't you have trusted me the way I trust you?"

He sat down on one of the chairs, looking up at her. "Because you never murdered anyone!"

Tears streaked her face. "That is not what I'm getting at. I know that couldn't have been easy to tell me, but you and I are to have a life together, for better or for worse. Does that sound familiar? I don't love you because you're perfect. I love you for the man you are . . . at least for the man I thought you wanted to be to me."

"I am the man you fell in love with; a man with a checkered past, that's all."

"You're a man who can't trust his fiancée, and that hurts me . . . that hurts me, Tim!"

He took her into his arms. "Brandi, I never meant to hurt you. You're the only one I've ever loved other than my own child. Let me make things right for us again. I'm begging you."

She wiped her tears. "I have a lot of thinking to do, so let me out of here." She pulled the door open and ran out.

"Brandi, please." He ran after her.

Students stopped to look, but she didn't care, and continued running until she was leaning against her car. She wiped away tears, but felt the coolness of the ring against her cheek and looked at it. *I finally get one of these and I don't even want it—not from him.* She knew her own thoughts were a lie.

She got into the car, starting it and not stopping until she was home. Her parents were still at work, and Brian was at school. That gave her plenty of time to cry her guts out in peace, without having to answer a ton of questions. She looked at the ring again, then took it off, wrapped it in tissue and put it in her purse to give it back later, when she could face him.

Tim sat in his empty classroom. Another failed relationship was weighing heavily on his chest. Passing students stared at him, but he didn't care. What he cared about was that a beautiful young woman had just run out of his life, probably forever.

CHAPTER 21

Brandi didn't know where the ring was. She had agonized for days before deciding she could face Tim again. She knew she had to face him and return the ring.

Mrs. Miles stood outside the door watching her daughter's frantic search. She knew what Brandi was looking for. "I put it in your bottom drawer."

Brandi pretended not to know what her mother was talking about. "What's in the drawer?"

"Don't be coy. I know what you're looking for. Any woman would know that from the looks of the ring."

Knowing now that it was safely inside the top drawer, she sat next to her mother on the bed. "Thanks for putting it away for me. I don't know how I could have been so careless."

"Indeed. It's gorgeous. Why was it under your bed? I walked in and saw it lying on the floor. Brandi, what's going on here?"

"Please, I can't discuss this now, if it's okay with you."

"Well, it's not okay with me. I find my daughter's engagement ring on the floor; and you close yourself up in this room for three days, refusing to see your friends. I don't understand you lately. Now what has happened?"

"Tim and I had a fight."

She smiled and patted Brandi's back. "Baby, is that all? Most couples have spats before they get married."

"This was not just a spat, Mom. I can't trust him."

"What? You can't trust him? Did he cheat . . ."

"No! He didn't do that."

"Then what is it?"

She put her face in her hands. "Mom; he's been lying to me. I was sent some information on him, and I confronted him about it. He lied to me about part of his life."

"Like what?"

"Mom, please. I can't talk about it now. All I know is that he never said those files were a lie. I knew about some of it, but he couldn't trust me with the other details of his life. I knew he didn't have a great childhood, but he withheld things from me." She retrieved the ring, holding it to the light. "All I know is that I have to give this back to him, and soon."

"Can't you two talk it out again? I've never seen you not want to talk to him." She saw the blank look on her daughter's face. It scared her. "I just hope you two can workout whatever this is."

"That takes more strength than I have right now." Brandi found the ring's box and gently placed it back inside.

Brandi pulled into Columbia's parking lot. She parked her car and took the little silver box from her purse. She hating giving the ring back; it was gorgeous, given to her by a man she still loved. She had to give it back, because hanging on to it was too painful. She would have seen Tim each time she looked at it. That was just too hard to do.

His lecture hall door was wide open. She knew he had third period free on Wednesdays. She started to walk, then stopped. Her feet tried to move, but it was as though they were glued to the floor. She knew she had to make that move eventually.

He saw her, and forced a tired smiled, hoping she was here to give him a second chance. She continued to stand there, looking as if she didn't know whether to come in or leave. So, he went to her. "Are you going to come in, or do you need an invitation?"

She walked in and put the box on his desk. "I just wanted to give this back. I left in such a hurry last week, I and forgot to give it to you."

He looked at it, then back to her, knowing she wasn't there to make amends. "I see. Sooner or later, I knew it would make its return." Quickly changing the subject was his best defense so she couldn't see his tears. "Are you okay?"

"Not exactly."

"I'm sorry for that. I'm sorry for everything."

"Tim, I know you don't understand what's been going on lately, but lack of trust is a big thing with me."

"Brandi, you knew I had a screwed-up childhood. I didn't hold anything back. How can I explain a lifetime of defeat and betrayal?"

"I just wish I had known more about your life."

"Would that have made you love me any less?"

"No . . . I don't know, Tim; probably not." She took the box and placed it in his hand. "All I know is that I need time to try and understand my own feelings about us now."

"Funny thing; I don't need time to think as you say you do. I know I love you, Brandi. I just can't understand why this is so messed up for us."

"I don't know what you might tell me next that I was supposed to already know. That sounds odd, but that's how I feel."

"What feels odd is that I finally fell in love. I can tell, because my heart is breaking."

Those words almost broke her down, and running back into his arms would be her next move if she didn't soon leave. But she was determined to stand her ground and work this out in her own head, in her own time.

She wiped her tears and walked out. There were no tears left for him to shed. He took the ring from the box and examined it as if it were still on her precious finger. "Designed just for you, but you'll never wear it."

A student approached and saw his worried expression. "Are you okay, Dr. Polaris?"

"No."

Tim needed to talk to someone who could understand, someone who wouldn't give him advice; someone who knew what he was going through: Monica. He called her number and waited for her to answer. He knew she only worked half-days on Fridays. She had piano lessons. "Monica, I know this is a bad time, but can we talk today? I really need your ear."

"Sure. I'm across town at my lesson and should be done shortly. Take the key from my patio mat and let yourself in."

"Great! May I use your computer and a spare disc in the meantime for something I need to copy from the Internet?"

"Yes, take what you want. The discs are in the top left drawer on the desk."

"Thanks, see you soon."

There were no discs in the top left drawer in Monica's desk drawer, so he searched further and saw two towards the back of the middle drawer. He put one in to see if it was used. Her lecture notes from months past were on that one, so he picked up the other one. The contents of the other disc flashed across the computer screen—Brandi's paper. "What the hell . . . ?"

He read parts of both papers, realizing these were the exact ones that the girls were to read at Niagara University. "Why does she have these? My God! What has Monica done?"

Brandi was no longer in his life, and now Monica was seemingly sabotaging everything. He was about ready to dive to the bottom of the first bottle he could find. He took the disc and left before Monica arrived.

Tim went home and sought refuge in sleep. Hours later, he woke clutching an unopened bottle of scotch and hearing the Hiroshima CD playing over and over again. In his other hand was a picture of him and Brandi taken at Coney Island weeks ago.

Brandi woke up from her dream at the same time, crying and calling out Tim's name. Her parents heard her screams. Mrs. Miles resumed her knitting while Mr. Miles looked up the steps, wondering what was going on with his daughter. Mrs. Miles stopped him before he went up the steps. "Jeff, don't go up there. It's the same thing as before."

"I knew that guy was trouble."

"Don't start the same old crap again about having arrested him after some fight at a boy's home. That was years and many stories ago. Let it go; he's a grown man now."

"He's dangerous."

"Talking trash about him won't help; now let her work through this."

He slowly walked back to the couch, plopping down next to his wife. "I hate seeing her so upset over him. I just wish there was something I could do to help her."

"If you like, I'll get your Superman cape from the basement."

He kissed her cheek. "Funny."

Brandi tried going back to sleep but couldn't. All she could do was think about him when awake, dream of him when asleep. All he represented was more drama in her life, but she still loved him, needed him in her arms, but he had destroyed that. She simply wanted what her parents had, a marriage that was in its twenty-third year. Everyone thought she was going to have it until things took a drastic turn.

Another hour passed; still unable to sleep. She thought she had heard someone call to her. Thinking it was her imagination, she turned over. She heard the call again, and it was Tim. She looked through her window and saw Tim standing on the wet lawn, drenched.

Tears came to her eyes when she saw how bad he looked. His clothing was ripped and wet. He was crying and on his knees, becoming seriously unglued. His voice grew louder and louder. Neighboring porch lights began to come on. Soon the entire neighborhood seemed to be gawking at Brandi's version of a Frankenstein monster. Brandi grabbed her robe and ran past her mother before she had a chance to confront her about anything.

She made it to the front door in time to see Tim break away from her father. He looked her dead in the face. "You come over here right now and tell me you don't love me, Brandi. Why are you doing this? I've made mistakes, that's all, mistakes. I can't help how my life started, but I have tried to fix it." He tried standing but fell back to his knees. "You know I love you because I'm losing it out here. Why can't you love me back? I've tried to be a good boy. Didn't I love you enough?"

Her father tried stopping her, and pushed Tim aside so he couldn't stand. Brandi ran to Tim's defense. "Don't do that to him, Dad."

"Brandi, he can't reason with you now. Look at him." He proceeded to lift Tim to his feet and push him across the lawn. "Get the hell out of here. You've caused my daughter enough pain. I wish I had been able to nail you all those years ago. You were a punk then, and you're a bigger one now. Get lost, Polaris!"

Again Brandi ran to Tim. "Tim, please don't do this."

"I . . . I just want another chance, Brandi."

"I can't talk to you like this, now just stop it! You've got to trust my decision, Tim."

He stared at her, contempt pulsing through his voice. "Trust you? How can I trust you, Brandi? You won't give me a chance. Look what I've become because I trusted another woman. I also trusted Monica, and look what she did to me."

"What's Monica got to do with anything?"

"Screw Monica, and screw you, too! You were something I thought was good and real. For the first time I thought I had that! All you did was toss me away like yesterday's trash!"

Mr. Miles took Brandi's arm. "Honey, he's drunk, let me handle him until the police arrive."

"The police! No, I'll handle him; you've done enough, thank you. You didn't have to knock him around, Dad. I'll handle Tim."

"I don't think you can."

"He's listening to me, at least. He may not be saying the words I want to hear, but he's listening to me."

"Honey, the neighbors."

"I don't care about them; let them look." She returned to Tim. "Let's go somewhere and talk; just you and I."

He stood on wobbly legs. "We've talked enough. Why would you want to continue talking to someone you hate?"

She reached for his hand, but he pulled away. "Brandi, if you loved me, my past wouldn't have mattered. I didn't mean to kill him, but he was always on me. I was dying inside with every blow that kid gave me. No one would help me." He looked at her father. "No one would believe me; that includes my brother." He heard the sirens in

225

the distance. "I'm leaving before the cops come. Don't worry, I'll never bother you again. Consider me history."

Brandi watched him walk off, all along feeling the metaphorical knife in her back. She called to him, but he kept walking.

Tim wanted to turn back, but figured she'd only toss him aside again when the going got rough. Hearing her cry made him want to take her into his arms and promise her that things would be better for them. He heard Brandi screaming at her parents as they held her back.

"I need to try and make up with him. He was right . . . he was so right, and I acted without thinking as usual." She looked at him. "Tim, please come back. I'm sorry. I was wrong, and I realize that now. It takes seeing you walking away from me to make me realize everything. Tim, come back!"

"You weren't wrong, Brandi. You're better off without me." He continued walking away from her crushing cries. Every step he took away from her killed him, but he knew that he could never truly make her happy with all of his inadequacies. Their love had only been a taste of temptation. She was temptation, and he had been weak for her.

The next morning, Mrs. Miles helped Brandi pack the rest of her clothes and put them into the car. Before closing the hatchback, she pulled her depressed daughter aside. "Are you going to be okay?"

"I don't know, Mom. I've never loved anyone the way I love him, yet I ruined everything."

"You don't have to leave, honey. Stay here and we can talk through it."

"What can I possibly say? I messed up, and Tim is gone. I haven't been able to reach him on his house or cell. His truck is never there. He has moved on, apparently."

"Maybe not. You can keep trying while talking it out with me. Honey, you shouldn't handle this alone."

"Aunt Theresa will be there with me. Besides, this is best. I've caused enough trouble around here. I can see the disappointment in Dad's eyes."

"Baby, that's not true. He's concerned about you."

"It's bad enough what I did to Tim, but Dad hitting and kicking him . . . I just can't be here knowing he did that. I can still see him doing that, and it hurts."

She saw her mother's tears matching her own and took her hand. "This will be better. With time away, maybe Dad and I can be civil to one another." She pulled her last suitcase into the car and closed the door. "Aunt Theresa and I can talk, but not right away. I don't even know how to talk about Tim anymore."

"If you need me, will you call me?"

"You know I will. I love you."

They waved good-bye as Brandi's car drove out of sight.

CHAPTER 22

Tim sat at his computer, staring at the screen as it displayed Brandi's and Dana's papers. In one hand was his cell phone, in the other, another bottle of scotch. His intent was to drink the day and night away, but only after he called Monica to get her over to look at the mess she had made of their experience at Niagara University.

He punched in her number and waited for a response. The minute he heard her mellow voice, the madder he became. He hid it though, because he was on a mission. "Monica . . . Tim."

"Hey, Tim. Weren't you supposed to meet me at the house last night? What happened?"

"I had things to do at the house, but I did borrow a disc; hope that's okay?"

"Sure. Is everything all right? You sound a little out of it."

He looked at the bottle in his hand. "I'm fine, but I have a computer problem, and was wondering if you could come over and take a look at it. I can't get into Windows XP, and you're a whiz at these things."

"Sure. You wanted to talk, anyway. Are you sure you're okay, because I can bring something for lunch and we can talk."

"I've got Chinese left over from the other night; we can have that. I really need you to look at this computer."

"Give me twenty minutes."

Tim left the door unlocked and waited for her. Twenty minutes later, Monica walked in, calling to him. They met at his computer room. She looked at the half-empty bottle of liquor dangling from his hand.

He held the bottle up. "Want some?"

"No . . . no, I don't drink. You know that." She eyed him. "You didn't drink all that this early, did you?"

"Not yet."

"Tim, what's going on with you? You called me Friday wanting to talk and never showed. Does that bottle have anything to do with it?"

"No, this is actually helping." He leaned against the wall. "Brandi and I aren't together anymore." He looked at her, hoping to see some sign of glee on her beautiful face. Nothing. She was just as calm as ever, an incredible actress. Her words were even more Oscar-worthy.

"I'm really sorry. When did this happen?"

"The other day."

"You want to talk about it?"

"First things first." He held open the door to the computer room. "I really need you to look at this."

They entered the room; she took a seat and looked at the Windows XP display. "Okay, what's wrong with it that you know of?"

He punched a key. "This!"

Brandi's paper appeared on the screen. "Look familiar, Monica?"

"What . . . what are you talking about?"

"Christ! In case you can't remember, which I doubt, this is the paper Brandi couldn't present at the Niagara competition."

"You had her paper on disc the entire time and didn't give it to her?"

"No, but you had it." He leaned over her, staring down at the most gorgeous dark hair he had ever seen; he couldn't believe her exotic look belonged to a maniac. "Monica. I looked in your desk drawer as you told me to, and pulled out what I thought was a blank disc. It wasn't marked, so I assumed it was usable. When I checked it on your computer, Brandi and Dana's papers smacked me in the face, the same papers they couldn't find, the same papers that they weren't able to pull up on the computers there. What did you do to those computers there, Monica? Tampering with equipment that's not yours could get you some real prison time."

She stood, facing off with him. "What the hell are you talking about? I did nothing like that. I don't know how those discs got into my desk. Maybe they got mixed with my other belongings."

"No way, Monica; you're so careful with your briefcase, you would never let anyone get near it." He picked up the phone. "Now, either you tell me what you did, or you can tell the cops. Of the two, I'm the less intimidating; it's your choice."

She tried to move past him, but he shoved her back into the chair. "Don't even try it, Monica. I may have had a few too many," he held up the bottle, "but I can still overpower you. I know you took the discs, Monica. You even acted suspicious—nervous all the time, needing to know where I was every second of the day. I thought you were nervous about the presentations. I never thought . . ."

"Okay! You want to hear the damn reason, Tim? I didn't want her to win, plain and simple. I wanted to add a little turmoil to her life."

"Why? Why do you have it out for her?"

"The way you rant and rave over her—I was sick of it! All you talk about is Brandi. Brandi this, Brandi that." She stood inches from him. "Are you that dense that you couldn't tell that someone else may have wanted a shot at you?"

"You really are nuts."

"You're the one that's nuts. How could you even look at someone like her? She's black, Tim! What would someone with your looks and intelligence want with her?"

"This is so 17th-century Anglo-Saxon. I can't believe it! Look at you; you're not exactly 'Miss White America.' You were born in Hong Kong, for Pete's sake. Where the hell do you get off . . ."

"What's going on here?"

Both Tim and Monica turned to see Brandi standing in the doorway. Tim retrieved his bottle. "Perfect, just perfect; the other person I least wanted to see today!"

Brandi approached him. "Tim, I wanted to see you and try making up. I heard you two shouting and . . ."

"Really, you wanted to try and *make up* with me? Why? I'm a murderer, a liar, and probably an alcoholic by now. What would you want with a person like me?"

"Tim, please. I was on my way to Aunt Theresa's house and felt the need to try once more."

"Actually, Brandi, you are the last person I need to argue with." His hand stretched out to Monica, as if he were introducing her. "What you see here, Brandi, is the main person who's been wrecking my nerves today."

"What wrong?"

"Lots. Remember your paper that you didn't get to present at Niagara? Well, guess who had it?"

Brandi stared at Monica. "You took my paper?"

Monica grabbed her purse. "I'm leaving. I don't care what you think, Tim. I didn't take those discs, but you know why I would have, had I been that stupid. Besides, you have no real proof."

"I have more than you know, Monica."

She shot past Brandi, who stood there in disbelief as Monica left. "Tim, you're just going to let her leave?"

"Yes. Why don't you leave with her?" He picked up his cell phone to call Dean Moore at Madison to inform him of everything. Brandi walked off, crying.

This time, he didn't care if she was hurting or not. He made the call, finished what was left of the scotch, and took another bottle from the liquor cabinet near his computer table. He walked into the living room to crash on the couch. Then he saw Brandi still there. "Why are you still here in my face, Brandi?"

"Because we need to talk."

"Talk about what? How you dumped me? How you blamed me for having a brutal childhood? What the hell would I need to talk to you for?"

She walked closer to him. "You need to hear me out . . ."

He yelled, scaring her. "I don't need to hear a damn thing! Just leave."

She had never heard him talk above a normal range, and it hit her that she had definitely blown it. Something in her still wanted to try again. So she reached for his arm, but he abruptly pulled away from her. "Tim, please listen to me. I know I hurt you."

Ignoring her, he took his bottle and walked to the basement steps. "Where are you going?"

"Away from you; now leave me alone, Brandi. Get the hell out of here."

She ran to the steps and grabbed his shirt as he staggered down the stairs. "Tim, I've got to explain everything to you."

He jerked away from her, losing his footing. She grabbed at his clothing, trying to stop the fall, but he tumbled down, landing head first against the cement.

"TIM!!!"

Brandi waited on pins and needles for two hours for Tim to come out of surgery. He was wheeled back into his room hours later, and she sat with him the rest of the night. Sometime that night, Dr. Hammond came in to see about Tim. Brandi was asleep, her head resting on the bed. The doctor cleared her throat, and Brandi's head popped up. She looked up at Dr. Hammond's face. "Who are you?"

"I'm Dr. Hammond. You must be Brandi Miles."

"Yes. He has mentioned you before."

"You're all he talks about."

That made her feel awful, because she suspected that all he had to talk about lately was her ditching him. "I'm afraid he hasn't had the best things to say about me lately."

"On the contrary. He feels he did everything wrong, and has had nothing but good things to say about you."

"I'm surprised." She heard Tim's labored breathing. "Dr. Hammond, what's wrong with him? No one has told me anything really, except that he has some fractured bones."

"He also has a concussion, and the hospital has to keep monitoring him because the injury is close to the brain. His medical doctor informed me that Tim was here and I wanted to check on him. You don't mind, do you?"

"Of course not. He needs people like you, someone who loves him. I love him, too, but I'm sure he won't allow me to show him after what has happened between us."

Dr. Hammond saw the terrified look on Brandi's face and tried to console her. "Not to worry, Tim is strong. He will pull through this, and you two will be together. But that was a hell of a fall he took."

"Before this happened, we had some problems, and I took off like a scared child instead of dealing with them."

"It couldn't have been easy hearing about his past life, especially after hearing about the incident in the facility he was in."

"Knowing that another child died wasn't easy to hear about, but it was an excuse that I used. I love him more than I can imagine loving anyone."

"Tim is lucky to have you, because there's no one else except for a brother and his mother, and he has no contact with them. I have counseled Tim for years now, and he has grown quite a bit, but his past still hurts him. Unfortunately, it is something I can't erase for him." She smoothed Tim's bedding. "It's late. You need to go home and rest. Tomorrow maybe you can bring some personal belongings, like a robe and slippers."

"Sure."

She entered Tim's house. Any reminder of Tim's fall down the stairs surely would make her sick. She also wanted to avoid the bedroom. She used to love it there; many a night she had laid on that bed in her lover's arms as they talked about their future, their marriage, children . . . a life full of love, but now that all seemed to be gone. His bedroom was also the same room he had made wild love to her, finally making her feel what it was like to be a total woman.

But she had to go in to collect things he would need for his hospital stay. When she looked under the bed for his slippers, she noticed a picture on the floor. It was of an unborn baby—a fuzzy, hazy picture of an infant. She turned it over and read: "*Our first. Isn't she beautiful? I love you, Tim . . . Charlotte.*"

Then it dawned on her. "Of course, his baby; the baby they lost." She tried to put it back in a box under the bed but it was stuffed with letters, all stamped, *Return to sender.* They were from Tim to Greg and had a Schenectady, NY, address. "Where the heck is Schenectady?" The postmarks on the letters were more recent than on the letter she had with the White Plains address on it. She just didn't know where to begin. Operator assistance was of no help, because there wasn't a Gregory Polaris listed anywhere. Her only choice was to drive to the address and hope she would make it there.

The next evening she stopped by the hospital, looked in on Tim resting, and kissed his lips. "Dream of me." Then she left for Schenectady.

"You must be Destiny."

The little girl looked at Brandi rather strangely. "Yes, and you are . . . ?"

"I'm Brandi Miles, a friend of your Uncle Tim's." Destiny had Tim's eyes. She was a lovely girl of twelve or thirteen, tall for her age, and had almost blue-black shoulder length hair.

Destiny continued. "You're here about Uncle Tim?"

"Yes."

"Good, is he here? I've never seen him."

"No, he isn't. He's sick right now. Is your father home?"

"Sick? From what?"

"Please, I need to speak to your father. It's very important."

"He's in the garage working on a Mercedes Benz. He's a mechanic, you know." She kept looking at Brandi, having never seen beauty like hers, let alone a beautiful black woman at their house. She kept questioning Brandi instead of going to get her father. "Are you Uncle Tim's girlfriend?"

"I am."

Obviously, Destiny had a very curious mind, but Brandi was becoming impatient with her questions. She had driven for hours and had coped with a flat tire, little money, and a lumpy bed in a fleabag hotel that had given her a terrible backache. The only thing she wanted to deal with now was the infamous Gregory Polaris. "Will you please get your father for me?"

"Sure. You can come with me, but he may be a little dirty."

Brandi read the sign on the door as they approached the two-door garage: GM-certified mechanics on duty. Gregory Robert Polaris, owner; Chris Mayers, Asst.

Destiny pointed under the car. "He's under there. Dad?"

A voice sounding much like Tim's, asked, "What is it?"

"There's a lady here to see you."

"Bring her over here."

Brandi turned to Destiny. "That's okay. I'll walk over."

Greg's voice echoed again. "You go inside and wait for your Uncle Chris. He'll be here soon."

Brandi watched her swish off. Taking her for a customer, Greg said he would be with her soon. "Just let me tighten this hose. What's wrong with your car? You can leave the keys with me and my partner will take you wherever you need to go when he gets here."

Brandi cleared her voice. "I'm not here about a car. I'm here about your brother, Timothy."

He dropped his wrench and quickly slid from under the car. "You're here about. . . ." Greg looked into her beautiful face, and then looked her up and down. Before him was what he thought a virtual goddess. She was a knockout from her shapely body, to her flawless café au lait skin. Realizing he was staring, he rose slowly walking toward her, and extending his hand. "I'm Gregory Polaris, and you are?"

She was disheartened by his non-reaction upon hearing his own brother's name. She extended her hand. "I'm Brandi Miles." As she stared back at him, she saw almost a replica of Tim, only darker and with green eyes. He was stockier than Tim but was still sexy in a pair of jeans and a torn t-shirt. She hadn't realized she was holding her breath until he took her hand.

"Brandi Miles, huh? You're here about Tim, did you say?"

She felt rising anger over his apparent indifference to his brother. "Yes, I'm here about Tim."

"Are you his social worker?"

"No, I'm his . . .

"Parole officer?"

"I'm his fiancée."

"You're kidding." He put his hand on his hip, backed up, and looked her over with those intense green eyes of his. "He always did have great taste in women, 'cept for Nikki, and of course, Charlotte, well, from what Mom has told me, but we all make mistakes." He wiped his hands on a towel on the hood of the Mercedes. "So, what's this about?"

She hadn't expected such terseness from him; he was Tim's brother after all. She had wanted so much to say something that would bring out his caring side, if he had one. But his words told her emotions were something he would have to buy at the local drug store. She got to the point. "Your brother's in real trouble."

"As usual. What's he done this time that would bring someone so pretty all the way up here to see me?"

She couldn't mask the disappointment on her face and in her voice. "He's in the hospital."

"What for, detox?"

His wisecracks were getting on her nerves. "I'm serious. He was injured in a fall, and he's in bad shape. He wanted me to see if you could come down, but I can see that you're too busy."

She turned to leave so Greg wouldn't see the tears welling in her eyes, but he took her arm. "I'm sorry. You're so teary-eyed. There must be something you're not telling me."

"Your brother needs you, Greg."

"Brandi, my baby brother hasn't needed me in years. What makes now so special?"

She hated getting into it, but it seemed Greg needed the whole story to be convinced. She sat down on the chair near the garage door. "Tim and I were to be married, but when I found out about his past I took off, leaving him alone to pick up the pieces. And then with this hospital thing . . . he just sounded so hopeless, Greg, like he was giving up and not even trying to live. He told me to find you and tell you he was sorry. What has he to be sorry for? That's what I need to know."

"A lot, but I can't get into it right now. I have this Mercedes to finish by six." He looked around nervously. "He's really bad off, huh?"

Streams of tears rolled down her cheeks, and he quickly handed her a clean towel. "I just don't know how to fix him this time. He's not really responding to me."

His eyes softened at the sight of her tears, but even her pain couldn't keep him from noticing how perfect she was, more beautiful than any woman he had seen in a long time. Then he remembered who that beauty belonged to—his damn baby brother!

Brandi gave him the towel and smiled sheepishly. "I won't waste any more of your time. I know you have that car to fix, and I'm sorry about everything. It's just that I love him so much, and I think I'm losing him."

His voice betrayed a trace of emotion. "I can tell you love him. He finally got lucky." His eyes lowered for a minute, then he remembered who he was—the unbreakable Gregory Polaris, whom emotions bounced from, or so he thought.

He moved to the door, facing her. "Look, I finish here around six, but where are you staying? Maybe we can get something to eat and talk about this."

"Could we? I'd really appreciate that. I'm at the Savoy off the interstate, room 216."

"Is seven good for you?"

She brushed her tears back. "That'll be good. That gives me time to look human again. I know I look like the living dead."

He wanted to brush away the fine strand of hair that fell against her wet cheek. He put that thought away, for he knew he would want to touch her elsewhere. He was known to be a fast mover, but this wasn't the right time, or the right person. He held the door open for her. "I'll be there by seven."

After she left, he closed the door and leaned against it. He was vulnerable for once; someone had finally penetrated his tough exterior, and it was Brandi. Her beauty haunted him, but her unavailability was like a knife in his chest. His main priority should have been his brother, but he hadn't had to think of Tim in such a long time he had actually forgotten how. But with Brandi Miles, well, he hadn't been so beguiled by a woman in years—not since Destiny's mother.

Gregory picked her up at precisely 7:00. He drove off at high speed and, for all Brandi knew, he could be driving her to hell and back. That was the kind of person he seemed to be, impulsive and fast. She didn't understand how two utterly different people could have come from the same womb. But Greg's fast life somehow attracted her; he was something different, maybe even a little dangerous. He was no Tim. Yes, she felt an attraction to her fiancé's brother, a big taboo. He oozed heat and fire, as if he would sizzle even in the rain. The attraction made her uncomfortable, half-regretting she had made the trip up there; half feeling that she was cheating on Tim just by looking at his brother. Anyway, she was on a mission, and intended to see it though, no matter what temptation got in the way.

They drove to the restaurant in silence, except for a casual word here and there. But there was nothing polite about him. He was just as rough around the edges in a Ralph Lauren sports jacket as he was in that greasy t-shirt.

After the waitress to took their orders, Greg searched her face and saw signs of her emotional day: eyes puffy from crying; brow creased with worry; lips tight with apprehension. He took a deep breath and plunged in. "Let's get to the good stuff. What happened to my brother?"

She decided it was now or never. "There are two things. First, he was in a fury and devastated by a co-worker's betrayal. He was angry with me, too, so he wouldn't let me console him. He started down his stairs to the basement to get away, and, well, he fell to the cement floor. He has a concussion."

"A really bad one?"

"Is there a good one? Yes, it's very bad. Look, he needs you to be there. I thought that hearing of his condition you would want to be there, too."

He changed the subject. "What's the other reason you're here?"

His lack of emotion after hearing about his brother's accident was killing her, so she kept her own voice cold and unemotional. "I'm here because of his bad family life when you both were kids. It has tortured him for years. Anyway, it finally caught up with him, and I don't feel that I'm helping the situation."

"What do you mean?"

"I bolted after finding out about his life, but I came back because I do love him, but I can't fix the real problem. You can, however. He needs someone other than me to be a stabilizing force in his life, Greg. I didn't know what else to do, so I came here."

"What has he told you?"

"Everything."

"Then he told you that he killed someone? That kid was my best friend, the only person who was ever there for me. Tim took that all away with one punch. So, I don't know how I can help either you or him."

"But Tim was *your brother*. You could have stuck with him, and you two could have had one another."

"But I never really had him. He was always in trouble for as long as I can remember."

"And why was that? He apparently needed someone, and wasn't getting it from home—where he should have been loved. The death of that boy was an accident; he would never willingly do that to anyone. You have to know that."

"You think you know so much about what went on in our lives, don't you? Well, you don't! I know my brother, Brandi, and I know what happened; you don't, and I think we need to drop this."

"I can't drop this. This is about a man I plan to spend the rest of my life with, Greg. What was a friend of yours doing bullying *your* brother in the first place?"

"That was just his way. He was a kid."

"Your friend's 'way' was to knock the hell out of your kid brother? How can you sit here and say that?" She had to calm down before she exploded.

Greg's voice was beginning to shake with anger, but he controlled himself. "Look, I was not there, and I was also not his or Tim's keeper. Neither one was my responsibility. I couldn't have stopped him, anyway. I wasn't there."

"But you knew about it."

"So did the staff, but they didn't fix the problem, either, and they could have."

Brandi smoothed the napkin on her lap and changed her tune, sensing there was nothing Greg was going to do about seeing Tim. "Well, it seems I have to fix things on my own."

"Now, don't go there, Brandi. I just don't know what to do to help him. He's a part of my life that I'd rather not revisit. I have a good business, a little girl I have to take care of, and I just can't go back to that!"

"It's okay, Greg. I know where you stand."

"Let me finish. I hardly see my mother because it reminds me too much of how she fell apart when both Tim and my father were no longer a part of her life. When Tim was with us, she mistreated him, blaming him for everything that went wrong in her life. That's all I heard as a kid. I know it's a stupid excuse, but it's all I have."

"Greg, I can't know how hard it was for you too, because you were also a child but . . ."

"Only someone who's lived it can know."

Their food arrived and they dropped the subject but Brandi was too sick over the situation to eat. She sat and watched Greg devour his salmon; her own steak sat untouched on her plate.

Greg spoke up again. "I can't see Tim and that's that. Besides, who's to say I won't remind him of the same awful things? He doesn't need that, either. Eat your steak."

The only thing she had left was her determination to help Tim by whatever means possible.

After he finished his chocolate cake, she asked him to take her back to the hotel. Not what he wanted to hear, but he honored her wish. He wanted to get to know her, to see the real Brandi as a person. He knew she wouldn't allow it as long as he refused to deal with Tim.

CHAPTER 23

The ride back to the motel was silent, cold. Neither had any inclination to say anything, there was nothing left to say. Tim was still in bad shape, Brandi was losing her mind with worry, and Greg . . . was still Greg, and nothing was going to change that!

They pulled in front of the Savoy and Brandi quickly opened the door to flee, but he stopped her. "I'll walk you in."

"Thank you, but I'll be fine."

"This is a bad area, and I'll feel better walking you inside."

She was not in the mood for a walk to her room. All she wanted was to go inside and have a good cry. She couldn't do that around him; he wouldn't understand. It seemed he hardly understood anything beyond his own life. Apparently, their father had stripped him of humanity. She was thankful that Tim was different. Tim was a bit headstrong, but had compassion nonetheless. Greg, on the other hand, seemed to have an empty hole straight in the middle of him where compassion used to live.

They walked to her room. She hated that they had accomplished nothing. Greg was adamant about not getting involved in the turmoil swirling around his brother.

To Brandi, it seemed as if he would never leave; he was comfortable around her. She didn't want Gregory Polaris comfortable around her, because he was of no help to her. Sure, he was sexy, but there was that empty hole in his being that she wasn't about to fall head first into.

The more she tried to entertain him, the heavier her heart became. Finally, she became so overcome with pain that she broke into tears.

He took her hands into his. "Everything will be okay."

"How will it be okay? His life is just so mixed up, and it'll take more than what I can do to turn him around."

Greg didn't know what to do. Crying women made him feel awkward. He remembered his mother crying over his father, and then Tim, and he had not known how to handle it. All he knew was that he was always the one left to try and pick up the pieces. Now, there were no pieces to collect-just Brandi. He didn't know whether to hold her or walk out. In the end, he gently wrapped his arms around her.

She needed a shoulder to cry on and willingly moved into his arms. He was so soft and warm, and he smelled so good . . . like Tim. Her own emotions were so intense that she had forgotten where she was or who he was and tenderly whispered, "Just hold me. Hold me, Tim."

Greg found himself in an awkward position, but he did what she asked and held her. She melted into him. Her scent intoxicated him, and he felt all control slipping away. He felt her skin against his, his lips against her neck. It felt so incredible that his body moved into hers, feeling her warm thighs, her slender hips; hearing her soulful voice as it tickled his neck. "I love you, Tim. I love you so much."

He stopped suddenly, realizing he was going way too far, taking advantage of a desperate woman. He brought her face to his then slowly backed away, dropping his hands to his sides.

Her eyes flew open. "What . . . what have I done? I'm . . . I'm so sorry, Greg. I didn't mean to . . . oh, God! I think I'm losing my mind, losing touch with reality."

"You didn't do anything, and I really need to get out of here before something does happen."

"I wouldn't let it."

"Somehow I know that. I need to get back to Destiny before her Uncle Chris has a coronary." He smiled that famous Polaris smile. "Don't worry, Tim will be okay."

"Then that means you're coming to see him?"

He raked his hands through his silky, dark hair. "I . . . I don't know. Maybe."

He was in a cold sweat by the time he got back to his car. He pounded the steering wheel. "Damn! Great move, Polaris; making moves on your brother's girl." He knew going to Queens was out of the question now, because a temptress would be there.

Brandi was on her bed, the pillow wet with tears. Nothing had been accomplished. She had cried in Greg's arms, and still his heart hadn't softened. The only thing left was to go back to New York and face Tim's dilemma. Whatever happens, happens.

Brandi thought Tim might not want to see her, but she felt compelled to sit in his room and talk things out with him, if he would listen. She had driven without stopping to get back to him. She had changed a flat tire, and gassed up at shady looking stations with no one knowing where she was, aside from Greg. To get help for Tim, she'd gladly do it all again. She was tired, more tired than she had ever been. When she arrived at the hospital, Tim was sleeping peacefully; she collapsed into a chair and was out like a light.

Tim tugged on the hem of her skirt, waking her up. When she opened her eyes, he whispered, "Where the hell have you been for the past two days?"

She managed a smile. "Tim, I know you don't want me in here."

"I do want you in here."

"You were so mad at me, and with good cause."

"I've had time to think. Look, honey, I had no right to turn on you the way I did, and I'm sorry."

"You were right. I overreacted as usual. You had every right to be mad." She straightened his covers and kissed his damp forehead. "I know I look a fright to you."

"You're the most beautiful thing I've ever seen."

"That's why I love you so much. You always see the positive in me. You make me feel beautiful when I know I look like hell."

"You'll never look like that."

"You think maybe we can work this out?"

"I want that. Maybe starting over is a good idea. We both know where to start; we can make this thing work for us."

"That's all I want, Tim, another chance to make things right with you."

"I couldn't have expected you to remain calm after hearing the gory details of my life. I should have told you sooner."

"That's in the past. Now that I have you again, the only thing I want to concentrate on is the future. Can we do that?"

"We can do anything we want, as long as we do it together. You didn't answer my question, though. Where have you been? I wanted to apologize to you."

"If I tell you, you'll only get mad."

"I'm through being mad at you. I was worried, thinking you went off somewhere never to return to me."

"I went to Schenectady."

Schenectady? "Why there?" Though he had a good idea that Greg was in the picture somewhere.

"The truth is, I went there to see your brother."

"I'm sure that was a bad move, because literally nothing is there."

"There is something there."

"What did you find, other than someone who hates me?"

"I found a man there who is just as scared as you are."

"I doubt that."

"He is scared, Tim. I was so distraught that I thought Greg was the only answer, and I didn't tell you because I thought you wouldn't listen to me. You would have told me not to go."

"Right, that's exactly what I would have said. Now, did you make any headway, or was it a waste of gas?"

"Not really."

"Figures."

"He isn't coming down, but I had to try. He said he was sorry about everything, but can't deal with it."

"Isn't that just like him?"

"He does love you, Tim."

"Funny way of showing it. He hasn't seen me in over twelve years."

"He's just scared, and doesn't want to get hurt again."

"But he doesn't mind me feeling the pain, huh?"

"This may be little consolation to you, but you still have me."

"That's the best news I've heard lately. Oh, speaking of news, Derrick came by yesterday and told me Monica was arrested."

"That's great! Also a little sad. I thought she had more sense than that."

"You never know people. She tried taking away your scholarship, destroyed computer and student files, and God knows what else. Anything she could do to break us apart, she tried."

"Unsuccessfully."

"That's the awesome part, because I still have you."

Thank God!

"I can't wait to get out of here and finish the last few days before the semester ends."

"I think the people handling your classes are more than prepared to fill in for you for the next few weeks." His eyelids began to get heavy, and she gently kissed his lips. "You go back to sleep. I'll be back later today. All I want now is to crash on Aunt Theresa's spare bed and sleep."

"Why there?"

"Tell you later."

The elevator doors opened, and out stepped Greg and Destiny. Brandi could hardly believe it; he was the last person she expected to see in Queens. "Greg?"

He flashed a sheepish grin. "Yeah, it's me and the rugrat!"

"I can't believe you're here."

"What can I say? Your words really made me think. I need my brother, and he needs me."

"I'm so glad you decided to come." She hugged Destiny. "You finally get to meet your Uncle Tim."

"He's all Dad talked about in the car."

Greg pulled Brandi's arm, looking at her with sad eyes. "I don't get a hug?"

"Of course you do." They embraced one another with a heartfelt hug. Greg pulled back, smiling. "Are you and Tim on better terms?"

"I have my Tim back. Does that answer your question?"

"The joy on your face tells it all."

Brandi pointed down the hall. "He hasn't been sleeping long, but I know you're anxious to see him. Destiny can't go in, though."

"You know the routine, Destiny." He pointed to the waiting room. "The only way I could bring her up here was to promise the nurse I would leave her in the waiting room . . . that and dinner with her tonight."

"Is she cute?"

"Not my style."

"Really? What is your style?"

You. "No one, lately." He turned in the direction of the room. "I guess I had better do this."

Brandi sensed his hesitation. "Don't be afraid of your brother."

"I'm not."

"You are. I can see it on your face."

"I'm just a little nervous. After all, I haven't seen him since he was about eighteen or something. I just don't know how he'll react to me."

"There's only one way to find out. Open the door and go in."

"Will you come with me?"

"Sure, but don't you want to spend some time alone with him?"

"Brandi, I don't know how to be alone with him. I mean, when he wakes up he's not going to want to see me, a stranger. He'll be looking for you. I'm probably not what he needs right now."

"You're exactly what he needs, so stop second-guessing yourself."

He slowly walked in, approached the bed and looked down at his brother—wanting to smile, wanting to hug him for the first time ever. Then he noticed the bruises. "Still a fighter, I see."

"He got those from the fall."

"Right." He inspected Tim a bit longer. "We really do look alike, don't we?"

"The eyes and personalities are different."

As if not hearing her comment, he kept talking, half to himself. "He really grew up on me. No more baby brother; look at those arms."

"No, he is not a baby. He turned thirty in January."

"I remember, January ninth. What I don't remember is what he's like. It's been so long, you know." He felt so ashamed getting that kind of information on his own brother from a relative stranger.

Brandi leaned over Tim and smoothed his hair back. "He's wonderful, kind, a good man. He always tries to do the right things, always sees the good in people despite how they act, at least until they betray him."

"That's a professor for you. Where does he teach?"

"Columbia. He teaches English lit there."

"Columbia! I knew the guy was smart, but I didn't know he was that smart. I guess I've let too many ghosts keep us apart."

"So you really didn't read any of his letters."

"No, that's why I don't know my own brother."

"But you will. You'll have plenty of time to do that. Speaking of that, where are you and Destiny staying?"

"Nowhere! But if you don't think he would mind, I'd like to stay at his house."

"Are you kidding? He would love that. Tell you what, after classes today I'll go over and clean up, have it all ready for you two. I'll even make dinner. But just stay here and visit with him; he'll wake up soon."

"Can't you stay?"

"You need time with him. There's so much to know, and you might as well start today. When you get to the house maybe I'll have everything done. Hey, maybe I'll invite my aunt. You'll like her."

Greg smiled, and then turned back to Tim with a concerned expression on his face.

After the dinner dishes were cleared, and Destiny shipped off to play on Tim's computer, she and Greg started talking, getting to know one another better. Greg sipped his piping hot coffee. "I'm glad you're in his life. Maybe you can give him something our family never gave him. That's why I'm here; I want a brother again. I actually missed the guy."

"He wants the same things. Didn't he tell you that today?"

"He didn't wake up. But like I said, I was trapped inside a ghost and it was hard getting away from it. As kids, we were taught to avoid emotions at all costs. Entertaining a humorous thought just wasn't done, but Tim was always a little different, always a free spirit, from what I remember. I guess our lives finally caught up with him, though. That's why I was actually glad for him when he turned eighteen and entered Princeton. I thought he could finally be happy, but I understand he wasn't."

"He's getting there, but it's a slow road, Greg."

"I heard his marriage to Charlotte was a sham."

"From what he told me, yes. I just hope I can make him happy. God knows he's had his share of disappointments."

"I can already tell by the look on his face as he sleeps that he's more at peace, and I think you're the reason."

"I want to be."

"The only time I remember being truly happy was when Destiny was born. She was so beautiful and perfect, and I knew it was my task to take better care of her than our parents had us. She is really all I have; But at twelve, she can really be something."

"That's a tough age for girls. I was hell on wheels at that age." She leaned back in her seat, her coffee mug held between her hands. "I guess I'm still boy crazy—but over one boy. I can't believe I almost lost him. Thankfully, I grew up, enrolled at Madison and got the scholarship."

"I had no idea all of this was going on with him. Pays to read the mail, doesn't it?"

"I doubt he had time to write about us. We spent every waking second together, outside his work and my classes. At first, he would hardly talk about you. I had to drag it out of him."

"When something bothered him, he always kept it to himself."

The doorbell rang and Brandi jumped up. "That's got to be my Aunt Theresa. She has this giant crush on Tim, so I know she'll go hog-wild over you."

"Why is that?"

She kept talking as she ran to the door: "Because you two are just about the spitting image of each other."

Brandi returned with her arm around the shoulder of a woman as pretty as she, but older. "This is my Aunt Theresa; she just got back from some conference in Boston. Theresa, this is . . ."

"Brandi, I already know Timothy. Who could forget him?"

Greg stood and kissed her hand. "Sorry to disappoint you, but I'm not Tim. I'm his brother, Greg."

Theresa's mouth flew open. "Oh, God!" She turned to Brandi. "Two of them? How delicious!" She immediately took his hand and walked into the living room with him, still speaking to Brandi. "You have one, and I have one. A cool deal, don't you think?"

Brandi saw the interested look in Greg's eyes and decided to let them get acquainted.

When Brandi walked into Tim's room the next morning, he and Greg were talking. That's when she knew for sure finding Greg was no mistake; the look on Tim's face confirmed it. She walked to the bed and kissed his waiting lips. He tried to put his arms around her, but the pain in his ribs wouldn't permit it.

His looked into her eyes. "You see who's here, don't you? Was this your doing?"

"Absolutely. I made the contact, but it was solely up to him to follow through. Glad he did."

"I've missed him, probably more than I could miss anyone other than you."

"I see my brother hasn't missed fighting, though." Greg pointed as if scolding him. "Very unattractive, Tim."

"He's slowly getting out of that. I've finally gotten him to accept the fact that it's okay to walk away. Right, Tim?"

"Umm, I'm working on it, honey. I just need someone young and beautiful to keep me in line."

"Is that invitation still open to me?"

"It was never closed; just put on hold."

She wanted to kiss him for that, but didn't want to embarrass his brother. "I should leave before we get into real trouble in front of Greg. I don't think he is the type who can deal with mushy stuff. You two need more time together, anyway, and I need to get a bite to eat."

Greg reached into his pocket and fished out a $10. "Can you take Destiny? She likes cheeseburgers, but no fries for her. She's getting too fat."

"No fries with a burger? Sacrilege, man!"

Once she was out of the room, Greg said, "That's some lady you have there."

"A dream come true. I never thought in a million years I would land someone as incredible as Brandi."

"Don't you think it's about time? From what I heard, your marriage to Charlotte was a disaster." He looked down. "I am sorry about the baby, though. I really am. I could have been an uncle."

"And you will be. The baby was the only tragic part of the marriage. Getting away from Charlotte was actually a relief. But the baby, well, that floored me; it still does. She would be ten years old this coming July twenty-third." He saw the sadness in Greg's eyes. "Hey, I didn't mean to go off on that tangent."

"It's all right. She was your baby and you'll never forget her."

"I would rather talk about you, about something more positive. What happened with you and Destiny's mother?"

"Carmen? There's nothing positive about that. She and I did eventually get married, but a year later she left me with a two-year-old baby to raise on my own. Good choice, wasn't she?"

"From what I remember, she wasn't exactly the picture of mental health."

"She wrote the book on what not to be in life. But I got Destiny out of it, and that makes everything Carmen put me through well worth it. She's beautiful, Tim, and she's 'growing' things, know what I mean?"

"That's the age, man." Tim thought about his own child. "Had she lived, she would be about the age to be 'growing' things, too." He lay back remembering the one time he saw Destiny. "I would love to see her. I think she was only a few months old, last I saw her."

"That you will. She's been pestering the hell out of me since we've been here. Brandi showed her your picture, and she's been carrying it around everywhere."

"Why? I look just like you."

"Not the same, man." Then he thought about it. "Hey, are you and that pretty thing going to have kids of your own one day?"

"Only if she wants to; I'd rather her graduate college first. She's got plenty of time, though it will be a lot of fun trying."

Greg thought back on her in his arms and how intoxicating she was. "Yeah, I'll bet!"

A week later, after Mr. Moore finished his speech congratulating the award recipients, he brought on a guest speaker. No one knew who it was. Brandi assumed it would be someone from Niagara University or from the Academy of American Authors. When Tim walked onto the stage, she stood with the others to applaud him; tears moistened her spring green suit. Tim had worked hard to make sure everything went exactly right, but it hadn't in the end, thanks to Monica's shenanigans. Tim looked good despite everything. In his navy double-breasted suit, he looked sexier than ever, not at all like a man who was recovering from a concussion. The surprise for her was not knowing he had been released from the hospital. She waved at him from the front row.

Tim announced Tiffany Jackson as the Madison student to receive the Norton Scholarship. Tiffany ran on stage, crying. She hugged him and then gave her acceptance speech, which Brandi had helped her draft. Tim's eyes met Brandi's, who seemed not at all upset about not winning; she looked happy. He was glad for her, for he selfishly had not wanted Brandi going even a mile away from him.

In the back row, Theresa nudged Greg. "Isn't he supposed to be in the hospital?"

"Destiny and I picked him up last night."

"Why didn't you tell me?"

He put his arm around her shoulder. "So you could blab it to the rest of the world? Tim wanted it to be a surprise. He, Dr. Moore and Columbia's dean of students arranged it so he could deliver the awards."

"You two did a good thing; look how excited she is. I've never seen my niece so happy, other than at her Barbie party I gave her when she was seven, but I digress." She looked down at Destiny, who was oblivious to their conversation. Her eyes were on her new-found uncle. "She is so happy he is in her life."

Tim left the podium, and went directly to Brandi and kissed her. "I'm glad you're not upset about losing."

"My best friend won; that's just as good. She worked so hard for it, harder than I did. Besides, I wouldn't want to leave you."

"Good, because I'm not worth a damn without you. Come on, let's join the others."

They slowly made their way to her parents. Tim kissed Mrs. Miles's hand. "It's very nice to see you again." He looked at Mr. Miles and added, "And you, too, sir." He still wasn't wild over the past bad blood between them, but he had made amends for Brandi's sake.

Mrs. Miles jumped in. "You're going to make a great son-in-law, Tim." She nudged her husband. "Right, Jeff?"

He looked Tim squarely in the face, his expression cold and still, then he smiled. "I've been wrong about a lot of things, and it took me almost losing my daughter to wake up."

"You were being a father. Who's to say I wouldn't have done the same thing. I know you love her; so do I. I promise to take good care of her."

Mrs. Miles eyes turned her attention to Theresa and Greg as they approached. "Now we have to get those two married."

Theresa spoke up, "Give me a break! I just met the guy."

Tim politely cut in. "If you'll excuse us, Brandi and I have loose ends to take care of. We won't be long."

Brandi winked. "Yes we will, so don't hold your breath!"

The minute his classroom door closed, he and Brandi were locked in an embrace. "I love you, Brandi, and nothing will ever change that. That's why I have to give this back to you." He took the ring box from his pocket. "You remember this silver box, don't you?" He slipped the ring back on her finger.

She gazed at it in the light. "How could I? It's perfect; so are you."

"Then please say yes to me again. Don't even think, just say yes, and we'll be on our way to heaven."

"Yes. I'm already in heaven, and I have a husband to take with me." She kissed his lips then asked, "When?"

"You really mean it?"

"I would be a fool to let you get away." She stared at her ring again. "When can we do this? I can barely wait."

"Anytime you want to—today, tomorrow, this very minute. I don't care when, so long as you're mine."

Her arms tightened around him, her voice mellowed, "Oh, I'm yours all right, Dr. Timothy Edward Polaris, now and forever."

EPILOGUE

Brandi could see miles and miles of water from their oceanfront window. She and her new husband frolicked on the small strip of beach below well into the early morning hours. She looked at the large diamond on her finger, then at Tim asleep on the bed. He still looked awesome to her, as much as he did the first time they met. Was he real or a figment of imagination? He yawned, and it was like music to her ears. Yes, he was real, very real. The mere sound of his voice still sent delicious chills through her body; his voice, his laugh, everything about him rocked her world. She let her sheer robe fall to the floor as returned to bed.

Brandi's gentle movements woke Tim. Smiling and dreamy-eyed, he welcomed his bride back with open arms. "Umm, have I told you lately how much I love you?"

"Only a few hundred times, but say it again."

"Showing is better than telling."

"As if you hadn't shown me last night, and again early this morning." She settled deeper into him. "I can't believe I'm here with you. I never knew Madrid was so romantic. How did you ever come up with it?"

"I simply thought of the most romantic place to bring the most romantic woman. I only hope you have no regrets about marrying a crazy, wacked-out man like me."

"Regrets? No way! I won, don't you see? I won over all those women mooing over you, especially the conniving Miss Monica Shang. She almost won, too. She came awfully close to breaking us up. But I have got the ring; I have you. I feel very blessed."

"So do I. I hope Greg and Theresa will be as happy as we are."

"My aunt deserves a good man. I think Greg may be it. Despite his rough edges, he's a good guy. Someone managed to get some good instincts into you two." Her smile brightened. "It was wonderful seeing you with your mother. How long has it been, fourteen years?"

"At least. The years have taken their toll on her. I think I was sixteen the last time I saw her. I talked to her a few times after my divorce and other failed relationships, but that was about the extent of our togetherness."

"She cried so hard when she saw you. It was sad watching her cling to you as if one hug could make up for all that time lost. Do you think you two will ever get close?"

"Maybe. It'll take some time though; a lot has happened."

Brandi studied his expression with an empathetic heart. His mother was still a painful subject, so she changed course, playfully poking his ribs. "Right now, I need you more than anyone does, including your mother. So, if you don't mind, Dr. Polaris. . . ." She pushed the sheets aside and straddled him. Her lips gently met his. "I'm never letting you go no matter what you say or do. You're mine for eternity."

"Eternity is a beautiful place to be with you, Mrs. Polaris!"

ABOUT THE AUTHOR

Renee Alexis is the author of several erotic and traditional romances. She loves writing romantic fiction, teaching elementary school, and making gemstone jewelry. Born and raised in Detroit, Michigan, she enjoys the arts and excitement of a large city.

Renee loves hearing from fans. You may reach her at: www. reneealexis.net.

Excerpt from:

EBONY ANGEL
by
DEATRI KING-BEY
Release date: February 2007

CHAPTER 1

The cold slap of an early-morning Chicago winter greeted Ebony as she stepped onto the snow-covered porch. She adjusted her scarf and hat, then gingerly made her way down the icy steps and on the sidewalk.

"You got class dis early?" drawled Meechie, one of the neighborhood lookouts. He stepped from behind a parked van and blocked her path. "It's still black outside, girl."

"I can't talk today. I'm late." She observed her self-appointed protector in his ragged field jacket and filthy gloves. Drugs had claimed him long ago. Now he spent his days looking out for the police. In exchange for shouting warnings to the drug dealers operating down the block, he received his daily dose.

She inched around him. "Go inside before you freeze your tail off."

He pulled one of her book bag straps, stopping her in her tracks. "Trae know you out here?" He pointed a bony, gloved finger in the direction of the alley she was headed. "It's too damn dark for you ta be alone. He ain't gonna like me lettin' you go down there. You better get in the house. It can't be five yet. He ain't gonna like—"

"I'm not worried about Trae," she cut in. "Thanks for your concern, but I'm late." Easing away she said, "Don't worry. I've lived here my whole life. I'm safe."

"Maybe I should walk with you?"

An amused smile touched her lips. Meechie moved slower than the line at the bank on the first of the month. How could he protect her? She'd seen dried twigs that weighed more and were stronger. "Thanks, but you'd better stay at your post." She trudged through the snow-covered lot into the alley with a heavy heart. Meechie was deteriorating so quickly, she wasn't sure if she'd be able to convince him to go to rehabilitation before it was too late.

As usual, most of the lights were out. She made a mental note to complain to the alderman, again. Someone appeared from between two garages, startling her.

"You got a smoke?" a crackly female voice asked.

Ebony stood under one of the few working streetlights. "Sorry, I don't smoke."

The bag lady cocked her head to the side as she crept into the light with Ebony. "Oh." She leaned forward, squinting. "You a good girl." She pulled the scarf down from her mouth and raised her ashy fingers, chastising, "Don't walk down no alley. All these nasty perverts 'round." She stuffed her hands under her armpits and bounced in place. "Don't do that no mo'." She pulled down on her hat and shuffled away.

"Wait a second." Ebony rushed to the woman. "Take these." She took off her gloves and handed them to her. "It's too cold to be outside without gloves."

The woman's eyes shot wide open. "Ooo, these dem good insulated ones." She slipped on one of the gloves. "Oh, there's fur inside." She held her hand down and out as she opened and closed her fist. "Warm, and looks good." Black eyes bright with gratitude, she shook her head. "No one ever gave me such nice finery. Bless you, chile'."

The woman's joy at receiving the unexpected gift warmed Ebony's heart. She smiled. Even if she missed the train, her day wouldn't be ruined. She resituated her book-bag, stuffed her hands into her pockets and ran down the ally, then cut across the park.

Half out of breath, Ebony looked up at the long metal stairway leading to the platform of the Laramie Street el station. Taking the steps two at a time, she suddenly remembered her monthly pass was in her other purse. Praying she wouldn't break her neck, she ran faster. When she reached the platform, to her surprise, someone was at the transit card machine.

She stood behind and to the side of the man, wondering why anyone would leave home in an expensive cashmere trench coat without hat or gloves in sub-zero weather.

He kicked at the machine. "What is wrong with this stupid thing? It won't take my cards! It won't take my money!" He drew the bill back, flattened it and tried to force it into the slot.

His wavy black hair half covered his reddened ears. *Probably frost-bitten,* thought Ebony. *And why is a white guy in this neighborhood, anyway?* She heard the train approaching. She stepped in front of the man with a $5 bill in hand. "Excuse me."

"Hey!"

"We'll freeze to death waiting for you." She purchased the transit card, then turned to him. "Here you go." She handed the card over.

Their eyes locked. She had never seen such beautiful smoky blue eyes in her life, and his sexy crooked grin raised her temperature high enough to need central air. The clickety-clack of the train pulling in snapped her out of her trance. "Get going."

Handing her the card, he shook his head. "I can't take this."

The rich timbre of his voice sent her heart racing. She crossed her arms over her chest. "If you don't move, we'll both miss the train." She pretended to tune him out while she dug through her purse for $5. "You still there?"

Richard Pacini swiped the transit card, then pushed through the turnstile and ran along the platform. At first, he wanted to curse-out the long-nailed, rude woman in the warm-looking parka. Then she set her stunning sepia eyes on him, and he melted. Memories of her sweet smell lingered; he inhaled deeply. The cold air burned his lungs, jolting him out of his daydream. He hopped on the train and stood in the doorway.

The conductor stuck his head out of his cubicle's small window. "Step fully into the train, sir."

Richard looked back at the turnstile for the young woman. She was still at the transit fare machine. He worried the machine was now giving her as much trouble as it had given him. "Can we please wait a few more seconds?"

"I'm on a time schedule. Step inside."

"I'm changing cars." Taking a risk that the man would leave him, Richard hurried along the platform to the conductor's car and hopped on.

"Next time you pull a trick like that, I'll close the door and pull off." The conductor poked his head out the small window, looked both ways, then closed the doors.

"I'm sorry. I was waiting for someone." Richard chose a seat near the front of the car and watched the streetlights as the train moved down the tracks. He hoped he hadn't caused her to miss the train. The way she crossed her arms over her chest, and the determination in her eyes, told him she wouldn't accept the transit card. His only choice was to make the train and stall. He would lay odds his great-grandmother had the same fire. His grandfather, Nonno, often reminisced about her beauty, intelligence, kind heart and fire.

"Where do I get on the Red Line?" he asked the conductor.

"Get off at the State Street station. There are signs. You can't miss it."

It was only 5:22. Already feeling the long day stretch before him, Richard yawned, leaned forward and dropped his face into his hands.

The automated message announced the next stop. He heard the doors sliding open, and then closing.

"Hola, Oscar." Ebony untied her hood, unwrapped her scarf.

"¿Cómo está, Ebony?"

She walked to the conductor's compartment, nodded slightly. *"Bien gracias, pero muy frío."* She held up her hands.

Richard heard bright joking and sat up straight. No matter what language, he would recognize her deep, confident voice and her plush charcoal parka anywhere.

"Where the heck are your gloves?" Oscar asked in English. "Don't make me call your mother." The train stopped and doors opened. Oscar leaned out the window and did a visual check both ways.

"If you want to dog me out, dog me out in Spanish, please. I want to be fluent." She held onto the edge of a seat as the train lurched forward and moved down the tracks. "For a minute there, I thought I had missed you today." She heaved her book-bag around, then plopped it on the seat. "I'm writing down our number. If I had of known giving away my gloves would get you to call, I would have given them away eons ago."

Richard watched her rummage through the bag for a pen. If she turned, he could see those exquisite eyes again. Oscar seemed a little short and old for her. Richard's eyes traveled from her boots to her jeans, then stopped at the end of her coat. He used his imagination to fill in the blanks for what lay beneath the parka. He guessed she was slightly over six feet tall.

"I have the number."

"So why haven't you called? I've told Mom all about you. I even showed her your picture."

Richard didn't realize he was smiling until Oscar shot him a knowing look. He stopped smiling instantly, but he couldn't stop the blood from rushing to his face. He pretended to study the advertisements along the walls of the train.

"I'll call. I promise. So why were you late?"

"Trolls reset my alarm clock for 4 P.M."

Oscar laughed. "Trolls?"

"We have a really bad troll problem. I think I need to call an exterminator." She unzipped her coat. "Thanks for holding the train for me. I had to switch cars, but I made it."

He shook his graying head. "You know I love you, but I didn't hold the train. Some maniac stood in the doorway talking about waiting for his friend." The automated system announced the next stop. "I need to get back to work. *Adiós*."

"*Adiós*." She turned and saw Richard. "Well hello there. I see you made it safely." She sat in the seat beside him.

His pulse raced. The contrast between her smooth dark skin and dazzling white smile was as captivating as her sepia eyes. He found himself staring.

She frowned. "Is something wrong? I can sit somewhere else."

"Oh no, no. Cat got my tongue for a second there. I apologize. I didn't mean to stare. You're just so beautiful."

Ebony covered her face with her hands, displaying at least two gold rings on each finger and long acrylic nails.

He gently pulled her soft hands from her face. He'd swear she was blushing. "Much better. I'm Richard, Richard Pacini."

"Ebony Washington."

He reached inside his coat pocket, took out his wallet and searched for a small bill. "Let me repay you now."

"No need."

He held out a $50 bill. "This is all I have." She laughed lightly and shook her head. He knew he'd never seen a brighter day. "What's so funny?" He brushed his hand over his dark, wavy hair.

"You tried to put a fifty in the machine. No wonder it was confused. You don't ride the train much, do you? And I'm not taking your money."

To keep from insulting her, he put the money away. "This is my first time. My car had not one—but two flats."

"I'm not trying to get into your business, but people like you don't usually come on this side of the tracks unless they're looking for drugs or a cheap trick."

"Like me?" He grinned. "You mean white."

Her lips tipped up at the corners. "Yes, white." She took off her charcoal fleece hat, allowing her blond microbraids to fall freely. "It's getting hot in here."

"Whoa, now that's a shock. Amazing contrast." He started to reach for a few strands to examine, but thought better of it. He didn't want to insult her. "This had to take hours to do. Extensions right?"

"About twenty to be exact, and, yes, I wear weave. Do you always get so personal with strangers?" The next stop was announced over the speaker system.

Expecting to see annoyance, he was relieved to see amusement dancing in her eyes instead. "It works for me." The doors slid open, a few passengers stepped on, then the door closed. "I'm not here *trolling* for women or drugs." A slight breeze brought a hint of her sweet scent. Like her, the scent made him wish for more.

"You've been eavesdropping." She wrapped the scarf around her hands.

"Who, me? I'd never. What happened to your gloves?"

"I gave them away." She unrolled the end of the scarf, offering it to him. "So how did you end up at the Laramie Street station?"

"A semi was stuck under the Austin viaduct, so I continued down to Central."

"Oh, I bet I know what happened. A water main broke on Central last night. I'll bet Central is still closed."

"So that's it! I continued down the road when my car started to lean. I drove down to the next street. For a second I thought the power was off in the neighborhood. You should call your alderman or someone and have the lights fixed. Anyway, I drove around the corner and parked under a streetlight to change my tire."

"Didn't you have a spa—" she stopped abruptly. "Wait a second. You said two flats."

"I should have known there was something wrong with the spot I parked in. The few other empty spaces had chairs and other furniture in them." The whole placing chairs in the street to reserve a parking space was new to him. Born and raised in Texas, he'd moved to Chicago in December. He was still waiting on a call from his sister to welcome him to her city.

"Well, if you had spent all that time shoveling, you wouldn't want anyone taking your space either. Even the mayor says to respect others' parking spots."

"Yeah, I guess that's why the spot I parked in was filled with nails. I didn't see them until I got out of my car."

"Ouch."

"Yep, ouch. I saw the train station on Laramie and went for it. I'll call triple A from work. No offense, but I didn't want to be sitting in that area any longer than needed."

"Smart move."

The automated message announced the approach to the State Street station. He had meant to ask for her number before they separated, but time flew by too quickly.

She stood slowly, zipping her coat. "I'm afraid this is my stop. I have to catch the Red Line."

The tinge of sorrow that colored her voice encouraged him. "You're not losing me that easily."

"You're transferring also?"

"I am today."

2007 Publication Schedule

January

Corporate Seduction
A.C. Arthur
1-58571-238-8
$9.95

A Taste of Temptation
Reneé Alexis
1-58571-207-8
$9.95

February

The Perfect Frame
Beverly Clark
1-58571-240-x
$9.95

Ebony Angel
Deatri King-Bey
1-58571-239-6
$9.95

March

Sweet Sensations
Gwendolyn Bolton
1-58571-206-X
$9.95

Crush
Crystal Hubbard
1-58571-243-4
$9.95

April

Secret Thunder
Annetta P. Lee
1-58571-204-3
$9.95

Blood Seduction
J.M. Jeffries
1-58571-237-X
$9.95

May

Lies Too Long
Pamela Ridley
1-58571-246-9
$13.95

Two Sides to Every
    Story
Dyanne Davis
1-58571-248-5
$9.95

June

One of These Days
Michele Sudler
No Contract
$9.95

Who's That Lady
Andrea Jackson
1-58571-190-x
$9.95

2007 Publication Schedule (continued)

<u>July</u>

Heart of the Phoenix
A.C. Arthur
1-58571-242-6
$9.95

Do Over
Jaci Kenney
1-58571-241-8
$9.95

It's Not Over Yet
J.J. Michael

$12.95

<u>August</u>

The Fires Within
Beverly Clark
1-58571-244-2

Stolen Kisses
Dominiqua Douglas
1-58571-248-5
$9.95

<u>September</u>

<u>October</u>

<u>November</u>

<u>December</u>

Other Genesis Press, Inc. Titles

A Dangerous Deception	J.M. Jeffries	$8.95
A Dangerous Love	J.M. Jeffries	$8.95
A Dangerous Obsession	J.M. Jeffries	$8.95
A Dangerous Woman	J.M. Jeffries	$9.95
A Dead Man Speaks	Lisa Jones Johnson	$12.95
A Drummer's Beat to Mend	Kei Swanson	$9.95
A Happy Life	Charlotte Harris	$9.95
A Heart's Awakening	Veronica Parker	$9.95
A Lark on the Wing	Phyliss Hamilton	$9.95
A Love of Her Own	Cheris F. Hodges	$9.95
A Love to Cherish	Beverly Clark	$8.95
A Lover's Legacy	Veronica Parker	$9.95
A Pefect Place to Pray	I.L. Goodwin	$12.95
A Risk of Rain	Dar Tomlinson	$8.95
A Twist of Fate	Beverly Clark	$8.95
A Will to Love	Angie Daniels	$9.95
Acquisitions	Kimberley White	$8.95
Across	Carol Payne	$12.95
After the Vows	Leslie Esdaile	$10.95
(Summer Anthology)	T.T. Henderson	
	Jacqueline Thomas	
Again My Love	Kayla Perrin	$10.95
Against the Wind	Gwynne Forster	$8.95
All I Ask	Barbara Keaton	$8.95
Ambrosia	T.T. Henderson	$8.95
An Unfinished Love Affair	Barbara Keaton	$8.95
And Then Came You	Dorothy Elizabeth Love	$8.95
Angel's Paradise	Janice Angelique	$9.95
At Last	Lisa G. Riley	$8.95
Best of Friends	Natalie Dunbar	$8.95
Between Tears	Pamela Ridley	$12.95
Beyond the Rapture	Beverly Clark	$9.95
Blaze	Barbara Keaton	$9.95

Other Genesis Press, Inc. Titles (continued)

Other Genesis Press, Inc. Titles (continued)

Echoes of Yesterday	Beverly Clark	$9.95
Eden's Garden	Elizabeth Rose	$8.95
Enchanted Desire	Wanda Y. Thomas	$9.95
Everlastin' Love	Gay G. Gunn	$8.95
Everlasting Moments	Dorothy Elizabeth Love	$8.95
Everything and More	Sinclair Lebeau	$8.95
Everything but Love	Natalie Dunbar	$8.95
Eve's Prescription	Edwina Martin Arnold	$8.95
Falling	Natalie Dunbar	$9.95
Fate	Pamela Leigh Starr	$8.95
Finding Isabella	A.J. Garrotto	$8.95
Forbidden Quest	Dar Tomlinson	$10.95
Forever Love	Wanda Thomas	$8.95
From the Ashes	Kathleen Suzanne	$8.95
	Jeanne Sumerix	
Gentle Yearning	Rochelle Alers	$10.95
Glory of Love	Sinclair LeBeau	$10.95
Go Gentle into that Good Night	Malcom Boyd	$12.95
Goldengroove	Mary Beth Craft	$16.95
Groove, Bang, and Jive	Steve Cannon	$8.99
Hand in Glove	Andrea Jackson	$9.95
Hard to Love	Kimberley White	$9.95
Hart & Soul	Angie Daniels	$8.95
Havana Sunrise	Kymberly Hunt	$9.95
Heartbeat	Stephanie Bedwell-Grime	$8.95
Hearts Remember	M. Loui Quezada	$8.95
Hidden Memories	Robin Allen	$10.95
Higher Ground	Leah Latimer	$19.95
Hitler, the War, and the Pope	Ronald Rychiak	$26.95
How to Write a Romance	Kathryn Falk	$18.95
I Married a Reclining Chair	Lisa M. Fuhs	$8.95
I'm Gonna Make You Love Me	Gwyneth Bolton	$9.95
Indigo After Dark Vol. I	Nia Dixon/Angelique	$10.95

Other Genesis Press, Inc. Titles (continued)

Indigo After Dark Vol. II	Dolores Bundy/Cole Riley	$10.95
Indigo After Dark Vol. III	Montana Blue/Coco Morena	$10.95
Indigo After Dark Vol. IV	Cassandra Colt/	$14.95
	Diana Richeaux	
Indigo After Dark Vol. V	Delilah Dawson	$14.95
Icie	Pamela Leigh Starr	$8.95
I'll Be Your Shelter	Giselle Carmichael	$8.95
I'll Paint a Sun	A.J. Garrotto	$9.95
Illusions	Pamela Leigh Starr	$8.95
Indiscretions	Donna Hill	$8.95
Intentional Mistakes	Michele Sudler	$9.95
Interlude	Donna Hill	$8.95
Intimate Intentions	Angie Daniels	$8.95
Ironic	Pamela Leigh Starr	$9.95
Jolie's Surrender	Edwina Martin-Arnold	$8.95
Kiss or Keep	Debra Phillips	$8.95
Lace	Giselle Carmichael	$9.95
Last Train to Memphis	Elsa Cook	$12.95
Lasting Valor	Ken Olsen	$24.95
Let's Get It On	Dyanne Davis	$9.95
Let Us Prey	Hunter Lundy	$25.95
Life Is Never As It Seems	J.J. Michael	$12.95
Lighter Shade of Brown	Vicki Andrews	$8.95
Love Always	Mildred E. Riley	$10.95
Love Doesn't Come Easy	Charlyne Dickerson	$8.95
Love in High Gear	Charlotte Roy	$9.95
Love Lasts Forever	Dominiqua Douglas	$9.95
Love Me Carefully	A.C. Arthur	$9.95
Love Unveiled	Gloria Greene	$10.95
Love's Deception	Charlene Berry	$10.95
Love's Destiny	M. Loui Quezada	$8.95
Mae's Promise	Melody Walcott	$8.95
Magnolia Sunset	Giselle Carmichael	$8.95

Other Genesis Press, Inc. Titles (continued)

Matters of Life and Death	Lesego Malepe, Ph.D.	$15.95
Meant to Be	Jeanne Sumerix	$8.95
Midnight Clear	Leslie Esdaile	$10.95
(Anthology)	Gwynne Forster	
	Carmen Green	
	Monica Jackson	
Midnight Magic	Gwynne Forster	$8.95
Midnight Peril	Vicki Andrews	$10.95
Misconceptions	Pamela Leigh Starr	$9.95
Misty Blue	Dyanne Davis	$9.95
Montgomery's Children	Richard Perry	$14.95
My Buffalo Soldier	Barbara B. K. Reeves	$8.95
Naked Soul	Gwynne Forster	$8.95
Next to Last Chance	Louisa Dixon	$24.95
Nights Over Egypt	Barbara Keaton	$9.95
No Apologies	Seressia Glass	$8.95
No Commitment Required	Seressia Glass	$8.95
No Ordinary Love	Angela Weaver	$9.95
No Regrets	Mildred E. Riley	$8.95
Notes When Summer Ends	Beverly Lauderdale	$12.95
Nowhere to Run	Gay G. Gunn	$10.95
O Bed! O Breakfast!	Rob Kuehnle	$14.95
Object of His Desire	A. C. Arthur	$8.95
Office Policy	A. C. Arthur	$9.95
Once in a Blue Moon	Dorianne Cole	$9.95
One Day at a Time	Bella McFarland	$8.95
Only You	Crystal Hubbard	$9.95
Outside Chance	Louisa Dixon	$24.95
Passion	T.T. Henderson	$10.95
Passion's Blood	Cherif Fortin	$22.95
Passion's Journey	Wanda Thomas	$8.95
Past Promises	Jahmel West	$8.95
Path of Fire	T.T. Henderson	$8.95

Other Genesis Press, Inc. Titles (continued)

Path of Thorns	Annetta P. Lee	$9.95
Peace Be Still	Colette Haywood	$12.95
Picture Perfect	Reon Carter	$8.95
Playing for Keeps	Stephanie Salinas	$8.95
Pride & Joi	Gay G. Gunn	$8.95
Promises to Keep	Alicia Wiggins	$8.95
Quiet Storm	Donna Hill	$10.95
Reckless Surrender	Rochelle Alers	$6.95
Red Polka Dot in a World of Plaid	Varian Johnson	$12.95
Rehoboth Road	Anita Ballard-Jones	$12.95
Reluctant Captive	Joyce Jackson	$8.95
Rendezvous with Fate	Jeanne Sumerix	$8.95
Revelations	Cheris F. Hodges	$8.95
Rise of the Phoenix	Kenneth Whetstone	$12.95
Rivers of the Soul	Leslie Esdaile	$8.95
Rock Star	Rosyln Hardy Holcomb	$9.95
Rocky Mountain Romance	Kathleen Suzanne	$8.95
Rooms of the Heart	Donna Hill	$8.95
Rough on Rats and Tough on Cats	Chris Parker	$12.95
Scent of Rain	Annetta P. Lee	$9.95
Second Chances at Love	Cheris Hodges	$9.95
Secret Library Vol. 1	Nina Sheridan	$18.95
Secret Library Vol. 2	Cassandra Colt	$8.95
Shades of Brown	Denise Becker	$8.95
Shades of Desire	Monica White	$8.95
Shadows in the Moonlight	Jeanne Sumerix	$8.95
Sin	Crystal Rhodes	$8.95
Sin and Surrender	J.M. Jeffries	$9.95
Sinful Intentions	Crystal Rhodes	$12.95
So Amazing	Sinclair LeBeau	$8.95
Somebody's Someone	Sinclair LeBeau	$8.95

Other Genesis Press, Inc. Titles (continued)

Someone to Love	Alicia Wiggins	$8.95
Song in the Park	Martin Brant	$15.95
Soul Eyes	Wayne L. Wilson	$12.95
Soul to Soul	Donna Hill	$8.95
Southern Comfort	J.M. Jeffries	$8.95
Still the Storm	Sharon Robinson	$8.95
Still Waters Run Deep	Leslie Esdaile	$8.95
Stories to Excite You	Anna Forrest/Divine	$14.95
Subtle Secrets	Wanda Y. Thomas	$8.95
Suddenly You	Crystal Hubbard	$9.95
Sweet Repercussions	Kimberley White	$9.95
Sweet Tomorrows	Kimberly White	$8.95
Taken by You	Dorothy Elizabeth Love	$9.95
Tattooed Tears	T. T. Henderson	$8.95
The Color Line	Lizzette Grayson Carter	$9.95
The Color of Trouble	Dyanne Davis	$8.95
The Disappearance of Allison Jones	Kayla Perrin	$5.95
The Honey Dipper's Legacy	Pannell-Allen	$14.95
The Joker's Love Tune	Sidney Rickman	$15.95
The Little Pretender	Barbara Cartland	$10.95
The Love We Had	Natalie Dunbar	$8.95
The Man Who Could Fly	Bob & Milana Beamon	$18.95
The Missing Link	Charlyne Dickerson	$8.95
The Price of Love	Sinclair LeBeau	$8.95
The Smoking Life	Ilene Barth	$29.95
The Words of the Pitcher	Kei Swanson	$8.95
Three Wishes	Seressia Glass	$8.95
Through the Fire	Seressia Glass	$9.95
Ties That Bind	Kathleen Suzanne	$8.95
Tiger Woods	Libby Hughes	$5.95
Time is of the Essence	Angie Daniels	$9.95
Timeless Devotion	Bella McFarland	$9.95
Tomorrow's Promise	Leslie Esdaile	$8.95

A TASTE OF TEMPTATION

Other Genesis Press, Inc. Titles (continued)

Truly Inseparable	Wanda Y. Thomas	$8.95
Unbreak My Heart	Dar Tomlinson	$8.95
Uncommon Prayer	Kenneth Swanson	$9.95
Unconditional	A.C. Arthur	$9.95
Unconditional Love	Alicia Wiggins	$8.95
Under the Cherry Moon	Christal Jordan-Mims	$12.95
Unearthing Passions	Elaine Sims	$9.95
Until Death Do Us Part	Susan Paul	$8.95
Vows of Passion	Bella McFarland	$9.95
Wedding Gown	Dyanne Davis	$8.95
What's Under Benjamin's Bed	Sandra Schaffer	$8.95
When Dreams Float	Dorothy Elizabeth Love	$8.95
Whispers in the Night	Dorothy Elizabeth Love	$8.95
Whispers in the Sand	LaFlorya Gauthier	$10.95
Wild Ravens	Altonya Washington	$9.95
Yesterday Is Gone	Beverly Clark	$10.95
Yesterday's Dreams, Tomorrow's Promises	Reon Laudat	$8.95
Your Precious Love	Sinclair LeBeau	$8.95

274

Order Form

Mail to: Genesis Press, Inc.
P.O. Box 101
Columbus, MS 39703

Name _____
Address _____
City/State _____ Zip _____
Telephone _____

Ship to (if different from above)
Name _____
Address _____
City/State _____ Zip _____
Telephone _____

Credit Card Information
Credit Card # _____ ☐ Visa ☐ Mastercard
Expiration Date (mm/yy) _____ ☐ AmEx ☐ Discover

Qty.	Author	Title	Price	Total

Use this order
form, or call
1-888-INDIGO-1

Total for books _____
Shipping and handling:
  $5 first two books,
  $1 each additional book _____
Total S & H _____
Total amount enclosed _____

Mississippi residents add 7% sales tax